FATED WINTER

ANGEL'S FATE: BOOK 2

TESSA COLE

Gryphon's Gate Publishing

Fated Winter

Cover Design by Melody Simmons

Gryphon's Gate Publishing

550 King St. N.

PO Box 42088 Conestoga

Waterloo, ON

N2L 6K5

ebook ISBN: 978-1-988115-78-8

Print ISBN: 978-1-988115-77-1

AMIAH

T<small>HE SHIMMERING LIQUID PORTAL SPAT US OUT INTO</small> F<small>AERIE</small> and jerked Sebastian forward who was still kneeling and holding me. The sudden jolt made him tighten his grip and shoot agony through my bruised and broken body, drawing a whimper that I struggled to hide. I didn't know why. There wasn't any point. They'd just seen me at my worst — and a lot more of me than I'd wanted — and I had every reason to be in pain.

A few feet away, Hawk stumbled and fell to his knees, and Cassius and Titus staggered but managed to keep standing.

We'd arrived at the back of a massive hall that looked like it had been carved entirely of ice even though I couldn't feel the cold. Pale glowing balls of light hovered above us, not even close to the vaulted ceiling, illumi-nating the space and reflecting in the semi-translucent pillars and walls.

But the sense of ice, gleaming walls, and vastness was all I could really register. Agony from the beating I'd taken at the hands of Balwyrdan, the Spring Court's seneschal, wracked my body along with the horror of what I'd gone through. I'd been taken. Again.

God, again!

And while I had a glimmer of healing power inside me, it wasn't enough to heal any of my broken bones, since healing myself took a lot more power than healing someone else. Even if I'd been at full, it still wouldn't have been enough because my thoughts spun, ripped apart in a whirlwind of fear and pain and I couldn't focus long enough to pull my power from my palms and direct it to my injuries.

All of my ribs were broken, my wrist was broken, my nose was broken, and a hairline fracture sliced through my cheek. I also had a concussion, which explained, in part, why I couldn't focus my magic. Most of my face and torso was one big swelling bruise, and I could only see out of one eye — the other had swollen shut — and my vision was blurry and dark while the room spun and lurched around me.

I wasn't sure if there was anyone else in the room other than us, the tiny woman with the gossamer wings who'd pulled us into the portal, and her massive ice guards with their ice spears.

I could only pray she wouldn't force me to stand. I wouldn't have been able to, no matter what I wanted.

"God damned fucking shit," Sebastian hissed, his body shaking and his heart pounding. But I couldn't tell if it was from the fight we'd just won or our abduction into Faerie to the Winter Queen's court. As it was, his complexion was gray from all the magic he'd been forced

to expend to save me, and I doubted he had anything left to use if we needed to fight our way free.

"We can't stay here," Titus growled softly, his claws fully extended — the glamour making his dragon claws look like wolf claws — and his hands and forearms covered in blood. Blood also dampened his ripped T-shirt and pasted his right pantleg to his thigh where he'd been injured. I couldn't tell what other injuries he might have had, but my magic didn't lock onto him so he couldn't have been in immediate danger, and with his amazing natural healing, whatever injuries he did have would be healed sooner rather than later.

The woman with the wings flew to the center of the room, leaving the guards who stood a few feet away to glare at us, and a murmur of voices on the far side of the room greeted her.

"Your majesty. The winter faekin to swear his allegiance," she said, her voice echoing off the icy walls.

Cassius shifted closer to us, his hands clenched but not a hint of smoke curling from his skin. He'd also used every last drop of his fire magic to save me in a terrifying display, burning Balwyrdan to ash in a matter of seconds, and there was no way he'd be able to fight us free, either. "Just swear your allegiance so we can go."

"It doesn't work that way," Sebastian said.

"Of course it doesn't." Hawk stood and tightened his grip on his wickedly curved knife. His T-shirt was also bloody and torn, and he had a nasty set of lacerations along his ribs, likely from a shifter's claws. He was going to need an influx of sexual energy to heal and I wasn't in any kind of condition to help him.

"Step forward, faekin," the woman called from her spot in the center of the room, "and bow to your queen."

Sebastian staggered to his feet, jostling me. I whimpered again and a tear I didn't want to cry rolled down my cheek. I hated that I was in pain and weak even though I had good reason to be at the moment.

Because I'd been taken.

I fought to shove that thought aside and think about anything else, the guys' injuries, concentrating past the whirling room, trying to breathe without slicing pain through my chest. Anything but what had happened.

Taken. Again.

And this time I'd been seriously beaten. I swore I'd never be anyone's prisoner ever again, done everything in my power for the last hundred years to keep that vow, but I'd been helpless to save myself. So damned helpless. I was tired of being helpless, but in a world of supernatural beings, an angel with a healing magic that could compel her to heal her enemy was weak and useless in a fight.

"Give her to me," Cassius said, holding out his arms, the muscles of his bare chest flexing with the movement. He'd given me his shirt because Balwyrdan had ripped my dress's neck strap.

I didn't want to think about that, either. All of the guys had now seen me topless. And if I didn't hurt so much, I would have been embarrassed.

"No," Sebastian said. "If I'm holding her, they're less likely to separate us."

"Right." The muscles in Cassius's jaw flexed at the reminder that Sebastian and I shouldn't be separated.

Sebastian had taken on Titus's half of the leash spell

that had bound us together and now I couldn't be more than a hundred feet from Sebastian or I'd suffocate.

I wasn't sure how I felt about that, either. The last time Sebastian and I had talked was just after having sex and I'd fled his bedroom, too stunned at what I'd just done. It had been amazing and surprising and completely out of character for me. Over a hundred years of celibacy broken in one amazing, confusing moment, and yet at the time, I'd desperately wanted him, wanted to be kissed and touched and filled in a way that I'd been holding back from because I'd been foolishly waiting for my soul mate.

"In fact, everyone stay close." Sebastian took a careful step forward, but even that sent blazing pain rushing through me and drew a whimper.

"They must know about T," Cassius whispered, falling into step beside Sebastian and keeping his gaze locked on the front of the room. "Why else would they come after you?"

I tried to make my breath as shallow as possible. But it didn't matter how slightly I breathed, every miniscule movement hurt.

"I'm hoping because someone from the Spring or Shadow Courts told Her Majesty there was a winter faekin in the mortal realm who most likely needs to vow his allegiance to the queen in an attempt to get us out of the way so they could have T to themselves." Sebastian's trembling increased. "I really hoped I'd never have to come back."

"Faekin," the woman snapped. "Disobedience is death."

Sebastian barked a quiet bitter laugh. "Maybe we'll get lucky and this won't take long."

"There's only one way to manage that," Titus said under his breath.

"I know." Sebastian glanced at Hawk, whose expression was pinched. "Can you give Amiah a bit of a distraction to ease her pain?"

"Ah... sure." Hawk brushed a finger down my bare calf and a warm sensual curl of his incubus magic unfurled within me. For a second, I was drifting in a heated ocean of desire, my pain a whisper at the edge of my senses, my fears and worries muted, my focus entirely on the bone-melting sensation coursing through me. There was no hall, no guys, just blissful nothingness.

Then light flared around me and Hawk's magic stuttered, jerking me out of my haze. Sebastian had released his hold on his glamour that kept the glow emanating from his skin at a low faekin level, letting it blaze at its full fae radiance. His ears, already with a small delicate point, grew pointier. But unlike the last time I'd seen him in his full fae form, his face also changed. His eyes became bigger, his nose narrower, his cheekbones and chin sharper.

I hadn't thought it was possible for him to be more stunning. He'd already had the looks to compete with an incubus. Now he wasn't just breathtaking, he was mesmerizing. Everything within me tripped, stunned, unable to think past his appearance.

"Kneel, fae—" The woman with the wings turned to us and gasped, which drew a big gasp from the people gathered at the front of the room.

A murmur rushed through the crowd and I strained to focus on them and see just who we were facing. There were maybe a hundred people in the room, a mix of men and women some with the full-body glow of fae, but others were small with wings, or tall and bulky... actually, they were all manner of shapes and sizes, although most looked humanish. The women all wore diaphanous dresses in white, silver, and blues and they all dropped into low curtsies. The men wore knee-length tunics and loose pants in the same colors, and they knelt on one knee, their heads bowed.

Behind them on a raised dais sat a tall, beautiful fae woman on a massive throne that looked like it was made entirely of ice. She had the same white and silver hair as Sebastian, although she wore hers half up with braids and half hanging past her waist instead of Sebastian's short and spikey.

A small, delicately spun ice crown rested on her head, the thin strands woven into a complex filigree, and she wore a shimmering midnight blue gown made of diaphanous layers of fabric tailored to perfectly accentuate her slim figure and tease with glimpses of pale glowing flesh beneath.

To her right stood another beautiful fae woman with striking black hair, the color unlike any other fae in the room. An intricate ice circlet held back her hair, and she wore a similar dress to the queen's in white as if she were the queen's opposite.

At their feet, were a dozen men, half of them fae like Sebastian, the rest a mix of shifters and demons. They lounged on thick blue rugs and cushions, dressed only in loose pants made of the same light fabric as everyone else's clothes, but in varying shades of red, each one of them with an exquisite physique.

All of them, the men in red and both of the fae women on the dais, stared at Sebastian with guarded expressions.

"Oh, shit," Hawk hissed.

"The day has finally arrived," the Winter Queen said, her voice breathy as a single, shimmering tear rolled down her cheek. "You've come home."

Sebastian slowly dipped into a shallow bow. I could tell he was trying not to jostle me, but the movement still made me whimper and the room darken and lurch. "Your majesty."

"Formalities? Really Seireadan? I haven't seen you in over three hundred years." The queen clapped her hands and a dozen people, a mix of men and women who looked like they'd been carved from ice like the two guards — although not nearly as tall or muscular — scurried from a small door behind and to the right of the dais. "Seireadan, prince of the realm, heir to the throne of the Winter Court has returned home. This calls for a celebration."

The men on the dais all bowed their heads, but the woman standing beside the throne continued to glare.

"Prince?" Hawk asked under his breath. "If I'd known you were royalty, I would have charged you more."

"Not any more. I abdicated and got the fuck out of Faerie," Sebastian murmured back, giving him then me a pointed look. "Your magic for Amiah."

"Shit. Right. Sorry." Hawk brushed his finger over my

calf again, stealing my breath with another sensual curl of power and sending me spinning, half in pain and half with desire.

"Yes," the queen cooed, her eyes bright. "This will be the biggest celebration in court since your betrothal. Bigger."

"Your Maj—" Sebastian started but the queen's eyes narrowed, and for a second it looked like something dark and ugly flashed behind her bright joy. But it happened so fast I wasn't sure I'd actually seen it.

"Mother," Sebastian corrected. "We're in no condition for a celebration."

"Of course you are." The queen leaned back on her throne and raised a hand. Most of the crowd scurried out of the room followed by half of the ice people, while the other half of the ice people knelt to the right of the dais and five women gathered demurely to the left — although all of them kept glancing at Hawk, unable to keep their eyes off him even though it seemed they were supposed to keep their heads bowed.

I couldn't blame them. Hawk was as handsome as Sebastian and with his magic oozing through me it was difficult to think of anything other than begging him to satisfy me. And while the other women didn't have his magic inside them, he, like all incubi, naturally radiated sexual desire, and I doubted he did much to hold it back.

"Oh, you look tired but I'm sure you're more than perfectly capable of handling a celebration in your honor and selecting a bride." She gave Cassius, Titus, and Hawk a dismissive wave. "Give your bodyguards and—" Her lips pursed and she studied me with a cold calculating look that made my insides churn. I hadn't imagined that ugly darkness.

The man closest to her, a werepanther with a sleek, lean-muscled body, leaned toward her and mumbled something, and her grip on the arms of her throne tightened.

"I see," she said, the darkness shifting to something else, something more... calculating? "Give your men and your concubine time to relax."

Cassius stiffened at her words, as Titus growled low in his throat and Hawk snorted.

Concubine? I wasn't his concubine... although I had slept with Sebastian — and with Hawk's magic heating me, I was starting to think sleeping with Sebastian again was a good idea despite my injuries. But that didn't make me his concubine. We weren't in a relationship.

"I'm not going to a party," Sebastian insisted, "and I'm not choosing a bride. I'm going home. Allow us to pass through the portal."

"But you are home, dear, and you must choose a bride." Actual darkness bled over the queen's eyes, and crackling frost rushed down the dais's three shallow stairs and across the floor toward us. "You'll be king. You must produce an heir."

"I don't need to produce an heir," Sebastian said. "Padraigin already has an heir."

The woman beside the throne stiffened and more ice crackled across the floor around Sebastian's feet. The temperature in the room dropped, making me shiver, and the agonizing blaze in my body devoured Hawk's magic.

"Padraigin isn't *my* heir," the queen said. "You are."

"Mother—"

"You just needed time to think after that silly business with Enowen." The queen sat forward and all the men around her straightened, ready for her command. "And now you're back."

I strained to breathe as darkness crept around the edges of my vision, and Hawk's magic fought to overwhelm my pain.

"Pick a wife." The queen gestured to the ladies who now openly stared at Hawk. I didn't know if he was purposefully letting his incubus magic affect them or not. He seemed oblivious to them, all of his attention on me, his expression tight with concern... or was that concentration? How hard was it to use his magic to distract me from my pain without making me ignore my injuries to satisfy myself?

"I'm not picking a wife."

"You are." The temperature dropped again and snowflakes lazily drifted from the ceiling. "And tell your incubus to pull his power back or I'll neuter him. The maids are for you. I'll not have him manipulating your future wife." The queen's smile turned wicked. "Not until you've made your vows. Then you can do whatever you like with her."

Sebastian shot Hawk a quick glance, who frowned and squinted at Sebastian before his magic evaporated.

The agony in my body surged — I hadn't realized how much he was actually muting my pain — and I tried to bite back a sob but it escaped, a pathetic, mangled whimper.

"You've had your fun, Seireadan." The queen stood

and all of her men stood with her. "Now pick a wife. Your whore can always remain in your harem. They all can."

"I can't do that," Sebastian said, his voice low.

"Of course you can." More ice crackled across the floor and the snow falling from the ceiling thickened. "If none of them appeal to you, I'll send for more."

"I can't. I..." Sebastian's almost-colorless blue gaze met mine filled with apology and resignation. "I've already made the vow to Amiah. You know it can't be broken."

"You vowed your fertility to a being you can't have children with?" The snowfall burst into a blinding freezing flurry. The flakes turned to ice pellets, stinging my already burning skin and sending tears streaming down my cheeks.

"I have," Sebastian yelled into the storm, hugging me tighter and hunching forward in an attempt to protect me from the storm. "Amiah is my wife."

The light in Cassius's eyes flared and he jerked close. "You better be lying."

"I'm not," Sebastian replied.

My heart skipped a beat and my thoughts whirled, caught between pain and confusion. "We're married?"

"Hey, man," Hawk said. "Just because you licked her, doesn't mean she's yours."

When did we get married? It couldn't have been because we had sex. I was sure in his very long life that Sebastian had slept with hundreds of women. He had to be lying. It couldn't be the truth. I couldn't be trapped like that. I couldn't be trapped, period. Never again.

Please, no.

Sebastian was supposed to be helping me remove my not-yet-awakened angelic mating brand and avoid the horrible fate of having a soul bond with a complete stranger, not trapping me to him. And if he couldn't remove my angelic mating brand, married to him or not, the brand was going to make me fall in love with someone else... and I wasn't in love with Sebastian. I didn't even know if I liked him.

AMIAH

THE WINTER QUEEN'S STORM PICKED UP, THE WIND howling around us, the temperature so cold my nose, cheeks, fingers, and bare toes grew numb even with the pain wracking my body. I huddled against Sebastian's chest, fighting to breathe.

I can't be trapped. I can't be. I can't—

"How are we married?" I gasped. How was this even possible? I didn't vow anything to him. We'd just had sex.

"I used the binding ritual and everything," Sebastian yelled into the storm, ignoring me.

"You what?" I yelled back as the storm vanished, my cry suddenly loud in the silence.

A flicker of sadness flashed across Sebastian's face before he jerked his attention away from me. "Check for yourself, Mother."

Icy magic swept into my chest, stealing my breath completely before I could deny that I was married to Sebastian, that I hadn't agreed to anything. My shivering increased turning my pain into an inferno. For a second, darkness filled my vision and the promise of unconsciousness taunted me, then the pain surged, making me cry out.

"I see." The queen's power tore out of me and she glanced at a stunningly handsome fae who stood at her right and slightly behind her. He gave a tight nod and she huffed. "Well then."

Tears streamed down my cheeks, and Sebastian hugged me closer, his pulse racing even faster than when we'd first arrived.

"Prepare a room for the heir apparent, his bodyguards, and his... wife." The queen spat out the word and the remaining ice people rushed from the room. "Out!" she snapped at Sebastian's prospective brides, who scrambled to leave.

"We're not staying." Sebastian glanced at Cassius who, from his expression, if he had fire magic left, would have been dripping flames onto the floor. "My wife needs medical attention."

"Take her to the pools," the queen said, and the ice guards who had been hanging twenty feet back stepped up behind us. They looked identical both big, muscular, bald, and wearing strange shimmering breastplates and loose white pants, and they towered over all of us except for Titus who was only a foot or so shorter than they were. "We'll postpone your return celebration until she's recovered. Can't have the princess consort of the Winter Court missing her own celebration."

The queen flashed a disturbingly sweet smile and

stormed off the dais. Her men followed, and the other woman jerked forward a step but stopped as Sebastian gave her a tight nod.

"Padraigin," he said.

"You shouldn't have come back." Her expression was as hard and icy as the queen's.

"I wasn't given much of a choice."

Her attention jumped to the ice guards then back to Sebastian. "Congratulations on your nuptials, your highness."

"Not any more," Sebastian said. "I left a note. I abdicated."

"Her majesty didn't accept your abdication." The woman, Padraigin, gave a shallow bow and marched out of the room.

"What the fuck?" Hawk demanded.

"You'll address his highness with respect." The guard on the left jabbed the butt of his ice spear at Hawk's chest.

Hawk jerked out of the way, and tensed, ready to slash the ice man with his knife, but Cassius grabbed his arm and jerked his chin at me. I wasn't sure what he was trying to tell Hawk, but after a moment with a pinched frown, Hawk seemed to understand and relaxed his fighting stance.

The other guard gestured to the back of the room. "Attendants are waiting for you in the pools, your highness."

"Dismiss them," Sebastian said, heading to the back with a confident stride, his back stiff, each step setting my body on fire. "My bodyguards are adequate protection and I wish to attend to my queen alone."

"Sebastian," I gasped. "I'm not—"

"Ready to discuss us staying here. I know, my love," he interrupted, a strange desperation flashing in his eyes. "We'll *talk* when we get to the pools."

My mind tripped over his emphasis of the word talk. Whatever he wanted to say, he didn't want these guards to overhear.

"Your highness, we can't leave you." The first guard stepped ahead of Sebastian and led the way down a wide, white hall while the other guard took up position behind us. "But I'll dismiss the attendants when we get there."

"And you'll wait in the hall," Sebastian said.

"Your highness—"

"Have I not made myself clear?" Sebastian asked, his voice suddenly low and dark, promising danger if the guard disobeyed. "I'll not have her majesty's constructs ogling my wife while she bathes in the healing pools. She's not fae. Her sensibilities are different and you'll learn to respect that."

The guard dipped his head with the sound of heavy ice creaking, but I didn't know if that meant he was embarrassed that he'd insulted his prince or upset at Sebastian's command. "Of course, your highness."

The guard led us down long icy hall after long icy hall that all looked identical. The floor was smooth but didn't seem slippery since none of the guys had problems keeping their balance, and the walls looked like they were carved with an intricate pattern. Except with the glow of the faerie lights in the semi-translucent white-on-white walls, it was difficult to make out the design.

No one said anything, and my pain continued to grow with every body-jarring step. Soon the world was dark and spinning and my breath shallow ragged pants. I wasn't going to last much longer. If we didn't stop, I was going to pass out and then I wouldn't be able to even try to focus what little magic I had to start healing myself. Which meant I'd be in even more pain when I woke, and that would keep the cycle of not being able to focus my power going.

"Sebastian, I have to stop," I gasped, fighting my tears. I didn't know why I fought them. It wasn't as if he and everyone hadn't seen me crying in the queen's hall.

"Almost there," he murmured. "We just need to get inside."

We rounded a corner and reached a large intricately carved ice door. Six petite ice women, all identical to each other, and if I thought about it, identical to the ice women who'd been in the hall, dressed in white flowing dresses, waited outside the door holding bundles of fabric. All of them bowed low as Sebastian approached.

"Set the towels and change of clothes on the bench inside and leave," the guard commanded as he pushed open the heavy door.

Sebastian didn't wait to see if the women obeyed or not. He strode inside, into a grotto nestled in a dimly lit cave filled with the gentle sound of flowing water. The floor was polished granite, but uncut rock also jutted out from the walls and floor, creating four different levels, each with at least one pool sunk into them. Holly bushes and evergreen shrubs added hints of privacy among the pools — and maybe more than hints since there might have been other pools I couldn't see because of them. Their scent filled the warm, humid air, and soft light from glowing orbs reflected off the floor and water, while starlight shone through a skylight.

"We'll be just outside the door if you need us, your highness," one of the guards said and the door closed with a resounding boom. Trapping us in.

Trapped. Again. God, again!

I dragged my attention to the skylight. Even on the verge of passing out, I needed sky and open spaces. I couldn't be trapped. I was now trapped to Sebastian. I couldn't—

Sebastian sagged to the floor and his glow stuttered, revealing an ashen complexion.

"What in the ever-loving fuck?" Hawk hissed.

"She's your wife?" Cassius demanded. "When did she become your wife?"

With a groan, Sebastian set me on the floor and activated a glyph on his hip, the one he'd claimed while we were having sex was a sound blocking spell.

"You shouldn't be using magic," I said. "You don't look well."

"No choice. We need to have a conversation and my mother's ice constructs will be listening." Sebastian squeezed his eyes shut. "Someone get Amiah in a pool. Any pool will do. The water isn't as effective at healing as angelic healing, and the body can't stand submersion for more than an hour at a time, but it'll still help."

Cassius grabbed the front of Sebastian's shirt and

hauled him to his feet, but Sebastian's legs didn't brace to hold him. "How the hell is she your wife?"

"Cassius, please," I gasped as I sat up with a sharp slice of agony that made the room darken. "Look at him."

Cassius turned his glare on me. "You married him?"

"What if I did?" I blurted out. I didn't know why I said that. I was just so sore and angry. He didn't have a say who I married, just like he didn't have a say who I had sexual intercourse with. And Sebastian had no right to do a ritual marrying us without my consent, trapping me.

My pulse stuttered, the memory of Balwyrdan beating me threatening to overwhelm me.

Don't think about it. Just don't think about it.

A wisp of smoke burst from Cassius's hands. "Amiah—"

"For fuck's sake," Sebastian groaned, managing to get his balance. "My mother wasn't going to stop until I picked a wife and she wasn't going to let us go. I needed to say something that kept us together until I can break the leash spell on Amiah."

"So we're not—?" A strange mix of emotions crashed through me, fear, regret, anger, relief.

"No. We're not. Jeez, you really think I'd marry you?" he asked.

My throat irrationally tightened at that. No, of course he wouldn't. It was surprising enough that he'd had sex with me given how he clearly hadn't been interested before, just teasing me. Now that he knew I'd been a virgin and was inexperienced, I doubted he'd ever have sex with me again.

Which sent another confusing mix of emotions rushing through me. It shouldn't have mattered that he didn't want to have sex again, but it did. He already knew the truth about me, knew about my partially formed mating brand, and without a doubt wasn't my soul mate. In this particular instance, he was the safest person to satisfy my desires, desires I was tired of resisting.

And the fact that this upset me just proved how sore and exhausted I was.

"You still shouldn't have told her you gave Amiah your fertility," Titus said, his pupils slitted, his beast close to the surface. "You've put Amiah in danger. The only way now that you'll be able to have offspring with anyone else is if Amiah dies and you perform the ritual again." He yanked off his shirt and pulled off his boots.

"Without the binding ritual, my mother would never have accepted Amiah as my wife." Sebastian tugged at Cassius's grip but wasn't strong enough to break free. "It had to be irreversible."

"Yeah, but it's *not* irreversible," Hawk said, also taking off his shirt and shoes and reaching to unbutton his fly. "Amiah's death fixes your mother's problem." He flicked open his fly and stepped out of his shorts. No underwear. I wasn't in the least bit surprised.

My breath and thoughts stuttered at the sight of Hawk's stunning physique and impressive... equipment. I barely even noticed the lacerations along his ribs and right biceps and the large bruise on his left side.

"Hey," Cassius snapped. "Put your shorts back on."

"I'm not going into a bath with clothes on."

Oh, wow. For a moment there was no pain, no fear, nothing, only heart-pounding bliss.

"—hoping we'll be out of Faerie before it comes to that," Sebastian said, now sitting on the floor and unbuttoning his dress shirt, time having stuttered while I was mesmerized by Hawk.

The shirt fell open revealing the complicated black tattoos still covering Sebastian's torso. They really had been real and not a part of the glamour he'd apparently had up hiding his true identity.

"At least the leash spell is good for something," he said. "My mother is powerful, but she's not a sorcerer, so she could feel Amiah and I were bound together, just not how."

"Shorts." Cassius grabbed Hawk's shorts from the floor and tossed them at the incubus.

"Don't be an asshole," Hawk shot back.

I heaved my attention away from them to focus on the closest pool. It lay about twenty feet away and was big enough for all five of us. Steam curled from its gently undulating surface, the movement coming from a small waterfall at the back where water from the previous level up fed into the pool.

I couldn't afford to stay in my current condition. Especially if we needed to flee the Winter Court at a moment's notice, so I gritted my teeth and started crawling the twenty feet to the pool.

But I'd barely crawled a few feet before my body was on fire and the world so dark I couldn't see my hands on the floor in front of me. The adrenaline I'd had during the fight with Balwyrdan was finally well and truly gone and all I wanted to do was curl into a ball and cry.

I will not think about it.

"You shouldn't be moving," Titus said as he gently drew me into his muscular arms. He looked at me with sadness and pity and a small hot ember of rage, and I closed my eyes, my throat tight with tears I was tired of crying.

I would get through this. I'd heal myself and the pain would end. I just needed to be strong. Just for a little longer. But it was so hard to concentrate, let alone be strong, especially with all the proof that I wasn't.

Titus carried me into the warm soothing water still fully dressed — or at least as dressed as I had been when Balwyrdan had kidnapped me in only a dress without shoes or underwear. Soft tingling magic sank into my skin and oozed into my veins and between my cells. It curled around my heart, seeped into my essence, and, for a heart-stopping second, heated the delicate lines of my not-yet-formed mating brand.

Panic stole my breath. *Is he the one? Please, not him. Not now. Don't trap me now.*

Then Titus shifted, sinking us lower until the water lapped against my jaw, and the tingling magic swept out of my brand and muddled my thoughts, leaving me still in pain and yet drifting.

I tried to concentrate on my power and pull it from my palms into my body, but my thoughts floated farther and farther away from me. Which wasn't good. If I had a concussion, I needed to stay awake for the next three to six hours before it was safe for me to sleep.

"Don't let me pass out," I said, my lips numb. "Not for a few hours."

But Titus didn't respond. He just kept looking at me with that frustrating mix of grief and pity and anger. I mustn't have said that out loud, and with the tingling magic of the pool dragging at my senses, I didn't have the strength to try again.

AMIAH

Every nerve in my body was on fire and my fingers trembled as I fought to undo the last button on my shirt. I'd spent too much magic just moving Titus's half of the leash spell to the resonance charm — and as a result to me — and had been in pain before we'd even begun our fight with Balwyrdan.

The demonic magic trapped inside me had coursed through my veins like acid, like it did now, and it had taken everything I'd had to stay conscious while that Spring Court asshole had been using the leash spell to suffocate Amiah and figure out which one of us was Titus. And while Titus's half of the spell hadn't had the same deadly effects as Amiah's half, it had still been excruciating.

And now we were trapped in Faerie, a realm I'd sworn I'd never return to.

"Jeez," Hawk said, tossing his shorts back to Cassius for the second time and hopping into the pool beside Titus. "You should have undressed her."

"She's fine as she is." Cassius yanked off his army boots and stepped out of his fatigues, which left him in black boxer briefs. He grabbed a small towel off the bench by the door and slid into the pool on Titus's other side as if he was unwilling to have the incubus between him and Amiah. And given how I was sure Cassius was in love with Amiah, that didn't surprise me. "I'm sure she wouldn't appreciate us seeing her naked. It's bad enough we've all seen her without a top."

"Well one of us is going to have to see her naked," Hawk said. "If she's going to heal herself, she'll need sleep to recover her magic and we can't put her to bed in wet clothes."

"And let me guess." Cassius shot Hawk a dirty look as he dipped the towel in the water and started gingerly washing the dried blood from her face. "You volunteer."

"I was thinking her *husband* should do the job. Surely being married to her means he's already seen her naked." Hawk flashed me a dirty grin then shrugged. "But if you insist."

"Stop trying to push my buttons. We need to get serious," Cassius said, carefully wiping at the blood crusted on her upper lip from her broken nose. "You know as well as I do that I didn't insist on you undressing Amiah, and Bane has already said he isn't her husband."

"She is Seireadan's though," Titus said, hugging her closer to his massive chest.

I bit back a groan and prayed Titus's possessiveness had everything to do with the fact that he was a shifter and took comfort from physical touch and closeness, and not because he, too, had feelings for her.

But then, he couldn't have real feelings for her. He didn't know her.

Except the fury in Titus's eyes when he'd seen Balwyrdan beating Amiah...

It had been the same fury in Cassius's eyes.

Which had been the same fury I'd felt. So no. Titus couldn't be in love with Amiah like Cassius. Seeing anyone beaten like that was enough to get my blood boiling, Titus's too, not to mention Hawk's. He hadn't even thought twice about joining us and killing Balwyrdan's thugs.

That had to be it. Titus's reaction to Amiah was sympathy for her injuries and a need to be touching someone because he was a shifter. There was also probably a big helping of sexual frustration because he'd been imprisoned for half a millennium and likely hadn't had any sexual contact in that time, either. Amiah was the first woman he'd come across, and he too had been fighting Hawk's magic from aligning our resonance with the resonance charm — and maybe still was since it took hours, sometimes days, for it to work its way out of a person's system if he didn't have sex to release it.

"She doesn't belong to Bane," Cassius said. "She doesn't *belong* to anyone."

Titus flashed his canines at Cassius. "She's his female. She bears his scent."

Oh, crap. He knew we'd had sex.

God, I was a moron. But of course he knew.

I'd still been lying in bed thinking about the amazing surprising sounds she'd made and how, even after she'd run from my bed, I wanted to make her let it all go again and scream my name. Titus had ripped open my bedroom door and would have smelled her and sex all over me.

"Because she slept in his clothes," Cassius replied. "She—"

"She's not mine," I interrupted before Titus could tell Cassius Amiah and I had slept together. That was something she definitely wouldn't want to get out even though, out of all of us, Cassius was the only one who didn't know — since Hawk would have felt us having sex with his ability to absorb sexual energy.

But in no way was Amiah mine. For fuck's sake, she'd freaked out and ran the minute she'd realized what we'd done.

And I had no idea why that bothered me so much. Even if she hadn't been a virgin — and holy shit I'd popped her cherry — she would have run. Having sex with me would have worked all of Hawk's magic out of her system and reality would have sunk in.

Except she'd considered paying for my help to remove her angelic mating brand with her body before she'd met Hawk. Had she actually been interested in me before then?

And that didn't matter. Clearly she'd realized sleeping with me had been a mistake, which, at the time, had been amusing — because oh, the things I could tease her about! One knowing look or the right innocent word and her cheeks would go red and she'd get flustered then angry.

But now the thought made me furious. If she hadn't run— if *I* hadn't given in to my need to release Hawk's magic from my system and slept with her, she wouldn't have been on the roof. Her beautiful face and body wouldn't be swollen and bruised and bleeding, and she wouldn't be in pain that even now, while unconscious, tightened her expression.

And now I'd told my mother I'd completed the fae marriage ritual with Amiah, making me fertile for Amiah and Amiah alone when angels could only have children with other angels.

We had to get out of the Winter Court before the assassination attempts started. Except there was no way we could fight our way to the Winter Court's portal to escape back to the mortal realm in our condition, and no matter how much I wanted to, I couldn't summon my own portal like my mother's seneschal could. Even if I wasn't in pain and infected with demonic magic, I still wouldn't have been able to make a portal. That just wasn't one of the things I could do despite my sorcerer's ability to weave the raw magic of Faerie to my will however I wanted it.

Biting back a groan of pain, I eased into the pool. At least the magical waters, unlike Amiah's healing magic, would help restore some of my magic.

But the warm water didn't relax me and the pool's magic, its soft tingling sensation seeping into my essence, set my nerves on edge.

I was back in Faerie and I'd brought Amiah with me.

"We just need to hold out until Amiah has recovered," I said to myself.

"You're going to need time to recover too," Hawk replied.

Crap. I'd said that out loud.

The incubus turned a pained gaze to me. Which was confusing as hell. His injuries hadn't been that bad and, unlike angelic healing that wasn't effective on incubi, the pool would heal him just like everyone else.

He squeezed his eyes shut and took in a shuddering breath and realization hit me.

He was a Sensitive, able to sense magic, and he was one of the most sensitive Sensitives I'd ever met. Faerie had to be overwhelming.

And while I was also on the sensitive end of the Sensitive scale, the magic that made Faerie *Faerie*, that seeped from the ground and drifted in the air, was a part of me. I accepted it and it me, at least in the courts, and I couldn't sense its full power. Hawk, a being from the Realm of Celestial Darkness, was a foreign body without the acceptance of Faerie's magic. He had to be sensing *all* of its power.

Jeez, I was missing everything right now.

"We need to get a shield on you first," I said. The demonic magic swelled and I bit back a groan.

"I can manage until you've recovered." Hawk jerked his thumb at Cassius. "That and it'll make Sparky feel better."

Cassius's eyes narrowed. "What will?"

"The fact I can't see shit. Faerie is so fucking magical it's like I'm staring at the sun. I'm surprised I haven't walked into a wall yet. At least people have different colored auras to differentiate them and I can sort of make out faces."

"So great. You're in rough shape," Cassius said to me,

missing the fact that Hawk couldn't get a good look at Amiah even if she was naked, "and you can't see. Anything up with you?" he asked Titus.

"Aside from the fact that we need to figure out what to call you since we can't use your real name?" I asked.

"I can't shift." Titus carefully brushed a strand of wet hair away from Amiah's bruised cheek, his pupils still slitted, his dragon still threatening to take over even though we weren't in immediate danger. "No glamour is going to make me look like a wolf if I do a full shift."

"And right now I'm out of fire." The muscles in Cassius's jaw flexed. "We need to recover. All of us. If we keep T's identity under wraps, how safe are we?"

"We're not," Titus said. "The Winter Queen wants Sebastian to produce an heir, which means she wants Amiah dead."

"Except we're in no condition to fight our way free," I forced out as the demonic magic flared again. "If we're careful and Amiah is never left alone, we should be okay for a while. My mother won't make her move right away and when she does, it won't be overt. If I have proof she attacked or killed my wife, I'll be able to demand a blood price."

"But only if you have proof," Titus growled, shifting to curl a little more around Amiah as if he was already trying to protect her with his body. "We can't count on the royal blood price to keep her safe."

"And it takes her longer to heal herself than others," Cassius said. "Her nose is broken, her wrist is broken, and I'd bet at least half of her ribs are as well. We're not talking a good rest and a few hours of healing. She's probably going to have to drain herself a few times and that's if she can concentrate past the pain."

"We'll supplement with the pools." I sank deeper into the pool so I could rest my head back against the ledge and fought to focus on the soft tingling magic flowing into my body and not the demonic magic burning through my veins. If I could just hold out, the pain would ease up.

Except it wouldn't fully ease up until I stopped channeling magic and released my sound blocking spell. God, how the hell was I going to break the leash spell between me and Amiah let alone remove her mating brand if just keeping something as simple as a sound block spell active hurt?

I wasn't.

If I could get back to full, I could probably manage the leash spell, but even with an external source, I wasn't going to be able to remove her brand. Not unless a miracle happened and someone pulled the demonic magic out of me — which was supposed to happen tomorrow... in the human realm.

Yeah, it looked like I was going to miss that meeting and piss off one powerful demon.

Someone else was going to have to remove Amiah's brand... although now that we were in Faerie, I might know someone who could... if he was still trustworthy.

"I'm not saying we stay here forever," I said. "Just long enough for Amiah to fully recover, and she's going to recover faster than my mother expects. As long as we can keep Amiah's magic a secret—"

"And we *are* going to keep it a secret," Cassius said.

"Only angels have the magical ability to heal others and if her power is revealed, she's in danger of being abducted again."

Something I prayed would never happen again.

"So what? Pretend Amiah is worse off than she actually is?" Hawk asked. "I'm not sure how that's much of an advantage."

"But it is an advantage." Cassius rubbed his face. "I'm just too tired to figure out how."

"My mother knows the pools will heal Amiah's cuts and bruises faster than her broken bones so we can convince her to put off my welcome home celebration until we've had time to get the lay of the land before we make our escape," I said.

"You don't trust that your knowledge of the Winter Court is still accurate, and you don't think we can just make a break for it." Cassius pursed his lips, his gaze growing unfocused with thought. "And you can't make a portal?"

"No," I said. "I have to use a preexisting one."

"Well, if we're going with that," Hawk said, "then the best plan is to use your party as a distraction for our escape."

Titus leveled a hard gaze at me, his golden eyes blandly brown, changed by the glamour hiding his identity. "We should avoid the court portal and go into the Wilds, find a portal there or sneak into one of the other courts and use theirs."

I bit back a groan. Going into the Wilds was a terrible, dangerous idea, and where Deaglan and Enowen had left me to die. But no one went into the Wilds because of how dangerous it was, especially to high fae like me. Which made it the perfect place to hide. "Agreed."

"And the Heart?" Cassius asked. "We can't forget that after Amiah's well-being, it's our top priority." Hawk opened his mouth and Cassius glared at him before he could speak. "No matter what you think of Amiah, she can keep us alive. That makes her more valuable than any of us."

And she'd do it at her own expense, no matter what anyone else wanted, or how it pissed off anyone else.

"I wasn't going to argue Amiah's usefulness," Hawk huffed. "I was going to say fuck the Heart."

"So you'd rather hide for who knows how long until the Heart goes back to sleep?" Cassius asked.

"This treasure hunt is going to kill at least one of us." Hawk's gaze jumped to Amiah then back to Cassius, his worry clear that the treasure hunt was going to kill Amiah. She was the least able to defend herself in a fight... and I had no idea what to make of his concern. "But hey, you want to go after it? That's fine by me. I'm good with keeping the pretty doctor company until this blows over. I'm sure I can keep her entertained," he said, his tone clear he was going to *entertain* her with his body.

The light in Cassius's eyes flared, smoke curled from his shoulders, and the water around him started to bubble.

Hawk flashed him a wicked grin. "You're welcome to join us if you'd like."

"I'm not having sex with Amiah," Cassius said, "and neither are you."

"Pretty sure that's her choice," Hawk drawled.

Cassius glared at him. "Only if you don't use your power to coerce her."

The demonic magic inside me flared and I bit back a groan. "We can't sit back and wait. We have to go after the Heart."

A part of me hated that I agreed with the uptight angel, but Cassius's original assumption was still right. Our best hope for survival was to get Faerie's Heart, the one magical thing that could destroy all of Faerie, and use our possession of it as leverage to protect ourselves.

"T—" Another agonizing flare stole my breath. Jeez. I'd hoped the pool's magic would have been more helpful easing the pain. "Can you sense any of the keys? Have any of them been empowered yet?"

Titus closed his eyes and slowly rubbed his hand up and down Amiah's arm, his palm never leaving her flesh. She looked small and fragile leaning against his massive body, the whole right side of her face an enormous swollen bruise.

I wanted to kill Balwyrdan again. Slower this time. Cassius had turned him to ash, but it had happened too quickly and the fae hadn't had enough time to suffer. He'd deserved to suffer.

The thought shocked me. Oh sure, if you wronged me, I got even. But I never set out to make anyone suffer.

Clearly I'd spent too much time around angels. There was a fine line between vengeance and justice... and I usually didn't give a shit about either. I certainly didn't give a shit about getting it for someone else. After my betrothed, Enowen, and one of my best friends, Deaglan, had tried to kill me, I swore I'd never be blinded by love or friendship again. No one and nothing took precedence over me, especially a woman. They were a good time and that was all. Including Amiah. If I was smart, I'd keep my distance from her before Cassius burned me for looking at her the wrong way.

Hell, if I was really smart, I'd find a way for Cassius to admit his love to Amiah so those two could finally get married, fuck, and make little angel babies like I'm sure Amiah wanted.

Except even if Amiah was in love with Cassius — which I also suspected — she'd never sleep with him until her mating brand was removed because she didn't want to get trapped in a soul bond.

And I couldn't blame her for that. I'd almost permanently bonded myself to a woman who'd only been marrying me to take the throne of the Winter Court. I still had no idea why she and Deaglan had jumped the gun and tried to kill me before Enowen and I had completed the marriage ceremony, making her the princess consort. Guess, Queen of the Shadow Court as Deaglan's wife was the better position. Although I didn't have any proof that she and Deaglan had actually married, that was just the most logical step for that power-hungry bitch.

Titus opened his eyes and for a second — because I knew what lay under his glamour and I was a Sensitive — his glamour wavered and they were strikingly gold, reminding me that he was the last dragon. The Heart had taken the lives of his entire species, and God help me, I didn't want it to take Amiah's life too.

"I can't sense any of the keys," Titus said.

"Which means what?" Hawk asked.

"It means we focus on using Bane's party to hide our escape," Cassius said. "If that changes, the plan changes. Until then, we protect Amiah until she's recovered."

Amiah, still unconscious, shuddered and whimpered, and Cassius's attention snapped to Titus, who froze as if he was afraid moving would hurt her.

"What did you do?" Cassius demanded.

"Nothing," Titus replied.

She whimpered again and threads of glowing faerie magic snaked through her cheek.

"It's the pool. We need to get her out." I didn't know why she was already showing the signs of being in the pool for too long. We'd barely been in the water for fifteen minutes. Perhaps it had something to do with her healing magic conflicting or augmenting the pool's magic.

Titus got out of the pool careful not to jostle her and headed to the towels and robes sitting on the bench by the door.

"Okay, so who's changing her?" Hawk asked, hopping out of the pool and striding to the towels.

The light in Cassius's eyes flared and a wisp of smoke curled from his shoulders as he got out. "Not you."

"You should do it, Cassius," I said. No way was I volunteering since he wasn't going to be happy with anyone else. And hey, maybe a little intimacy would start to break the ice between them.

Cassius stared at me as if I'd suggested he'd run naked through the halls or something. Then his expression grew pinched and he gave a tight nod.

Jeez. That man had so many issues. I staggered out

of the pool, agony still burning through me. The pool's magic had done little to ease the acidic burn of the demonic magic, and I pushed aside the niggling worry that the demonic magic was a bigger problem than I feared. At the moment, there wasn't anything I could do about it, so I was just going to have to push through.

Titus sat Amiah on the bench but didn't let go of her shoulders when Cassius approached.

"T," I said, grabbing a towel from the pile on the bench and offering it to him.

Amiah groaned and her eyelids fluttered open, but her breath picked up with short sharp painful gasps and her gaze was unfocused.

"Hawk, a little distraction," I said as I eased onto the bench beside her, leaning close to Titus's arm since he refused to move.

Hawk brushed a finger across her neck then stepped back, allowing Cassius to draw closer.

Her eyes rolled back and her expression softened with the seductive slide of Hawk's magic, reminding me of the look she'd had when I'd first pushed into her tight hot sheath and making me grateful I'd kept my pants on so no one could see my reaction. And I made a point of not looking away to see Hawk's expression, too. He knew I wanted to sleep with her again. There was just no getting around that. But given how she'd reacted, I doubted she'd let her defenses down long enough to return to my bed.

"Guys?" she asked, her voice too soft for the stern, desperate-to-be-in-control angel that she was. At least her eyes were clearer as her gaze slid from Hawk to Cassius to Titus to me.

"Cassius is going to help you change out of your wet clothes," I said.

She bobbed her head for a second in agreement then her eyes flashed wide. "I— ah... I can manage myself," she gasped.

"You can't," Cassius said, his expression hard and icy. He gave Titus a nudge, who snatched the towel from me and strode to the far side of the grotto to get out of his wet pants and dry off.

"No. I'm good with Hawk's magic," she insisted. "See." She sat forward and managed not to make a sound but it was clear she was in agony.

"Stop being stubborn." Cassius crossed his arms and glared at her, the light in his eyes blazing. "You're in worse shape than the last time and I can't just take you home."

Last time? Good Lord, had she been beaten before?

"You're not changing by yourself," Cassius said, "and I'm pretty sure you'd rather I saw you in your underwear than T, Hawk, or Bane."

Her eyes widened even more. "I'd rather Sebastian."

"You what?" Cassius looked at her stunned as if he couldn't believe what she'd just said.

And hell, I couldn't believe it either. I probably hadn't heard her correctly, what with the demonic magic burning through me.

"Sebastian can help me change," she said.

Smoke burst from Cassius's hands and with a growl, he yanked it back under his skin. "I see." His stunned expression vanished behind a hard, icy mask, and he gave me a tight nod before grabbing a towel and joining Titus and Hawk on the other side of the grotto.

"Are you that afraid of your brand awakening you'll refuse his help?" I asked, keeping my voice low so the others couldn't hear. "The mark is so pale he won't be able to see it. Hell, Hawk wouldn't be able to see it unless he actively looked for it. Pretty sure just seeing you in your panties won't do anything." I rolled my eyes at her, trying to ease the fear still in her expression by making light of the situation. "Those panties weren't even much to look at."

"And those panties are still somewhere in your bedroom," she said, refusing to make eye contact with me. "I don't want Cassius thinking Balwyrdan raped me. It's bad enough I was— Again—" She grabbed the hem of Cassius's T-shirt with her one good hand to pull it over her head but clutched the fabric instead, her hand trembling. "I swore I'd be strong, swore—"

Her breath hitched and a tear rolled down her cheek.

"But I'm not strong," she whispered. "I never was."

Frustration and anger squeezed my heart even as relief flooded me at the fact that Balwyrdan hadn't raped her. His usual M.O. was beating to achieve maximum pain, but there'd always been a chance he'd try something different or already given her to his men for their entertainment.

"And no one else... you know?" The words slipped out before I could stop them. *Please, no... Because Cassius will lose his shit if she's been raped, and I don't want to deal with a rampaging angel. Really.*

"No." She raised her gaze to meet mine, her angel

glow dim in her shockingly bright blue eyes revealing just how exhausted she was. Then, with an effort that made my chest hurt to watch, she slid her icy mask of professionalism into place. "And feel free to tell Cassius that so I don't have to have this conversation again. Now. All of my ribs are broken so I might pass out. Be ready for that," she said, her tone brusque. "And don't let me stay unconscious. I need to deal with my concussion first. *Then* I can pass out."

Jeez. And she didn't think she was strong.

AMIAH

I WOKE WITH FIERY AGONY FLOODING MY BODY AND IT TOOK me a terrifying moment to focus my whirling thoughts to remember where I was and what had happened. We'd been dragged to the Winter Court in Faerie, Sebastian had told his mother — the Queen! — that we were married, then after a momentary dip in a magical pool that made my own healing magic stutter and flare uncontrollably, Sebastian helped me dry off and change.

And I wasn't going to think about him seeing me naked again, or the fact that I'd refused Cassius's help because I didn't want him to know I'd lost my underwear. As it was, Cassius had barely said more than a few words to me, which might have had something to do with me barely hanging onto consciousness... but probably not, and I was sure I was going to have to give him an explanation as to why I'd chosen Sebastian to help me and not him.

After that, Hawk had sent another bone-melting swell of his seductive magic into me, somehow making it easier to focus past the pain, and I concentrated on healing my concussion. Thankfully my magic recognized it as the worst injury since it hindered my ability to heal anything else.

Then Titus carried me to the suite the Winter Queen had assigned us. The big shifter had tucked me into a massive plush bed big enough to hold all of us, and the guys argued about who would stay with me. Sebastian had suggested Hawk so when I woke he could ease my pain enough for me to use my magic again. Cassius had said absolutely not.

In the end, they'd all stayed, Hawk in a chair pulled up to the side of the bed, Sebastian in another chair on the other side of the large bedroom, Titus on the floor by the door, and Cassius perched on the far side of the bed as far away as he could get from me.

Shortly after that, I expended the last drop of my magic and passed out.

With a groan, I cracked open my good eye — my right one was still partially swollen shut — and a gentle wave of seductive magic unfurled low within me as a warm body lying beside me shifted closer.

My heart picked up. Someone was in bed with me. For a second I ached for whoever it was to wrap his arms around me and just hold me. I missed the comfort of being in a warm strong embrace and feeling the soft pulse of life force from someone. But as much as I craved that, my body wasn't ready for that kind of contact. It was a miracle I hadn't punctured a lung or my heart or any number of organs while being carried around the Winter Court.

I turned my head, my muscles screaming at the movement, and came nose to nose with Hawk. He was under the covers with me and I had no idea if he still wore the clothes he'd changed into after bathing in the pool or not.

Heat flooded my cheeks.

He could be naked.

I could be naked.

Just because Sebastian had helped me put on a robe, didn't mean someone hadn't undressed me while I was unconscious. And even if I was still in the robe, only a soft silky tie held it together.

"Why are you in bed with me?" I squeaked, my reaction embarrassing me more than realizing I was in bed with the sexy incubus.

"Why not?" He traced a finger along my jaw, sending another swell of magic heating my insides.

"Didn't Cassius tell you no?" I was pretty sure that had been part of their argument, which was why Hawk had ended up in the chair.

"He's not here. It's just you and me and what Cassius doesn't know won't hurt him." He flashed me a wicked grin, but it didn't reach his eyes. In fact, the hellfire in his unusual blue irises was banked and his expression was pinched. He was still breathtakingly handsome, but he also looked exhausted and in pain.

Had he been hurt worse than I thought? I'd been in too much pain and hadn't checked him or anyone else for serious injuries.

I eased my good hand out from under the thick white comforter and rested it on the side of his neck, pushing a small thread of magic into him to assess his injuries.

Nothing more serious than what I'd seen before. The lacerations on his ribs and right biceps were scabbed over but still painful and the bruise on the left side of his torso — that curled around his back to his left kidney — was still tender.

My compulsion to heal kicked in and, before I realized what I was doing, I pushed a stronger thread of power into him, even though logically I knew it took more power to heal an incubus than it did to heal myself. The best way to heal him would be to kiss him — which I wasn't going to do because my face throbbed.

"Whoa," he said, gingerly grabbing my wrist and pulling my hand from his neck. "What are you doing?"

A small snap of backlash from being disconnected from him jolted through me and my thoughts stuttered. What *was* I doing? I was in worse shape than he was and it was a waste to use my magic on him.

His hellfire swelled and so, too, did his sensual magic seeping through my veins. "There are more effective ways to heal me."

"I'm not up for *that*." As much as a part of me was starting to think it was a great idea.

"Oh, I know. But I'm not that hurt. A few naughty thoughts will do the trick." He gave me his wicked smile again and this time it did reach his eyes. The look sent a small shiver of desire racing through me that reignited the agony in my chest, which he melted away with another surge of magic.

This was a bad idea.

And yet when I'd been with Sebastian, just for a

moment, I'd been free of worry, of my need to be in control, of everything.

And I'd been taken again.

I shoved that thought back. I wasn't going to think about it. Ever. And Hawk pleasuring me would be the perfect distraction.

"What if I want more than just thoughts?" It wasn't fair if Hawk was just going to tease me. I was done with being celibate and he'd already proven more than capable of satisfying me with his magic. Hadn't I decided before Balwyrdan kidnapped me that I'd take control of my desires?

My pulse stuttered, and the part of me that screamed for control demanded I take it back and never be a victim again. Asking someone to pleasure me meant they controlled my pleasure. I couldn't allow that and even if there were sexual situations where I had control, I was in no condition for that and I still needed to ask someone to do that with me.

"Hey." Hawk hooked a finger under my chin and drew my attention back to him. "Whatever you're thinking, it's not a naughty thought." His hellfire dimmed. "Bane said Balwyrdan didn't force himself on you."

"He didn't and I don't want to talk about it." I didn't ever want to think about it. I'd tried to escape and been helpless against Balwyrdan's control of the leash spell. And even if he hadn't controlled the leash spell, I'd still have been helpless. I was just so damned helpless and pathetic. After being kidnapped by that human all those years ago I'd vowed never to be foolish and helpless again, and yet I'd spent my life letting my mating brand control me, waiting for a soul mate who'd then control my life.

And with the brand, there'd be no escape and no one to save me. Especially if Sebastian couldn't remove it before it fully formed. Once formed there wasn't even the hope of being free.

How could I keep control of my life when my loss of control was inevitable?

I struggled to shove those thoughts deep down inside me as well. There wasn't anything I could do about it and if I wanted to be useful — not the pathetic helpless angel that I was — I needed to heal myself. I was only useful as a healer and I wouldn't be able to heal anyone in my condition.

Focus on Hawk. Let him distract you. After this mess was done, I'd never see him again. He, like Sebastian, couldn't possibly be my soul mate so there was no fear of my mating brand awakening. That, and I didn't know if Sebastian would welcome me to his bed again after running out on him last night. He'd had a strange look in his eyes when he'd helped me change, but I could have imagined that since I'd barely been conscious. Hawk, however, survived on sex, and if he was going to be stuck with us, we were going to have to figure out a way for him to feed.

"Let's get you healed," I said.

His lips quirked and a flicker of his hellfire danced in his eyes. "Because you get nothing out of it."

"Only if you just tease me. But you wouldn't do that," I replied, my heart pounded with the fear that he'd reject me. *Please. I need this.* I needed it more than he needed healing. "You said you're generous. Was that a lie?"

"Oh, I am." His magic swelled, rushing heated desire through me. It wasn't the powerful bone-melting hunger when he'd kissed me in the abandoned bathhouse, but a softer, languid need. "I just need to be careful about this. And you need to lie there and enjoy it."

"What makes you think I wouldn't?"

"I barely know you and I already know you're terrible at letting others do things for you." He slid a hand between my knees and shifted closer. The demonic heat radiating from his body seeped into my skin and swirled with the warmth of his magic. My body grew heavy, my senses drifting on a gentle sensual ache. "You gave it up for Bane and then freaked out."

"I didn't freak out."

"Baby, from the sexual energy radiating off him, he would have fucked you all night long." Hawk's fingers teased up the inside of my thigh, and the languid need intensified in my core and my aching grew into insistent throbbing. "And from the energy radiating off of you, you would have let him, but your mind got in the way."

"I didn't expect to sleep with him. I needed to figure out what that meant?"

"Amiah." He leaned close, his breath feathering against my tender, bruised neck, swirling with his sensual heat. "It didn't have to *mean* anything. All you had to do was let go and enjoy it."

The thought sent a frozen snap of fear cutting through Hawk's sensual heat. Letting go meant risking I'd do something foolish, that someone could hurt me again.

And yet that was all I wanted. To let go of my fear and my desperate need to be in control. I wanted my mind to turn off, just for a little while, and to just feel.

"You know you want it." He brushed a finger through my folds and sent another rush of heat into me, melting my fear. "You want his cock inside you again. You want mine."

He flicked my clit and sensation shot through me. I gasped, spiking pain through my chest, but his power billowed, softening the agony, turning it into a shocking, exquisite pleasure.

"You want both of us at the same time."

I shuddered at the memory of Sebastian's heated gaze while Hawk had used his magic to make me orgasm in his tent yesterday, and my breath picked up. Watching Hawk seduce me had turned Sebastian on, and the idea of him watching Hawk slide into me turned me on. God, the idea of both of them filling me, moving inside me, sent the whispering ripples of an orgasm through me.

I wanted their hands and lips on me, their bodies pressed tight against mine. I wanted to give up my desperate, exhausting need for control. I wanted them to — God, I wanted them to pleasure me until I couldn't think straight.

"Now that's a naughty thought." Hawk hummed low in his throat, dipped a finger inside me, and rubbed the slickened tip over my clit, drawing a soft moan from me. "When you're all healed up, we're going to have so much fun."

Another whispering ripple of an orgasm swept through me.

"And we'll make Bane watch."

He pushed two fingers inside me and ground his thumb against my clit. His magic sharpened to a pinpoint inside me at the perfect spot where his fingers rubbed again and again, faster and faster. My breath picked up and he melted the pain of each inhalation into a desire that built inside me until I couldn't contain it any longer.

Hot, sensual pleasure rushed through me, infused in my cells, teasing my essence, and my muscles clenched around his fingers. The orgasm wasn't shattering like the ones with Sebastian. My body wouldn't have been able to handle that. But it still filled me with overwhelming, breathtaking bliss, and I rode the sensation, letting it steal my thoughts. There'd be time to worry about everything later. Right now, I felt amazing. I felt free. And I never wanted the feeling to end.

AMIAH

Hawk cleaned up in the en suite bathroom and left, and I, still warm and drifting on my orgasm and his magic, pulled my power from my palms and focused on knitting my broken bones back together.

I didn't know how long I lay there with my eyes closed concentrating on the slow agonizing process of healing myself, but it was long enough to drain every last ounce of my magic, which was only enough to partially heal my ribs.

Now I lay, still under the covers, the bliss of Hawk's magic a memory, staring at the softly glowing, translucent ceiling. Because of its plain surface, it was the only place I could look where the room's spinning didn't nauseate me even though the walls with their hint of swirling glyphs were pretty plain as well. They, too were translucent and softly glowing, giving the suggestion that I could see through them without actually being able to see through them. Which I appreciated since I didn't want people watching me. But there also weren't any windows, and that made my heart pound. I didn't like being unable to see the sky. I needed—

I squeezed my eyes shut and struggled to slow my breathing against the pain of my partially healed ribs. Even with my eyes closed, I could feel the room whirling and the walls pressing close.

I had to find space and sky. I couldn't just lie there in the closed off room. I needed to think, focus, figure out... everything.

Except exhaustion dragged at my limbs from having drained all my magic — and I wasn't even moving. And while my mind screamed to run, the rest of me dreaded the thought of getting up.

But no matter what my body wanted, at some point, I was going to have to rise. I wouldn't be able to restore my magic without eating and then sleeping again, and before I did that, I wanted to clean up — *and see sky. Please.*

The dip in the healing pool had helped my cuts, bruises, and achy muscles a bit, but it hadn't been completely cleansing, and my insides squirmed with the need for a more open space as much with the need to scrub the grime of last night's events from my body — some physical but most of it emotional grime.

Biting back a moan of pain in the hopes that the guys, wherever they were, wouldn't hear me, I sat up and slid my legs over the side of the bed.

The room lurched and darkened and I sucked in more, painful breaths. I really didn't want to vomit with broken ribs, but I also needed to prove to myself that I could do this, that I wasn't completely helpless.

After being rescued from that human faith healer, it had taken years to get Cassius to stop looking at me and treating me like I was fragile, and that time I'd just been a little beaten up and drained of all my magic. He was going to be impossible now.

I stood on shaky legs and shuffled over to the wall to keep my balance. At least my legs hadn't been injured. And while draining my power had left me dizzy and exhausted, I was still able to move without help... although I was sure that was something Cassius would also disagree with.

I was halfway to the bathroom — really only a handful of feet away from the bed — when the bedroom door opened.

"For the love of—" Cassius growled. "What are you doing?"

I didn't even try to look at him. Moving my head that much would make the room whirl and my stomach was already threatening a revolt. "I'm going to the bathroom."

"You should have called for help." He strode to my side and reached for me, but I waved him off as best I could with my elbow since my good hand held me steady against the wall and my broken one was drawn protectively close to my chest.

"My legs aren't broken. I'm just a little dizzy."

"And if you fall and injure yourself worse?" he asked. He wore a loose white tunic that hung to mid-thigh and loose white pants, a match to what the fae men had been wearing in the Winter Queen's throne room.

"Then you'll be able to say I told you so."

"What's gotten into you?" The angel glow in his eyes

flared, revealing his concern. Not that I needed it to tell me he was concerned. "You know this isn't practical."

I bit back a sigh and shuffled a few steps closer to the bathroom. He was right. Me trying to do this on my own wasn't practical... and yet I had to do it, had to prove I could do *something*.

God, when had I become that person? The one who willfully did something that went against common sense?

And if I was being practical, it wasn't safe for me to take a shower by myself, not until I was steadier on my feet. Which meant no matter how much I wanted to scrub off the memory of the pleasure in Balwyrdan's eyes every time he'd hit or suffocated me, I needed to eat first and get the room to stop spinning. Because I really didn't want to shower with Cassius or anyone else watching me.

Jeez, I really just want a shower.

Cassius stiffened and a wisp of smoke curled from his hand. "I'll get Bane then."

"You'll what?"

He turned on his heel and rushed from the room, leaving the door partially open and letting me see into what looked like a sitting area. The walls were the same as the bedroom, translucent and glowing — although the glow was much brighter out there than in the bedroom — and I still couldn't see a window. A dark blue couch sat with its back to me, and I could see the front edge of an armchair.

"Bane," he barked. "Help Amiah."

"What?" Bane asked as he sat up on the couch and rubbed his face — had he been sleeping there? For a second his complexion was gray, then his full-body fae glow flickered back to life.

"Amiah wants to shower," Cassius said, "and she's not doing it by herself."

Guess I'd said that thought out loud.

"You didn't need to announce it." Sebastian rolled his eyes at him. "Have fun."

"She's already made it clear which of us can see her naked," Cassius ground out.

"She *is* his female," Titus said from somewhere out of sight.

"She's not my female," Sebastian insisted.

"If none of you want to help her—" Hawk said, sauntering into sight, oozing sex and sin and flashing me a wicked grin. He too wore the loose white pants, sitting dangerously low on his hips, and no tunic, showing off his amazing physique. "I wouldn't mind more alone time with the pretty doctor."

"Absolutely not." More wisps of smoke curled from Cassius's hands.

"We're going to have to figure out how he's going to feed," Sebastian said. "Especially if we don't trust anyone in court."

"He's not doing it while Amiah is naked," Cassius said.

"Well if you want to be naked, I roll that way, too," Hawk purred, walking his fingers down Cassius's chest.

Fire sparked up Cassius's forearms and he slapped Hawk's hand away. "Why don't you seduce information out of the fae? That should keep you going for a while."

"We agreed, no one leaves this suite alone," Sebastian said, "so unless you want to join Hawk with his seduction, that option is off the table."

Cassius stiffened.

"And it still doesn't address who's helping Amiah," Hawk said, his grin deepening.

"Her mate," Titus replied.

"For fuck's sake." Sebastian threw his hands up in exasperation. "I'm not her mate."

"She chose you to help her change," Titus said.

This was ridiculous.

"I can handle it just fine on my own." I didn't want any of them to help me shower, and I certainly didn't want them arguing over who I belonged to or who could sleep with me or who my mate was.

"No, you can't," Cassius shot back, his eyes filled with that worried, pitying look I hated.

I wasn't going to win this argument with him. No one was. He'd dug his heels in, determined to *protect* me whether I wanted his protection or not, commanding me like I was one of his agents.

"Fine. Sebastian, if you would." I shuffled the last few steps to the bathroom and clutched the smooth stone counter to wait for him.

The door to the bedroom clicked closed, and Sebastian, in a dark blue version of the tunic and pants with silver embroidery sewn around the neck and cuffs, walked toward me.

"You're going to get me burned alive," he said, stopping in the doorway.

"Cassius wouldn't do that."

I purposefully avoided looking in the mirror in front of me and turned my attention to the rest of the bathroom. It looked a lot like a smaller version of the healing grotto with natural rock and winter greenery. The sink was a bowl carved in a wide stone pillar jutting from the floor and the toilet was also stone. Beyond that lay a pool sunk into the floor large enough for all of us — like the bed — and a waterfall, its flow gently tumbling into a shower-like area. A second, thinner waterfall diverted from the first and trickled down the wall to fill the pool.

"You didn't see him trying to get to you last night and he's been pissed since we got you in bed."

"He's been upset since he thought his brother's soul mate was a human who endangered his life." If I thought about it, he'd been upset for the last twenty-three years. Ever since his youngest brother had been killed in the war.

I reached for the tie on my robe, my thoughts stalling on the shower. No curtain to hide behind. Sebastian couldn't just wait in the bathroom to ensure I was okay. He was going to see me naked. Again.

I'd been in too much shock in the healing grotto for that to really register... him seeing me naked... again. Now my pulse picked up with uncertainty and embarrassment heated my cheeks.

"That doesn't make me feel better," Sebastian said. "The next time you need someone to see you naked, don't pick me. Pick him."

"I don't *need* for anyone to see me naked now." My

throat tightened. It was an irrational reaction, but his words still stung. He didn't want to see me naked again. Of course, I didn't want him to see me naked either. Not to mention I'd run from his bed. That had probably stung as well. And really, we weren't even friends. Just two people forced together by horrible circumstances who'd had a momentary lapse in judgment. "And why would I pick Cassius? I'm not adding anyone else to the list of men who've seen me naked."

He snorted. "You might want to tell Hawk that in front of Cassius. I'm sure he's convinced Cassius that he wants to see you naked, and Cassius doesn't know him well enough to know he's not going to risk his life and do something."

My cheeks grew hotter at the memory of Hawk's magic and fingers inside me.

Okay, so maybe I *did* want to add to the list of men who've seen me naked, and I would beg to differ on the incubus not doing anything. But that was none of Sebastian's business... unless we invited him to participate.

The thought sent a shiver rushing through me and I gasped, which shot agony through my chest and forced me to clutch the counter to keep standing.

"Fucking hell." Sebastian rushed up behind me, grabbed my hips, and gingerly drew my back against his chest to help steady me.

His breath feathered against my neck and my pulse picked up even as a part of my essence sighed at his closeness. I didn't know what I craved more. Just being held or being satisfied.

"He's determined to protect your virtue," Sebastian said.

"I never asked him to, and it's not the Dark Ages. I can do whatever I want with my virtue."

"Not if it's going to turn me into a pile of ash. It's obvious he's barely in control, but fuck— I had no idea he was that powerful. Did you?"

"No." I knew Cassius's magic was stronger than most angels and I'd seen him create a wall of fire to keep people away from us, but I'd never seen him make anything that burned as hot as the pillar he'd encased Balwyrdan in.

"If I'd known he was that powerful, I'd have never slept with you."

Fantastic! So now Cassius was controlling me just by being Cassius. I couldn't get away from it. God, I wanted to scream. I was free. I was strong. I was in control. And maybe if I told that to myself enough times it'd be true.

"Well, then," I said through gritted teeth as I pulled out of Sebastian's embrace and staggered the rest of the way to the shower then turned to glare at him. "I suppose it's a good thing I left your bed when I did. Wouldn't want Cassius to know two consenting adults had sexual intercourse. I didn't think you were a coward."

The muscles in his jaw flexed and something dark flashed across his expression. "It's called self-preservation and I wouldn't talk about being a coward."

"What's that supposed to mean?"

"That you're in love with Cassius, but you're too scared of your mating brand to admit it."

"I'm not in love with Cassius. We're friends." And I'd

never allowed myself to think of him in any other way because my mating brand hadn't woken when we met, and at the time, I'd been waiting for my soul mate.

Was I in love with Cassius?

I'd ached to be closer to him when I'd healed him in Sebastian's bathroom. But that had just been my yearning for sexual release and my lack of willpower because Sebastian had kept teasing me and reminding me about sex. I hadn't really wanted Cassius, just sex.

And could I love someone who didn't see me as an equal? In Cassius's eyes, I was a pathetic, weak angel he had to keep protecting. He'd never be able to stop seeing me as the angel he'd rescued all those years ago.

"You don't look at him like he's a friend," Sebastian said. "You look at him like you want to fuck him."

"I'm sure I look at all of you like that, no thanks to you and Hawk." I dipped my hand into the waterfall, unable to hold his piercing gaze. The water was cool. It wasn't going to be the warm relaxing shower I wanted, but it was better than nothing. "I'm over a hundred and twenty. That in itself is a strain on a vow of celibacy, and then I met you, and…"

"So it's my fault you broke your ridiculous vow? I gave you more than enough opportunity to say no. I warned you. Told you to get the fuck out of my shower," he snapped.

"You did. But that's—"

"You angels are unfucking believable. You have a glimmer of humanity, freak out, and blame it on someone else. You and Cassius deserve each other. You're so God damned uptight."

"I'm not in love with—" There was no point in denying it, and it didn't really matter if my love for Cassius was deeper than just a friendship or not. Sebastian and I weren't friends.

Why was that so hard to remember?

Because I'd liked the way he'd looked at me last night, like I was the most beautiful woman in the world, like I was, in that moment, even with all my flaws, perfect. And I'd loved the way he'd made me feel.

I wanted him to look at me that way again, to feel that way again.

Except was it him I wanted or just *someone*?

Well, it was clear, it was never going to be him again.

"I realize we were just getting something out of our system. I know it will never happen again." The water sluicing over my hand started to warm up. Guess the magic of Faerie warmed the water when someone wanted to use it. Thank goodness, because with my broken ribs and throbbing face, I didn't want to be shivering through my shower.

"Once you've removed the leash spell and this situation with the Heart is resolved, I expect you to keep your word and attempt to remove my brand. Now please," I said, not giving him a chance to respond, "wait for me in the bedroom. I didn't ask for your help and it's not needed."

"Of course you didn't. You don't need anyone," Sebastian said, his voice low, his words stinging yet again.

I didn't understand why the idea of never sleeping with him again hurt so much, why not needing him made me feel lonely, or why I couldn't close my emotions off like I used to be able to.

But then Sebastian was the first and only man I'd ever slept with. Even if I didn't want a romantic relationship with anyone, the surprising, amazing moment with Sebastian last night would be forever branded on my soul.

CASSIUS

THIS WAS A NIGHTMARE. *PLEASE LET IT BE A NIGHTMARE. Please let me wake up and everything be fine. Let Amiah be fine, not bruised and broken. God, she has to be fine.*

But she wasn't, and I didn't know, even after she'd healed her injuries, if she ever would be again. Abducted twice. Hurt twice— this time worse.

I didn't know how I could have protected her from Balwyrdan, but I should have. I should have paid more attention to her, not assumed she'd be okay when she'd left the kitchen last night to check on Bane. So much had happened in just one day. Hell, I was still reeling from it all and I'd seen heavy combat during the war. Amiah had only ever seen the results of combat, she'd never had to deal with anything like—

My throat tightened and fire snapped up my forearms before I could control my magic and suck it back under my skin.

Hawk, who'd taken Bane's place stretched out on the

couch, raised his eyebrows. "You know staring at the bedroom door isn't going to make their shower any faster."

Their shower.

She'd wanted Bane's help.

Not mine.

And I had no idea why.

Sure, our relationship had never been more than friends, but out of all of us, I would have thought she'd have trusted me the most. The friend who'd been by her side for a hundred years, not some sex-craving fae she'd met only a few weeks ago.

What did that say about us? About my hopes to be more than friends?

Another spark burst from my hands and hissed on the floor that felt like marble but looked like ice, reminding me why I couldn't be anything other than a friend to her. I'd hurt her if we got intimate and I couldn't live with that.

God, I could hurt her just standing too close.

My magic burned under my skin, scorching through my veins, and I couldn't get it to calm down. Seeing Amiah beaten by that monster had been the final straw. I'd been struggling all day and that horrible moment on the roof where Balwyrdan had been hitting her and I'd been helpless to stop it had been more than I could take. Whatever had been inside me holding back my inferno, the fire that I had let roar to life during the war and hadn't been able to extinguish, had shattered, and now all I had was a tenuous strength of will keeping me from constantly dripping a stream of molten flames on the floor.

And I hadn't even gotten a full night's rest. I wasn't at full power yet. How the hell was I going to keep it in once I was?

I'd have to find the time to release it. Except letting go last night and letting my power rage hadn't burned it out. Probably because my rage and fear still squeezed my heart.

She could have died.

And my failure to protect her was clear as day, red and swollen on her body.

Bane had said the pool would heal her from the outside in — unlike her magic which worked inside out — but she hadn't looked any better clinging to the bedroom wall in a stupid, headstrong act to take a shower without help.

Now she was in the shower with Bane — Bane! — who without a doubt, even in her broken condition, was going to hit on her. He'd hit on her every chance he got, seeing her naked — and this time while she was more coherent — would be an opportunity he wouldn't be able to pass up.

Another spark leaped from my hand and hit Hawk's bare shoulder.

"For fuck's sake." He jerked up, his hellfire blazing and his unique healing making the minor burn vanish between one blink and the next.

God, was he getting sexual energy as we waited?

I tried to shove that thought aside. As Amiah had

pointed out, she was her own woman, she could do as she pleased with whomever she pleased. But there was no way she was thinking straight after last night, and someone had to watch out for her until she was.

I jerked away from the bedroom door and dragged my attention across the sitting room. It looked like a sitting room from the mortal realm with a couch and three chairs and a table, and I didn't know if that was normal for the fae realm or if the Winter Queen had provided us with furnishings we were more familiar with.

Probably not. All she cared about was Bane— or rather Seireadan. I doubted she'd put us in a suite where her son's bodyguards would be comfortable, and given what Titus and Bane had said in the grotto about her wanting Amiah dead, I doubted she'd put us in a room to make Amiah comfortable.

Aside from the sitting room and the main bedroom, there was one other bedroom with a dozen cots, presumably for a few guards and servants, and another simple, adjoined bathroom.

And no windows.

In fact, I hadn't seen a window since we'd gotten here.

My insides squirmed at that, even though my need for sky and open spaces wasn't as strong as other angels... as Amiah's.

"Would you just take a breath," Hawk said.

I glared at him and realized I was smoking with little flecks of fire dancing up my forearms. Jeez.

"I know angels are high-strung," Hawk said, "but man, you're going to burn yourself up if you don't relax."

"My fire doesn't burn me. Not unless I want it to." Most of the time. I took a deep breath and heaved my smoke and fire back under my skin.

I could handle this and my out-of-control emotions. I had to handle this. I just needed to wrap my heart and mind in ice and freeze the blaze inside me into submission. It was the only way I was going to be able to think straight.

"You mentioned the Wilds in the pool last night," I forced out, turning my attention to Titus who'd squeezed his massive frame into one of the armchairs. "Tell me about them."

"The Wilds is the space between the Faerie Courts where the magic of every court has no control. At times it's a wasteland, at others a wild untamed jungle." Titus shrugged. "It all depends on what it feels like at the time."

"So even the Wilds are semi-sentient?" Everything I'd been told about Faerie — which hadn't been much — implied that the realm itself was alive... sort of. That sentience was muted in each court, the Monarch's will taking over their bubble of existence in the realm, but everything else was wild and free, and—

And that was everything I knew about Faerie. Less than two dozen fae sorcerers had come to the mortal realm to help the Angelic Defense fight Michael and save humanity and earth's supernatural beings, and they'd pretty much stuck to themselves with the exception of a few dalliances that produced about a dozen faekin worldwide.

"The Wilds are the soul of Faerie where it's the most

free and unrestrained from the courts and it doesn't like most high fae, that's what Seireadan is, so they avoid it."

"So there's less of a chance the Winter Queen will send her men after us." I could see why the Wilds was our best option. "How dangerous will it be for us and Bane?"

"I don't know how it will react to beings from other realms, but it will try to take back the magic inside Seireadan," Titus said. "My ancestral nest is in the Wilds. If we can get to it, we'll be safe within its magical walls for a while."

"How long is a while?" Hawk asked.

Titus shrugged. "I don't know. Depends on how much Faerie wants Seireadan."

The door to the outside hall flew open and I jerked to face it, my fire flaring, searing my insides and blazing around my hands. Titus and Hawk also jumped to their feet, ready to fight, as a pair of identical looking ice women in white flowing dresses carried in two large platters of food and set them on the table.

Outside, the two guards who'd been watching us since we'd left the throne room, stood statue-still on the other side of the hall, not watching out for trouble but watching in at us.

"Her majesty is concerned. His highness hasn't requested food yet," one of the women said, her gaze searching the room, clearly looking for Bane.

"His highness is with his wife," Hawk said, the words screeching against my soul. His wife. As if she'd ever marry a man like Bane. As if she'd ever be interested in a man like him—

Except right now she was naked in the shower with him.

"Tell her majesty, he'll eat when he eats," Hawk flashed a wicked grin at the woman, who didn't respond to his seductive nature. In fact she didn't even seem to notice he was half naked as he ushered her and the other woman out the door.

"Hmm," he said, pressing his back to the door his expression tight. "I can't affect the servants with my magic."

"Because they're constructs," Titus said, examining the trays of food. "They're beings made of ice and controlled by the queen's will. They live only to serve. They have no other desires."

"Well, shit," Hawk said, "I can't even flirt out a snack with the servants. I *am* going to have to get my meals from Amiah."

My fire flared and I gritted my teeth, managing to keep even my smoke inside. *Frozen blizzards. Encased in ice. Hard and cold.*

Hard and God damned cold.

"You can go a few days without a meal. We'll be out of Faerie by then." We were *going* to be out of Faerie by then. I would not have Amiah offering herself up to feed Hawk. And she'd do it, too, because she always gave everything she had to help someone.

And I wasn't going to let Hawk or anyone take advantage of that.

"Or," Hawk said, drawing out the word and leveling his gaze on me as his hellfire flared, accentuating the wicked gleam in his eyes. "You could relieve some of that stress and sleep with her. A little secondhand sex will also keep me going. You and she have a thing going, don't you?"

"A thing?"

Hawk shrugged. "Yeah, you want to sleep with her and she's waiting for you to make your move, and neither of you are doing anything about it." He rolled his eyes. "Because angel courtship is so fucking complicated and awkward and uptight."

"You think I want to—? No, I—" My gaze jumped back to the bedroom door and my inferno seared around my heart. "After what happened she can't be thinking straight. I'm not going to— That would be—"

Terrifying.

Amazing.

Wrong.

So very wrong. She wanted someone with a ferocious passion. Not someone who couldn't fully show her how he felt. She'd never want someone like me. We'd known each other for almost a century. If she wanted someone like me, I would have known by now. It didn't matter that I hadn't even known my true feelings for her until only twenty-five years ago. Surely she would have said something. Which meant we weren't meant to be. The best I could hope for was friendship.

"She's like a sister," I forced out, praying my hard tone ended this conversation.

I wasn't going to discuss my love life or lack thereof with an incubus, and I sure as hell wasn't going to let him take advantage of Amiah.

"You keep telling yourself that," Hawk drawled.

I jerked my attention away and reached for the first thing on the platters of food that my gaze landed on, an apple nestled among a pile of grapes. Even if I wasn't going to allow Hawk to eat, the rest of us should, and whenever we could since I had no idea when we'd get our next meal.

But Titus grabbed my wrist, stopping me before I could take it.

"It could be enspelled," he said. "We wait for Seireadan to check it out. He can sense spells."

I opened my mouth to ask if the Winter Queen would actually enspell food and give it to her son, but given that she'd demanded he take a wife the moment he'd returned to her court with barely a welcome home, it wouldn't have surprised me if she did.

"I'll check." Hawk dropped back onto the couch, leaned close to the food, and closed his eyes. The muscles in his jaw flexed and his eyelids squeezed tighter with pain. "You're good."

"Are you sure?" Titus asked. "Seireadan would be able to tell."

"I'd be able to tell what?" Bane asked, standing in the bedroom's doorway with Amiah leaning against him.

My heart clenched at the sight of her. She still wore the robe Bane had helped her put on in the grotto, the fabric closed all the way up to the base of her neck and the belt tied tight, and she looked exhausted and in pain — both of which were natural since it was going to take more than one session to heal her broken bones, and it'd been clear when I'd walked in on her that she'd already expended all of her magic healing what she could.

And God I *did* want to make my move and tell her how I felt. Except she'd never accept me and that would ruin our friendship.

"If the food is enspelled," Titus said.

"Hawk is more sensitive than I am," Bane said, helping Amiah to the couch. "If he says the food is safe, it's safe."

Amiah sagged onto the couch beside Hawk and he grabbed a hank of grapes and offered them to her.

The grapes were a good choice, bite-sized and didn't require a lot of chewing, but she still struggled to pull one free with just her one good hand.

I shifted forward to help, but Hawk noticed the problem right away and plucked a grape from its stem and fed it to her.

Damn. Biting back a growl, I grabbed the apple I'd originally wanted to take, viciously bit in, and paced to the front of the room and back again. This really was a nightmare. Now the incubus was hand feeding her!

"How many more sessions do you think you'll need?" I asked her, fighting to keep my emotions cold.

Hard and cold. Hold it together.

"It depends on how much the healing pool helps," she said, her words half-mumbled because of her swollen face. "At least one session, more likely two to be sure my bones are properly healed."

"And how many are broken?" I asked, determined to keep my tone steady and professional. I didn't want to know, but I needed to if I was going to properly assess the situation and come up with a plan.

The light in her eyes flared.

I could see her pride warring with her practicality in her gaze. She'd never wanted to be the one being cared for, always determined to be strong and put others first. It was one of the things I loved about her *and* that drove me crazy at the same time. *I* wanted to help her, wanted to do things for her, even silly little things that she could do herself. But she never let me and she never asked for help unless it was absolutely necessary.

"If things go sideways and we need to run, I need to know what your condition is," I said.

Her gaze dropped to her lap. "He broke all of my ribs. Half are mostly healed. My wrist and nose are also broken, and there's a hairline fracture in my cheek," she said matter-of-factly as if she wasn't talking about herself but a regular patient... except she didn't raise her gaze, didn't look at any of us, and that made my inferno flare. "But that's as serious as it gets. It could have been worse."

Titus, back in the chair, stiffened, and release a low, barely audible growl.

I wanted to growl with him. It could have been worse? God, it shouldn't have happened at all.

"We should get back in the healing pool," Bane said, grabbing a roll and sitting in the chair farthest from Amiah. "My magic is still low and I want another dip before I remove your half of the leash spell."

"You sure you want to do that?" Hawk asked. "It's what's making your mom think you and Amiah are married. You break it, she notices, and she's going to make you marry someone else."

"And punish Amiah for your lie," Titus added.

"Fuck," Bane hissed, raking a hand down his face, looking gray and almost as exhausted as Amiah.

I'd known he'd expended a lot of magic yesterday, but I hadn't known a sorcerer, someone able to tap into the primal magic of Faerie, could be drained like me or Amiah, whose power came from an internal source.

"Fine. We wait until we're out of the Winter Court. I'll warp the spell so it looks like a marriage bond just in case," he said. "There aren't a lot of sorcerers in the Winter Court, but I don't want to risk one of them getting curious and taking a serious look at it."

"No." My fire flared and I fought to keep it under my skin. "It's too dangerous. You need to break the spell. If you're separated, she could die."

"If the Winter Queen learns Seireadan lied, she'll die," Titus said, his voice low.

"I can stretch the leash and adjust its side effects, but I can't disguise it *and* change it at the same time. I don't have the power at the moment." Bane stood, dropped the roll back onto the tray, and knelt in front of Amiah.

Without asking for permission, he pressed his hand over her heart, drawing a small gasp that could have either been pain or surprise.

I gritted my teeth. *Icy cold. Hard. Frozen. God damned frozen.*

He closed his eyes, and Amiah's breath picked up. Her angel glow — terrifyingly weak, exposing how little magic she had left — fluttered brighter and this time her gasp was one of pain.

"Bane?" I asked. I didn't want Amiah in danger, but I also didn't want her in pain.

"Let him concentrate," Hawk said.

Amiah squeezed her eyes shut and her body trembled. A tear leaked from beneath her lashes and rolled down her cheek, and she released a strangled whimper, one she'd been trying to hold back.

My fire churned, boiling my blood. I clenched my hands, fighting to stay put, fighting to hold my magic back, fighting every instinct I had to yank Bane away and beat the shit out of him for hurting her.

Bane began to shake as well, his fingers over her heart digging into her robe and the soft flesh of her breast, his other hand clutching the couch cushion beside her.

"Almost there, man," Hawk murmured, squinting as if he was looking into a bright light.

Amiah's breath turned ragged and another tear rolled down her cheek, but she clenched her jaw tight, keeping in any sound.

Her strength tore at my heart. She didn't deserve any of this and I should have been able to stop it.

The apple in my hand burst apart, my grip crushing it, covering my hand in juice while little fiery pieces fell on the floor.

"Fuck," Bane groaned. His glow flickered, dimmer for a second, and he sagged forward.

Hawk caught him before he fell against Amiah and helped him sit on the floor then pressed a hand against Amiah's neck. She groaned and sagged back, her body going limp with the flood of Hawk's power, her ragged breath evening out as her pain melted into pleasure.

I tossed the crushed apple back onto the tray and paced back to the front door.

Ice. Hard. Frozen. Frozen. Frozen.

"Amiah and I need to make a trip to the pools," Bane groaned. "Cassius, you come with us while T and Hawk do some recon."

"Agreed." I paced back to the couch.

Frozen. Just be frozen. Don't burn Amiah.

AMIAH

Pᴀɪɴ ᴡʀᴀᴄᴋᴇᴅ ᴍʏ ʙᴏᴅʏ ᴇᴠᴇɴ ᴡɪᴛʜ Hᴀᴡᴋ's ᴍᴀɢɪᴄ flooding me, making me feel boneless and achy. What-ever Sebastian had done to the leash spell it had hurt and I just wanted to breakdown and sob. But Cassius already looked like he wanted to punch Sebastian, and the other guys stared at me with concern and pity, and crying would just make the situation worse.

So instead, I tried to eat another grape. But my face hurt too much and after chewing one, I gave up. Here was hoping the pools would ease some of the pain and I'd be able to get down more food before I passed out because being hungry made it harder to replenish my magic even if I slept.

Hawk put on a tunic, and he and Titus left — although for a minute Titus's expression grew dark and angry and it looked like he was going to argue with Sebastian about staying — then Sebastian insisted Cassius carry me to the pools.

"It's not far, but at the pace you walk, it'll take us

forever to get there," he said, and I couldn't tell if he wanted Cassius to carry me because he was too weak to hold me or if he wanted nothing more to do with me so Cassius wouldn't hurt him.

Which made me want to scream. At both of them.

As I'd requested, Sebastian had waited in the bedroom while I'd showered and changed, and he'd only made a move to help me when I shuffled out of the bathroom and admitted I needed help. Just showering and trying to dry off with one hand had sucked away what little energy I'd had and had left me exhausted and dizzy, forcing me to cling to the front of my robe with my good hand and lean against the wall to stay upright.

But he hadn't seemed happy about helping me and now he was out the door without waiting to see if Cassius was going to pick me up or not.

With a huff, his expression hard and imposing, Cassius carefully picked me up.

He was back to the cut-from-stone angel who'd stood on Operations' rooftop with me two nights ago. If I hadn't known his power was fire, I might have guessed it was ice from all the emotional warmth he was giving off. I wasn't even getting comfort out of my magic sensing his life force.

The two guards from the throne room fell in step behind us as we walked down a long wide hall to the very end and down another hall back to the large, intricately carved ice door of the healing grotto.

"Stay here," Sebastian commanded to them, "and no, we don't require assistance."

"Your highness—" the guard on the left started.

"Have the towels and robes been replaced?" Sebastian asked, although I suspected he already knew the answer.

"Yes, your highness," the guard on the right replied with the same voice as the one on the left.

"Then obey me." Sebastian pushed the heavy door open and strode inside.

Cassius followed and one of the guards pulled the door closed behind us, trapping us in the humid, steamy grotto.

"There's a pool at the back that's better for restoring magic," Sebastian said, grabbing a towel from the bench by the door. "The first pool is better for Amiah. It seems you can't stay in it for long, so when glowing threads start snaking through your skin or it gets painful, get out."

He strode up three wide steps cut into the rock wall and disappeared around a rough rock pillar and a narrow blue spruce that reached all the way to the ceiling.

Cassius stared at the wide pool ahead of us, its water gently rippling and lapping against the sides. "I'll call him back to help you undress and..." For a second his hands grew warm then his angel glow flared and he was back to cold and stern. "And I'll keep my eyes closed while you're in the pool."

Heat swept across my cheeks, and Hawk's power swelled low within me. How *was* I going to bathe? Even if Sebastian had stayed and Cassius didn't look, I wasn't going into the pool naked, no matter how impractical that was. Sebastian had made it clear he didn't want to see me naked again, and Hawk's magic still surged through me. The irrational desire that I'd thought — had prayed — I'd squashed when I'd slept with Sebastian, that I shouldn't have had because of the pain I was in, taunted me. And Hawk, bringing me to a gentle climax with his magic, fingers, and words less than an hour ago hadn't helped.

I ached to go back to bed. Although I wasn't sure if it was for sex I was too tired to have or to be held and feel the warmth of someone's body, their life force humming against my senses. None of which I was getting from Cassius at the moment.

"I'm sure we can manage without him. There are extra robes," I said, trying to ignore my aching desire. "I'll just go into the pool wearing this one so you can keep an eye on me. I can change into a dry robe when Sebastian returns." If he'd even be willing to help me again since he'd made it clear he wasn't even interested in that. Maybe I could manage untying the knot and drying myself off one-handed again.

"Right." Cassius's gaze slid over the pile of towels on the bench and the robes hanging on hooks on the wall behind it.

There wasn't a change of clothes for him unless he wanted to wear a robe. He wasn't going to be able to go into the pool still clothed like I was.

Would he strip to his briefs like he had last night? He certainly wouldn't strip all the way down like Hawk had.

My pulse picked up, need throbbing between my thighs. I ached to feel Sebastian filling me again, or Hawk teasing me with his fingers. What would Cassius be like as a lover? Cool? Reserved? Or would he finally release his hold on his emotions and join me in the consuming sensations, letting it burn away all the fear and heartache until there was only bliss?

He strode the few feet to the closest pool, knelt while still holding me, and eased me into the pool's warm soothing waters. My robe billowed up, exposing my thighs and the large bruises and scrapes on my knees, and I clutched at the front of it, holding it down between my legs so I didn't flash him.

His gaze locked on my hand between my thighs and a hint of embarrassment, but not enough to quell my desire, heated my cheeks. Then my rear end reached the submerged bench ringing the pool and he pulled away, both his body and his gaze, looking anywhere but at me.

The glimmer of magic I had left, that flickering core of power that I could never consume but wasn't powerful enough to even sense someone else's injuries, stuttered like a small flame in a strong wind, and the pool's tingling magic sank into my skin, rushing straight to my heart.

I gasped as it curled around the organ, no longer the lulling power from last night, flooded my veins, and gathered, cool and sharp along the lines of my mating brand, making its ache stronger than the rest of my injuries for a terrifying moment. My pulse pounded faster, fear consuming my desire, and I yanked my gaze to the skylight, seeking comfort from that small square of clear blue sky.

I won't be trapped. I can't be trapped. Not even by love. Especially the uncontrolled love of a soul bond. I didn't want my brand's cruel magic making me fall in love with someone I didn't know, making me lose myself in their soul. I didn't want the terror of knowing they were hurt or the inability to control myself when they were.

It was bad enough my magic compelled me to heal people. What happened if my soul was locked on my mate while my magic was locked on someone else? Who would I pick? Would I even be given a chance to pick or would my soul bond and my magical backlash tear me apart?

I fought to shove those thoughts aside, adding them to the list of things I didn't want to think about. I didn't know how long I'd be able to ignore them and prayed it would be long enough to get through this situation... even though I had no idea how long this situation was going to last.

"How are your burns?" I asked, jumping on the first thing that popped into my mind and gritting my teeth against a painful flare of magic in my palms. Yesterday, after the fight in Left of Lincoln, the illegal off-the-books market, Cassius had cauterized his wounds with his fire, leaving ugly, painful burns all over his torso. I'd managed to heal them enough that they were no longer painful, but I hadn't had enough power to eliminate the thick scars, and if I didn't get to them soon, they'd be permanent.

"I'm fine," he said. "Save your magic for yourself."

"I'm aware that your scars are less severe than my bones," I replied, my tone sharper than I intended. How many times were we going to have this conversation? "Stop assuming I don't know how to best use my magic."

"That's not what I was saying." His gaze jumped to me and slid down my body. Heat simmered in his eyes for a second, making my pulse thrum faster, before they widened and he jerked his attention away again.

Jeez. Did I look that terrible?

Except he'd already seen my battered face.

I dipped my attention to my body and my heart froze as a hot flash of embarrassment flooded my entire face and scorched down my neck. The white robe clung to my curves, leaving nothing to the imagination, and had turned see-through, exposing the ugly red bruises covering my torso... as well as my nipples. Thank goodness I was holding the robe down and my hand was in the way, or he'd be able to see a whole lot more.

"I'm saying stop worrying about us for a minute and worry about yourself," he said, his voice gruff.

Except if I worried about myself all the thoughts I didn't want to think would come crashing in. I couldn't just sit there and wallow. I had to keep busy, not think, do something.

"Cassius, please. Let me do my job." *Let me do something I know how to do. Let me be useful, not helpless and pathetic. Let me be an equal. Don't let this nightmare change our friendship, because I need you. You're all I have.*

A wisp of smoke curled from his hands then vanished.

"The pool last night helped them along," he said.

"Then let me see. I think my injuries are too severe to get a good sense of how this pool heals," I said, hoping that if I turned his examination into an educational experience for me I'd get him to take off his tunic and show me his scars. "How far along are they? Would another dip finish the job?" I asked, clinging to the questions of how effective the healing pool actually was. "You could change into a towel and join me and we could find out."

"No," he said, appalled. "I'm not— Not while you're —" He gestured at me, his gaze starting to slide back to me then jerking away as his back stiffened. "Out of all of us, why him? Why Bane?"

Because there's no chance he's my soul mate and he doesn't feel obligated to start a relationship. The memory of Sebastian's mouth on me made Hawk's power surge again. I just wished it had been more than a one-night stand.

Except I knew what Cassius was really asking. Why not him? Didn't I trust him? Weren't we friends?

But it was because we were friends, because there was a chance he could be my soul mate, that I couldn't let him get close. Not until my partially formed mating brand was gone.

"After this, I'll never see him again," I said, saying the first thing that came to mind. "Don't you think seeing me naked would make things awkward between us?"

The pool's tingling magic flickered with my power, sending tiny painful bites through my skin, and I sucked in a shallow breath, focusing on Hawk's magic still seeping through me instead of the pain.

Hot and sensual. Achy thrumming need.

God, his fingers pumping into me, bringing me to climax.

"You're a physician," Cassius said. "I'm sure you see naked people all the time. How would me seeing you naked be different?"

Because it was different. My robe had turned see-through and I was blushing and so was he. Except I couldn't say I didn't want to show him my body because I was attracted to him — because I ached for sex with anyone, not just him. Really — that would open the door to a conversation I wasn't ready to have. Not until my brand was gone. And I wasn't telling him about my brand either. He'd think it was wonderful and magical like every other angel, not the nightmare I knew it to be.

"You're right." I bit the inside of my cheek, my heart pounding, my core throbbing. If I didn't feel anything for him, hiding my body was illogical, and eventually he'd come to the same conclusion. If I didn't want him to think I felt something more for him and have a relationship conversation forced on me sooner than I wanted, I needed to be coolly professional about the whole situation. Right now, he was able to help me and I needed help. Nakedness shouldn't matter.

Fine.

"You might as well strip and get in the pool then," I said. "A body is just a body, be it mine or yours."

AMIAH

HEAT FLOODED MY FACE. *WHAT IS WRONG WITH ME? WHY did I just say that?* I'd just told him to strip and get in the pool with me.

"Amiah—"

"There's no point in you having scars or me wasting power removing them when you can just join me in the pool," I insisted, doubling down on my argument unable to stop myself.

"I'm not joining you in the pool," he snapped back.

"Agent. If you're shy, wrap yourself in a towel. But it's not like I haven't seen a man's genitalia before." And recently. I shuddered at the memory of Sebastian's hard and thick erection pushing into me. "You've briefly mentioned your romantic relations in the past, I'm sure you've a seen a woman's before as well. Don't be foolish. Take this opportunity for free healing."

He glared at me, his angel glow blazing.

"Fine." He marched back to the bench and pulled off his tunic.

Oh. My. God! Something was really wrong with me. I was supposed to be keeping our friendship a friendship, not invite him to strip and sit mostly naked—

He pushed his pants and briefs off his hips, giving me an amazing view of his glutes and muscular thighs.

Fully naked!

My mouth went dry and Hawk's power made the muscles between my thighs clench. Cassius was stunning with his sculpted arms and shoulders, his broad back tapering into a narrow waist, and the ripple of flexing muscles in his back and shoulders as he bent, grabbed a towel from the bench, and wrapped it around his hips.

Then he turned back to me and my heart dropped into my stomach. His expression was icier than before, almost pained, as if he hated the idea of joining me in the pool, but didn't want to argue with me.

I forced my gaze to his chest and studied his scars as he slipped into the pool on the far side, far enough away that our feet wouldn't accidentally brush. The scars were in better shape than I'd left them, and a few were no longer bright pink just rough shiny discolorations in his skin as if I'd already spent extra time working on him.

"How long were you in the pool last night?" I asked as the tingling snaps from the pool's magic grew sharper.

Focus on learning about the pool and the pain. Nothing else. Not what happened to me and not how much I want him.

My gaze dipped lower to his hands, one holding the towel closed, the other holding the front of it down, aching for just a peek.

Jeez. Focus.

Embarrassment heated my cheeks again and I

wrenched my attention back up to his eyes. Except he wasn't looking at me. He'd locked his gaze on the skylight above us, the muscles in his jaw tight. His whole body tight, actually.

"We couldn't have been in the pool more than fifteen minutes," he said.

"So not as powerful as me, but still impressive." It would have taken me only a few minutes — faster if I didn't care about hurting him — to do that amount of healing, but fifteen minutes in the water was still good. Maybe I should have looked at myself in the mirror. Perhaps I didn't look so bad. Except I felt horrible. Broken bones aside, my face didn't feel like I'd spent any time healing my bruises. "What rate would you say my bruises have healed?"

"They're maybe a day or two old." His gaze remained locked on the skylight.

"So the pool isn't as effective on me." I let my gaze wander back to his hands, the throbbing between my thighs increasing and my insides hot... or was that the water?

This was a mistake. A huge mistake.

"Bane thinks it has something to do with your healing magic." Cassius's breath picked up and he shifted his hips, trying to get comfortable.

I jerked my attention up and found him staring at me. His bright blue gaze, a match to my own, captured mine, and for a second I could see wild, seething emotions in his eyes. Fire and fear and an aching—? Was that desire?

No. It had to be my desire reflected back at me.

Still, my breath caught and a heavy tension filled the

air between us. Maybe Sebastian was right. Maybe I was in love with Cassius.

And maybe I'd just spent over a hundred years without sex and my libido wanted to make up for lost time.

That had to be it. I'd commanded Cassius to get in the pool because my subconscious wanted this moment, wanted to feel this burning need of being near a naked man, wanted more. I yearned for Cassius to cross the distance between us, yearned for the courage to cross to him.

Would it really hurt if I just kissed him?

My thoughts stuttered.

What was I thinking?

Of course it would hurt if I kissed him. That would ruin everything. If he didn't reject me, he'd want a commitment I couldn't give him. I was destined for someone else, and even if he was my soul mate, I didn't want to be trapped in a permanent magical bond.

Fear sliced through my desire, and the memory of last night flooded my mind. Terror. Pain. Helplessness.

I swore.

I started to tremble and fought to clamp down on my emotions. Not now. Not when Cassius was looking at me. Not ever. I wanted to pretend it had never happened, pretend I hadn't broken my vow to never be a victim again, pretend—

My throat tightened.

I swore.

The pool's magic snapped with a sudden biting sting,

and grew into a painful electric shock, searing through my body.

I swore. I swore. I wasn't going to think about it.

Cassius frowned. "Amiah?"

"I'm fine." *Fine fine fine.* It hadn't happened. I wasn't weak. I was strong. So strong. *Please, I have to be strong.*

"You don't look fine."

Another agonizing bite from the pool and my magic flared. The pressure built inside me, a mix of magics fighting for control, each surging to gain dominance even while I was drained, and there wasn't anything I could do about it.

So don't think about it. Think of something else. Anything else.

Except it was getting harder and harder to think past the pain and fear. Not even Hawk's magic and Cassius's nudity were helping.

I heaved my gaze up to the skylight, but the square in the ceiling was too small. Even the sky felt crowded and the walls of the grotto were closing in on me.

"I can do this." I had to do it.

"It's not a matter of whether you can or not," he said, his voice suddenly close, the water around me getting hotter.

I turned to look at him as the edge of his towel brushed my arm. So close. Would he kiss me? *Please kiss me and take it all away.*

"Bane said you couldn't spend a lot of time in the pool." The muscles in his jaw flexed and consideration flashed across his expression, then he released his towel, picked me up, and set me on the edge of the pool.

I tried not to look at him. I really did. But my gaze leaped to his sculpted chest and sank lower.

He grabbed his towel before I could see anything, the now-bubbling and steaming water billowing the fabric forward, unfortunately hiding everything.

"If you can hold on, I'll dry off first then help you."

The pool's magic snapped again, thankfully not as strong as before now that I was just wet, not immersed in its waters. "If you help me stand, I think I'll be okay."

In fact, while I was still tired and in pain, I felt a little stronger. But Cassius had already hopped out of the pool, steam rising from his skin, and rushed to the bench, his back to me and his wet towel in a heap on the floor, giving me an amazing view of his glutes again.

"You're just going to let her sit here?" Sebastian asked as he came down the stairs, fully dressed, his wet hair, the towel in his hand, and the healthy glow radiating from his skin the only indications he'd been in a pool.

I shifted to face him, not ready to stand just yet. His gaze dipped to my chest and his eyebrows raised.

"Ah," he said, drawing close and holding out his hand to help me. Desire dilated his pupils and his eyes raked over my body again, making me ache with need. "Decided to be cruel to him."

"Hardly. I doubt the bruises are attractive." I took his hand and he helped me rise with a tug that toppled me into him, although thankfully not forcefully enough to spike pain through my ribs or broken wrist. My good hand slid out across his muscular chest to his shoulder and my breasts pressed against him.

His pale blue, almost colorless gaze captured mine,

just like Cassius's had a moment ago, stealing my breath and making my pulse pound.

He'd kissed me like he'd desired me. He'd looked at me like I was beautiful. He'd taken the time to satisfy me with a passion I hadn't expected from a one-night stand kind of guy like Sebastian, as if I'd been important to him.

He was the only one who knew my secret, knew how terrified I was of my mating brand, and knew I'd never been with a man before.

And now he wanted nothing to do with me.

"Now who's being cruel?" I breathed.

"So fuck him," he whispered, his breath heating my skin and sending a shiver racing through me. "I bet he left you sitting here to hide a raging hard on."

"Remove my mating brand and maybe I will," I murmured back, making his eyes widen in surprise.

"Can you untie the belt?" Cassius asked, his voice gruff as he approached, now fully dressed.

I fought the urge to see if Sebastian was right about Cassius desiring me. *Not until my brand is gone.*

"Sure." Sebastian stepped back, slung the towel over his shoulder so he had the use of both hands, and reached for the belt's wet knot, his gaze on my breasts.

He licked his lips and my nipples hardened. I wanted his mouth on them again, teasing me, building the heat within me. I didn't care that most of my ribs were still broken and I looked horrible. I needed him, needed to forget about being trapped, being taken, being—

Oh God, please. I needed to have sex again to forget it all. I was going to lose my mind, break down, and start sobbing, and I couldn't do that. That would be admitting it was all true, that it had happened, that I'd been helpless.

But I certainly wasn't going to ask either man for intercourse, and I doubted my body could handle that. I was just going to have to wait until Hawk and I were alone again and beg him to use his magic to satisfy me.

Sebastian jerked his attention back to my eyes, untied the belt around my waist, and slipped the robe off my shoulders then hurried back to the bench to get another robe, as Cassius gently helped me dry off while keeping his gaze averted.

The whole moment was tense and awkward, and if I was being honest with myself, a little thrilling. I had two gorgeous men helping me change my clothes. If I hadn't been hurt and they hadn't been... well, if they hadn't been *them*, I might have found the courage to embrace the throbbing desire inside me. I might have been bold enough to ask for what I wanted.

And I wasn't going to acknowledge what a mess I was, being worried about Cassius and Sebastian seeing me naked while at the same time fantasizing about being intimate with both of them... at the same time.

"You should carry her," Cassius said stepping back and leaving Sebastian to tie my robe closed.

"I'd rather you did," Sebastian replied, tying the belt and also stepping back.

Jeez. Really?

I headed for the door. I didn't know if I'd be able to swing it open — it looked pretty heavy — but I wasn't going to stand around and wait for one of them to give in and pick me up. Yes, I was exhausted, and yes, I was still moving slowly, but the pool had helped and I no longer felt like I was going to fall over or pass out.

Thank goodness most of today's awkward problems would be solved by tonight — and I wasn't going to think about my fears or my desires. A little food and eight to ten hours of sleep, and I'd have restored enough magic to knit the rest of my ribs and my broken wrist back together. Then I could breathe easier and I'd be able to dress and undress without help.

Cassius hurried past me and opened the door, making Sebastian roll his eyes and sigh.

"Fine." Sebastian scooped me into his arms, jarring my broken ribs and making me gasp, which made Cassius glare.

"Hey, I told you," Sebastian said, "you should carry her."

Cassius's gaze jumped to the ice guards as they fell into step behind us and his body stiffened. "If your highness would prefer it."

"I would," Sebastian replied, a wicked haughty gleam lighting his eyes.

"Just don't," I insisted before Sebastian handed me over which would jar my ribs again. "I'm not a sack of potatoes. Every time you move me, it hurts."

Cassius's expression grew harder as if for a second he'd forgotten about my injuries and the gleam in Sebastian's eyes vanished.

"I just want to eat something and go back to bed," I said... with Hawk.

No!

Not with Hawk.

To sleep. Alone. And restore my magic.

"We can do that," Cassius replied, pity sliding into his expression and making my stomach churn.

I wished he'd stop looking at me like that.

I wished I hadn't given him another reason to look at me like that again.

Don't. Think.

Sebastian turned the corner to the hall leading to our suite and stopped. The door was open, two more ice guards stood on guard in the hall, and ice servants scurried in and out carrying empty dishes, silverware, crystal glasses, and table decorations.

"What's happening?" Cassius asked, his voice low.

"My mother, that's what." Sebastian stiffened and glanced at the glyph on the inside of his wrist that alerted him to the presence of shadow fae. It flashed a soft white glow then dimmed. "And trouble."

He squared his shoulders and strode confidently to our suite's door, stopping in the doorway.

Inside, the living room furniture was gone, replaced with a large wooden dining room table that was being set with fancy china, crystal, and silver place settings, along with lit candelabras, decorative floral arrangements of winter greenery, and bottles of wine. Half a dozen wide high-backed matching wood chairs, generously spaced out, surrounded the table, and at the far end, on a wide couch, tall enough for her to sit properly at the table sat the Winter Queen.

She wore another diaphanous gown, this one in blood red, cut low to draw the eye to her cleavage. As if the cut of the dress wasn't enough, a large diamond pendant surrounded by gold filigree hung on a delicate gold chain between her breasts. Two of the gorgeous men who'd been on the floor around her throne — one fae, like Sebastian with red and silver hair, the other the werepanther — sat on either side of her, still not wearing shirts, their pants still red now matching the queen's dress.

The woman who'd been standing beside the throne, Padraigin, sat stiffly in a chair to the queen's left. She wore the same simple white tunic Cassius did, and while I couldn't see her legs, I suspected she also wore the same loose pants. The delicate ice circlet that had been holding back her long black hair was gone and her locks were now only held back with two simple braids at her temples.

On the queen's right sat a breathtakingly handsome shadow fae, the shadows under his pale skin undulating, slowly, seductively. He wasn't the same shadow fae who'd attacked us in the park ring or in Left of Lincoln, even though he had the same shoulder-length black hair pulled back at the nape of his neck. The lines of the fae's face were sharper, more refined, and more beautiful, but that didn't make me feel safe because he wore a similar black leather outfit as the other fae, and behind him stood the demon-vampire, his cold lifeless essence making me shiver.

The demon-vampire still wore black leather pants and a long black wrap tunic. It was similar but not the same as the clothes the seated shadow fae wore, hinting at an East Asian style where the seated fae's clothes seemed more modern-day North American. His black hair hung halfway down his back and was half pulled back in a ponytail and half loose, and while his katana was sheathed at his hip along with a matching wakizashi, I knew how fast he could draw his weapon and slice someone down.

This was the man who'd tried to kill me in the park ring, decapitated someone in Lincoln without a second thought, and then given me a knife when I'd been Balwyrdan's captive. I had no idea why he'd given me a weapon when he'd tried to kill me earlier, and there was no hint of emotion on his face or in his black eyes — his hellfire banked to small red embers — indicating he thought anything about me or even recognized me.

"Seireadan," the Winter Queen purred. "Look who came to visit. His Majesty of the Shadow Court, your friend, Deaglan."

The shadow fae flashed a warm friendly smile that sent a chill racing through me. I didn't care how friendly he smiled. This was the fae who'd cast the horrible leash spell on Titus and had held him prisoner, trapped in his human form unable to shift and fly and satisfy his beast's needs, for five hundred years. This was a monster.

AMIAH

Sᴇʙᴀsᴛɪᴀɴ's ɢʀɪᴘ ᴏɴ ᴍᴇ ᴛɪɢʜᴛᴇɴᴇᴅ, ᴀɴᴅ ʜᴇ ꜰʟᴀsʜᴇᴅ ʜɪs own warm smile with no indication to Deaglan that he knew what he'd done to Titus or any fear that Deaglan would recognize that our marriage bond was actually a warped version of his leash spell.

"What an unexpected surprise," Sebastian said, striding the few remaining steps to the chair at the end of the table opposite his mother but not sitting.

"I heard you were back in court and married, your highness," Deaglan said, his voice warm and enticing, nothing about it implying darkness like the undulating shadows under his skin or the fact that he was the King of the Shadow Court and an all-around monster.

"Come, Deaglan," the Winter Queen cooed, "no need to be overly formal. You and Seireadan grew up together."

"And I'm no longer a prince of the Winter Court." Sebastian jerked his chin and one of the ice maids pulled out the chair in front of him. He sat, still holding me, and settled me in his lap.

Cassius took up position behind us, mirroring the demon-vampire's stance with his hands behind his back and his feet slightly apart like a soldier at rest.

"You still are a prince of the Winter Court," the queen said. A delicate mist curled around the table legs and a whisper of cold swept across my skin. For a second that something dark and dangerous that I'd seen in the Winter Queen's expression in the throne room returned to her eyes.

"Although you have made it challenging to produce an heir," Deaglan said, "what with marrying an angel and all."

"Because I don't need an heir." Sebastian pressed a kiss to the top of my head, sending a shiver of desire slipping down my spine even though the kiss was about as chaste as a kiss could get. "Once my bride has recovered, I'm returning to the mortal realm."

Deaglan cocked an eyebrow and pursed his lips, and the hellfire in the demon-vampire's eyes sparked, drawing my attention to his hard, emotionless expression.

Why did he help me? Why give me a weapon? It didn't make any sense—

Except it did. The demon-vampire had seen me with Titus and if he hadn't seen Titus come to my rescue, he'd probably been hoping I'd lead him back to Titus...

But he could have just as easily let me die and kept watching Sebastian or Cassius or even Titus-in-disguise in the hopes of finding Titus.

Another shiver of desire breathed down my spine, reminding me of the ache between my thighs that I'd been trying to ignore since seeing Cassius strip in the grotto— No, since seeing Sebastian standing over Titus's broken body in the park ring two nights ago.

"Now Seireadan, don't be foolish. You're not returning to the mortal realm. The future king of the Winter Court must *stay* in the Winter Court." The queen waved at no one in particular and maids scurried to pour wine and bring in plates with food, setting them on top of the plates already in front of us. "I'm sure the Winter Court will grant you fertility with your angel like the other courts do with all the other species."

She turned and captured the mouth of the werepanther in a deep passionate kiss, moaning when he teased his palms over the top of her breasts and cupped them, kneading them through her dress's gauzy fabric.

Padraigin picked up her fork and stared at her plate, while Deaglan's smile darkened, openly appreciating the sexual display.

"Angels are certain they can only have children with other angels," Sebastian said, smoothing a wrinkle in my robe along my thigh and resting his hand on my bare knee, not reacting to his mother making out in front of us. "I'm in love with Amiah. I didn't marry her for children."

My chest irrationally ached at his words. Oh, how the lie just slid off his tongue and how he touched me as if there really was something between us.

A part of me yearned for that, his— No, *someone's, anyone's* affectionate touch, his warmth, his thrumming life force near mine, his desire. I yearned with a need almost as strong as my need before I'd slept with Sebastian even though we were in a dangerous situation and surrounded by strangers and most of my body still hurt.

The Winter Queen broke off her kiss, but her hand dropped below the table, reaching out — for her lover's lap? — and the werepanther pressed sensual kisses against her neck as the other man joined in, kissing the other side of her neck. "Angels only *believe* that they're only fertile with other angels. The Winter Court tells me no angel has tried to become pregnant with a high fae in Faerie."

Sebastian tensed. "You asked it?"

"You are a royal and a full sorcerer," Padraigin said, her gaze jumping to the red-haired fae then to Deaglan then back to her untouched plate. "Her majesty says the Winter Court will grant you an heir."

"And there's already a precedent for a half-breed becoming heir." Deaglan caught Padraigin's gaze when it jumped back to him, and the heat in his eyes grew.

She stiffened, a hint of pink coloring her cheeks, and she dropped her attention back to her plate, stabbing a small white square that could have been a piece of potato or apple or something-only-found-in-Faerie with her fork.

"The heir to the Autumn Court is a half-breed," Deaglan said, "and his court has already claimed him and granted him royal privileges."

The werepanther's breath picked up and he slid a hand inside the front of the Winter Queen's bodice, roughly palming her breast.

The sight of their rising desire made my pulse quicken and my own aching need throb hotter between my thighs.

Deaglan took a long slow sip of wine, turning his heated smile to me. "Still, you're usually more affectionate with your lovers. I'm not sure I believe you love her."

"I made the vow." Sebastian's hand on my knee inched higher and shifted to the inside of my thigh.

Heat pooled low in my core and I leaned in to him, savoring the feel of my body pressed against his, broken bones and everything.

"I can see the bond." Deaglan shrugged. "Maybe all isn't right in your wedding bed? I could always work her in for you like I worked in Enowen." His gaze dipped to my chest, and I realized the robe had slipped open and was no longer pulled up to my neck, revealing a generous amount of cleavage.

My pulse beat faster, but I couldn't tell if it was with fear or desire at the thought... which was crazy. Deaglan was a monster. I wasn't attracted to him, and yet it felt as if my body didn't care what the rest of me wanted.

Another whisper of cold tickled under my skin and the mist curling around the table legs billowed. The demon-vampire's attention slid to mine and his hellfire sparked again, a sharp flash of red in his black eyes.

For a second, he looked hungry, in the way a predator *and* a man looked at a woman, sending another shiver of desire and fear sweeping through me. Then he blinked and his cold, emotionless expression returned. Except his gaze remained locked on me.

"You used to share all the time," Deaglan said, his voice dark, dangerous, terrifying, and sensual.

"I didn't share Enowen."

"You would have, eventually." The heat in Deaglan's eyes grew. "Just cut to the chase, Seireadan. Her majesty doesn't care what you do in bed."

"Only that I get a grandchild, and the Winter Court will only give the heir to you. It doesn't matter who else fucks her," the queen said, making Cassius stiffen and the light in his eyes flare. "Whatever fixes your problems in bed."

"I have no problems." Sebastian's hand slipped higher up my thigh, the tip of his fingers a breath from my slick heat.

The ache inside me grew and I squirmed my hips, shifting just enough in his lap to slide his fingers against my folds, showing him just how much I wanted him.

Sebastian pressed his lips against my neck and softly groaned into my skin as two of his fingers dipped inside me.

My desire spiraled tight, making my pulse race and my breath pick up.

The demon-vampire's hellfire swelled, now actual miniature flames in each eye instead of just red embers, and the heat in Deaglan's eyes grew, as Padraigin's hands trembled, her attention still on her food. The queen leaned back, her smile smug, and Sebastian groaned again and tensed.

"Fuck," he murmured against my neck as he withdrew his fingers, clutching the inside of my thigh. "Amiah is injured and an angel. She doesn't have the same sensibilities as a high fae."

"If she's going to be queen, she'll have to get used to it," Deaglan replied.

"Yes," the queen purred. She jerked her chin at the fae man who slid off the couch and went under the table, while her hand was still in the werepanther's lap, his jaw clenched as he fought to control his breath — and presumably his release for some reason. "You should start now."

"Is that why you've made the Winter Court fill the air with an aphrodisiac?" Sebastian's fingers dug painfully into my flesh and I reached under my robe and grabbed his hand, urging him to slide his fingers back to my core.

God, surely I had more control than this. Surely I could wait until we were alone. But just that thought made my yearning twist tighter. I needed him. Needed him inside me. *Oh, please.*

Then my thoughts tripped over what he'd just said. The Winter Court had released an aphrodisiac. That was why I couldn't seem to control myself.

"You clearly needed some encouragement," the Winter Queen said.

"I don't need help sleeping with my wife."

"The guards said you were distant toward her on the walk to the pools. I can't have that," the queen said, her voice thick with need. "I want a grandchild."

"You have one. Padraigin's son," Sebastian replied through gritted teeth.

"That child is a half-breed," the queen moaned, "and the court hasn't claimed her."

"Mine will be a half-breed as well." Sebastian's hand inched closer to my core again and I bit back my own moan, fighting to keep my expression as neutral as his.

"But yours will be the rightful heir and the Winter Court agrees." The queen's eyes fluttered shut and the werepanther groaned.

Her eyes snapped open and she glared at him, her expression filled with icy danger. "Did I say you could come?" she asked, her voice suddenly dark.

The man's eyes rolled back and he trembled. "No, your majesty."

"Good." The queen leveled her glare at Sebastian. "But you, Seireadan, should. Now and often until your wife—" she spat out the word "—has made me a grandchild."

My heart skipped a beat. I desperately wanted to sleep with Sebastian again, let go of everything and feel that amazing bliss. I wanted it so much I feared I'd shatter.

"Fuck your wife." The queen tipped her head back, her breath coming fast with whatever the man under the table was doing.

The heat building inside me surged with the memory of Sebastian's mouth bringing me to climax. Without a doubt, that was what the man under the table was doing.

And that was what I wanted. Now.

No.

"No," I forced out, "I'm in no condition to have sex."

"I don't care what condition you're in. You're the princess consort. Your duty is to my son and my court. You just have to lie there and get pregnant."

She waved at the bedroom door and it magically opened by itself with a rush of cool wind. The bed had been made, the white comforter replaced with a dark blue one to show off the shimmering, diamond-like snowflakes scattered over its surface like rose petals, and a soft white light pulsed around it. Four women in see-through gowns knelt in a row at the foot of the bed facing us. I didn't recognize them from the throne room, but I'd barely been conscious so they could have been in the group the Winter Queen had presented for Sebastian to choose his bride. Their heads were bowed, their breaths too fast, and their bodies trembling as if they, too, were affected by the Winter Court's aphrodisiac.

In fact, it looked like everyone in the room except the ice maids, Cassius, and the demon-vampire were being affected. Unless the queen always had sex at her dining room table, and Deaglan always looked at women like that. Padraigin certainly looked like she was trying to hold herself together.

I glanced at Cassius. He trembled and smoke curled from his hands. No, he fought some great internal battle. The court was influencing him too.

My gaze slid to the demon-vampire whose hungry look had returned, sending another confusing shiver of fear and desire rushing through me. A vampire's bite caused sexual euphoria. Some people threw themselves at vampires in the hopes of being bitten.

And now all I could think about was being bitten while having Sebastian push inside me.

"We don't need help," Sebastian said, his voice gruff, "and I'm not going to have sex with her right now."

The Winter Queen stood, drawing the werepanther up with her, her hand still in his pants, the fae man still on his knees under her skirt. "You can't resist the will of the Winter Court. My will."

Two ice maids picked up the couch and took it into the bedroom.

"Oh, no," Sebastian said, his fingers digging painfully into my thigh. "You're not watching."

"You're going to watch?" I squeaked before I could stop myself.

"Queen's prerogative." The Winter Queen gave me a wicked smile. "If it bothers you, Deaglan and his body-guard can watch... or help." She pumped her hand inside the werepanther's pants, drawing a strangled groan. "But I want proof of your heir's conception."

My gaze jumped to Deaglan, who had the same dark hunger in his eyes that I'd seen in Balwyrdan's, except instead of getting off on just hurting me, I had the sickening sense that he wanted me screaming, crying, bleeding, *and* be inside me.

Fear sliced through my desire, but didn't completely diminish it, which only made Deaglan's smile deepen. Behind him, the demon-vampire shifted, anger bleeding into his hungry expression.

"No," I gasped. I wasn't even sure if I said the word out loud. I wouldn't let anyone hurt me like that again. I couldn't—

"No," I said more forcefully, and Sebastian's grip on me tightened.

A sharp flash of pain cut through my hip where my

sleeping mating brand lay and the aching need inside me vanished, fully consumed by fear.

Oh my God! Was Sebastian—?

No, he couldn't be my soul mate or my brand would have formed already... when we'd had sex... wouldn't it have? Except the bond from a mating brand could form at any time. Surely sex was enough of an intimate act to make a bond form between us... if one was going to form.

And God, I wanted to have sex with him again, feel him fill me, sink into the bliss of sensation without thought or worry—

"No. I'm not having sex with Seb— Seireadan for your entertainment."

A gust of freezing wind blasted through the room and everyone's eyes widened, the queen's, the werepanther's, Padraigin's, Deaglan, the demon-vampire's, *and* Sebastian's.

I gritted my teeth against the Winter Queen's power.

She wasn't going to trick, coerce, or force me to have sex with Sebastian. "And I'm not asking the Winter Court to give me a child so your heir can have an heir."

The wind gusted again, sweeping around me and Sebastian as if we were in the eye of its storm.

"Well, that's interesting," Deaglan said, as the demon-vampire inched closer to Deaglan and the muscles in Padraigin's jaw flexed.

The Winter Queen's glare turned dark and frozen. She flicked a finger and the wind died. "The Winter Court responds to you. It's made its choice. Seireadan is heir apparent and you're his queen." Her eyes narrowed. "You will fuck my son. Now."

"Pretty sure I get a say in this, too," Sebastian drawled, his trembling belying his confident tone. "She's in no condition for sex. I won't risk hurting her."

"Fine then." The queen's glare turned wicked. "I'll make the appropriate arrangements for you to consummate your marriage at your party when she's healed up. All of court will witness the impossible conception and know you, my dear, belong to the Winter Court." She strode from the room, her men, and the four maids in the bedroom following her.

Padraigin stormed after her as Deaglan leaned back in his chair.

"You should have just let me watch," Deaglan said with a shrug. "Now everyone gets to see your milky white angel ass."

No no no no.

I wasn't having sex with Sebastian and no one was seeing anything. We were leaving before it came to that. *Oh, God. Please.*

"The Winter Court's wind gusted for her, Seireadan. Just like it gusts for her majesty and like it used to gust for you. It hasn't gusted for your sister in centuries." Deaglan's gaze raked over my body, making a mix of desire and nausea churn in my stomach. "Guess you really did marry her."

He flashed me a wicked smile and strode out of the suite. The demon-vampire shot me one last hungry look, the hellfire in his eyes licking across his cheeks, before he schooled his features back to coldly emotionless and followed Deaglan.

"What. Was. That?" Cassius growled as soon as the door closed.

"My God damned fucking mother," Sebastian groaned, yanking his hand out from under my robe.

"We're leaving before the party." My pulse was racing too fast and I couldn't catch my breath, each quick gasp shooting agony through my chest. "I'm *not* having intercourse with you with the whole Winter Court watching."

And we're not married. We couldn't be married. Please, don't let us be married.

I pushed out of his arms and stood, trying to put some space between us, but my hip bumped the table, making me stumble, and Sebastian grabbed my waist, steadying me, his touch searing through the thin robe.

His pale blue gaze captured mine, and time stuttered for a second, caught on my stalled breath.

"I'm not having intercourse with you, period," Sebastian said, jerking away from me.

Cassius moved toward me, but stopped and crossed his arms instead as if he didn't want to touch me. "Can the Winter Court really make you conceive with him?"

"How am I supposed to know?" I squeaked. "As far as I know no angel has ever tried to get pregnant with a fae." Yes, at some point I thought I'd want a family... if my soul mate had been an angel since I wouldn't be able to conceive with any other species, but not now and not with Sebastian. It was clear he didn't do commitments. Without a doubt, he'd run the minute I got pregnant and I'd never see him again.

"It can't," Sebastian said, "no matter how much magic

my mother uses. I haven't vowed my fertility to Amiah so I'm still shooting blanks."

The door to the suite banged open and we all jerked to face it. Fire rushed over Cassius's arms then vanished as Hawk staggered inside with Titus close behind him.

"Holy fuck," Hawk said, his words slurred and his hellfire blazing.

His gaze locked on me with a hunger that made my pulse trip, and he stormed toward me. Before I could stop him, he cupped my face with his hot hands, shooting agony through my fractured cheek, and dipped in to kiss me. But Cassius grabbed his shoulder and yanked him back before our lips could meet.

With a groan, Hawk turned on Cassius, grabbed his head, and captured his lips in a searing kiss instead.

AMIAH

CASSIUS FROZE, HIS EYES WIDE WITH SHOCK AT HAWK'S LIPS locked with his. The incubus hummed low in his throat, a sound of pure masculine desire, and leaned into Cassius, not caring that Cassius wasn't kissing him back. A curl of his seductive magic somehow swelled in my chest even though he wasn't touching me, and I fought to keep back a surprised gasp.

Then horror flashed across Cassius's expression and he jerked back, holding Hawk at arm's length. "Back off."

"Oh come on, hot stuff," Hawk moaned. He leaned into Cassius's grip, and grabbed for the hem of Cassius's tunic at his thighs but couldn't quite reach. "I want to see you let it go and light the bed on fire."

Another swell of Hawk's magic rushed through me, this one even stronger than the last, teasing me with the promise of an amazing climax. I tightened my grip on the table, my legs wobbly.

"Fuck," Sebastian hissed, his body trembling.

Cassius's eyes rolled back and smoke swelled from his hands. "Would you pull it back? You're bleeding magic."

And excessive amounts as if he had so much power, he wasn't able to contain it.

"Because— Fuck—" Hawk squeezed his eyes shut and clenched his jaw. His expression fluctuated between playful and pained as if he couldn't figure out what he was feeling and his breath grew ragged. "I need to— Fuck. Someone. Anyone. Hell, if you don't want to fuck me, Sparky, let me give you and Amiah a boost. Trust me. You'll thank me in the morning."

Titus stiffened, his gaze jumping to me, the same sexual hunger in his eyes that I'd seen in Sebastian's kitchen the other day.

"I'm not having sex with Amiah," Cassius snapped.

Another rush of Hawk's magic tightened hot and needy between my thighs. Where had all this extra power come from? I doubted Titus had helped Hawk get it or waited around from the incubus to seduce I-don't-know-how-many-women to gather that much power. It was like he had too much, was overflowing with it—

Oh, no.

Whatever the Winter Queen had done to try and get me and Sebastian to have sex, had to have affected Hawk. That sexual energy had to have broken through Hawk's shields and flooded his system.

"Come on," Hawk cajoled. "You know you want to."

"No one is having sex with anyone," Cassius said, his voice gruff, his attention on my cleavage, his gaze adding to the heat building inside me.

In fact, all of the guys were looking at me with a hunger that made my pulse pound.

Jeez. The Winter Queen hadn't had to come here to try and force me to sleep with Sebastian, she just had to flood Hawk with too much sexual energy and let nature take its course.

"What did he get into?" Cassius asked. "How can he be this... high?"

"My mother mustn't have specified our suite when she made the Winter Court release the aphrodisiac," Sebastian said.

"You mean *everyone* in court was feeling that?" I asked. "Why didn't you dispel it?"

"Because it wasn't a spell." Sebastian took an unsteady step away from me and crossed his arms. "It was her will on the Winter Court making it turn us on, and her will over the court is stronger than mine. She's the queen and the court hasn't claimed another, not even me."

All that sexual energy must have overwhelmed Hawk. And how many in court had actually given into their feelings and had sex? His natural shields that regulated how much power he took in wouldn't have been able to withstand that, not if he hadn't known it was coming and hadn't consciously bolstered them ahead of time. That surge had probably torn right through them and drowned him in power. Which meant he could be ODing and I had to do something. *Hawk* had to do something.

"He has to release his excess power," I said as his magic churned hotter inside me. "Hawk, look at me."

I needed to know how bad his condition was. If he

was just high, he could carefully bleed off some of the excess and sleep off the rest. If he was ODing, I'd need to do the equivalent of pumping his stomach, forcing as much of the excess magic out of his system as fast as possible before it killed him.

I reached for him but managed to stop myself before making contact. It was bad enough that I was about to orgasm, touching him could flood me with too much power.

Hawk turned to move toward me, but Cassius held him tight, his fingers digging into Hawk's shoulders making him shudder and groan.

His eyes rolled back and his breath grew ragged. "Jesus fucking Christ, someone fuck me."

I gritted my teeth and shifted closer to Hawk. "Open your eyes, Hawk."

He did. His hellfire flared erratically, indicating an OD. But before I could figure out what to do, another blast of magic shot into me, this time making me come with a powerful wave that stole my breath and made my legs give out. I tried to cling to the table but couldn't support myself and managed to sag forward instead of dropping to the floor, knocking over a crystal wine glass and spilling a pale yellow liquid over the white tablecloth.

Oh my God, oh my God, oh my God.

Sebastian jerked forward to catch me and ended up pressed against my rear, his erection grinding into me. I pushed back against him before I could stop myself even though I'd just climaxed, desperately seeking another one, and his fingers dug into my hips, his body trembling.

"Take it," Hawk murmured and his power exploded inside me again, twisting me to the edge but not crashing me over again. "Please."

"No." Sebastian heaved away from me.

This had to stop. Even if the guys wanted to sleep with me, I was still injured. It was just so hard to remember that with bliss blazing through my veins. With this much out-of-control power, Hawk had to focus it away from them or they wouldn't be able to control themselves and end up hurting me — not to mention that would make everything more complicated.

My desire swelled at the thought of all of them pleasuring me, worshiping me.

I gritted my teeth and fought to think beyond their powerful gorgeous naked bodies pressed against mine.

Jeez.

I wasn't going to have sex with them.

Which meant Hawk needed another way to release his excess power.

He could just release his power into me, but even if I wasn't hurt, I didn't know if I was strong enough to take the full force of it all without it killing me. And it wouldn't be pleasant. It'd be painful.

Come on, think. Do something,

Hawk groaned and heaved against Cassius's grip. His hellfire snapped and flared and his breath turned to short sharp gasps. He was running out of time. He needed to release the excess. Now.

Another wave of pleasure crashed through me, ripping a moan from my throat.

Smoke curled from Cassius's hands and he stared at

me, hungry and desperate. Titus snarled, dropped to his knees, and dug his claws into the floor, his massive chest heaving.

Think.

Maybe Hawk could find someone else in the Winter Court.

No. If I sent him into the hall, he might not find a good target fast enough before his power burst his heart.

Crap. The best solution was to take his power into myself and just deal with the pain. But he'd still need to bleed some off first to be safe—

"Cassius, burn him," I gasped.

Cassius's eyes widened. "What?"

"Burn him, make his power redirect itself to healing him until its low enough that I can take the rest."

"You're not taking any of his power," Cassius growled. "I'm burning it all off."

Hawk heaved in Cassius's grip, his eyes too wide. "I'd rather have sex."

"With who?" I asked, using the table to hold me up as I inched toward him. "I'm in no condition to take the full force of your power, and if none of the other guys are bisexual, you'll just make them unable to stop themselves from coming after me."

"Come on, Bane," Hawk begged, closing his eyes and panting. Sweat slicked his brow and hellfire snapped from beneath his lashes. "Surely you swing both ways."

Sebastian wrenched another step back from me. "I'm always up for a *ménage a* whatever, but you've used your power on me enough times to know if you flood me with your magic, I'll want Amiah over you or any of the other guys."

"Your body won't be able to take this for much longer," I gasped. "Look at me, Hawk."

Hawk's eyes snapped open, and his power surged inside me with the promise of an excruciating climax, drawing another throaty moan.

I fought to keep standing and hold his gaze. "I've got you. You just need to lose enough so you don't kill me. Cassius will make it quick."

A fiery tear rolled down Hawk's cheek and he shuddered.

"Take a deep breath and let it out," I ordered.

Hawk drew in a ragged breath and I gave Cassius a tight nod. He switched his grip from Hawk's shoulder to his bare forearm and, as Hawk released his breath, molten flames exploded around Cassius's hand with a sudden flash.

All of Hawk's muscles jerked taut and his head snapped back. He screamed with gut-wrenching agony, the sound tearing at my heart. Every instinct inside of me howled that I had to stop this, had to heal him. My compulsive need to heal twisted tight as his power stuttered inside me, freezing and burning with painful sharp flashes.

His knees gave out, and Cassius eased him to the floor. I sank with them, cupped Hawk's cheeks with my palms — now that the redirection of his power made it safe — and forced his gaze back to mine.

"I've got you."

Heal him. Stop his suffering.

His hellfire tears stung my hands and his body shook, but I wasn't going to let go. Even if my compulsion would let me, I still wouldn't — and thank God for being completely drained of magic or, without a doubt, I would have locked onto him making this whole mess more complicated.

Heal him, heal him.

"Take another breath," I said, trying to sound calm and soothing despite the urgency to heal him and his seductive magic still building inside me. "You're almost done."

I flicked my gaze to Cassius and — thank goodness — he sucked his fire back inside his body.

The sickening smell of charred flesh filled my nose and bile burned the back of my throat.

My fault. His suffering is all my fault.

Hawk's right forearm and hand had been burned down into his muscle and bone, his flesh charred and waxy. The assault had happened so fast, he hadn't even bled.

"Just breathe," I murmured, reconnecting our gazes, trying to keep him lucid through the pain so he'd heal faster.

"It doesn't help," Hawk snarled, agony and anger and betrayal in his eyes. "I fucking hate you all."

"You're almost done."

His hellfire still blazed bright, snapping and flaring erratically, and I hoped he'd used up enough power because there was no way I'd be able to tell Cassius to burn him again. Just thinking of the words tightened my throat and sent panic surging through me.

Blood oozed from Hawk's burn, splattering onto his pants, the red stark against the white fabric, ironically a sign he was healing. His magic turned his fourth degree burn into third then second, mending muscle and flesh.

With a groan, he clenched his jaw and his hellfire stuttered, flared, snapped, and flared again. He hadn't lost enough. He was still in danger of ODing. But then I knew that would be the case. I strained to keep my breath even, but my pulse was racing.

His bleeding, blistered skin, turned pink, his magic healing him fully, his flesh now just smeared with blood, the only indication he'd been injured.

I didn't want to do this, didn't want to experience the need and pain of his power. But better me suffering than him again.

"Now release the rest," I said, letting the words rush out before my fear choked me.

Cassius tensed and smoke rushed around his hands as if he was going to burn Hawk again.

My heart lurched. I couldn't let Cassius stop me and take control. This was my call to make. I was the only woman in the group and the only healer, and I needed to be in control of this. I had to be in control. I wasn't in control of anything else and I was barely holding it together.

I pulled Hawk's mouth to mine before Cassius could reignite his fire.

A shot of pain from my fractured cheek made me gasp and a flood of Hawk's power poured into me, rushing down my throat.

Need wrenched into a sharp painful ball around my

heart. It shot agonizing threads of power through my veins, along the lines of my mating brand, then swept into my cells and sliced into my essence.

I couldn't think, couldn't breathe. Hawk's magic had sucked all the oxygen out of my lungs and replaced it with desire, burning, searing, screaming desire. It consumed me, like Cassius's fire had consumed Hawk's flesh. Fast, ferocious, and without mercy. My soul wailed. I was pretty sure I wailed. But I couldn't hear anything past the roaring in my ears... my head... my whole body.

All my muscles contracted in the mockery of a full-body orgasm as my body and essence burned. Hawk's power consumed it all until all that was left inside me was an agonizing bundle of twitching raw nerve endings.

I collapsed onto Hawk, sobbing, each breath slicing into my body and soul.

It hurt. Oh God, it hurt. I didn't know where the pain ended and I began, and I couldn't stop crying, not even in an attempt to ease the agony, let alone appear strong.

Hawk pulled me into his arms and held me tight. Too tight.

"I could have killed you," he gasped, pressing his forehead against mine and rocking back and forth. "I could have killed you."

He kept repeating the words over and over again, his grip getting tighter and tighter. But I didn't care. It didn't matter that he was squeezing broken and tender ribs. My soul was on fire.

"She can't stay on the floor," Sebastian said, his voice close and soft.

"I could have killed you."

"It was her choice," Sebastian replied.

"Next time it won't be," Cassius snarled. "Now let her go."

"I could have killed you. Why the fuck would you do that?" A fiery tear plopped onto my cheek. "You don't even know me."

"Let her go, Hawk," Sebastian pressed.

Strong hands pulled me out of Hawk's arms and smoke curled around me. Cassius. His heart pounded and he shook, clinging to me almost as tightly as Hawk had as he stood.

"Come on, man," Sebastian said, his voice getting farther away... except it was really me and Cassius who were getting farther away, heading to the bedroom. "You should sleep the rest of it off."

"Don't you ever do that again," Cassius growled as he laid my burning body on the bed.

I curled into a ball as if that would somehow protect me from the pain. But of course, it didn't. Not unless I could separate myself from my flesh, and that wasn't my angel power.

"I swear to God—!"

Something snapped and hissed. Cassius's fire hitting the floor?

"I hate— I— God damn—!"

Blazing hot air rolled over me and Cassius screamed, a gut-wrenching cry of rage and frustration and pain.

HAWK

Why? God, why? Why?

I was stuck on that word, my thoughts whirling and my stomach churning. My whole body was raw from that sudden, uncontrolled blast of magic, and I couldn't stop shaking.

Why had she taken all that power? Why risk her life when Cassius could have burned me again?

I could have killed her.

"Why?"

"Because she's a fucking angel," Bane said as he helped me stagger into the servants' bedroom.

"You still should have stopped her, Seireadan," Titus growled.

Someone should have stopped her.

I should have stopped her.

Except I hadn't stood a chance. I'd been wasted on that massive surge of sexual power that had blasted through my magical shields as if they hadn't been there. My heart had pounded so hard I thought it'd explode and my body had been on fire from Cassius burning me, and then Amiah had kissed me.

Any hope of control erupted the moment our lips touched. My power had found its release and there hadn't been a damned thing I could have done to control it.

My knees hit a cot that I could barely see through the blazing glow of Faerie, and I collapsed onto it, my power still rushing through me setting my nerves on fire. "I could have killed her."

Out in the living room, Cassius howled a wordless scream of rage and frustration and pain. A door crashed shut and the angel stormed into the room bringing with him a ferocious heat. Fire roared around him, somehow not catching on his clothes, and dripped on the floor, crackling and hissing.

He barreled toward the back of the room, snapping fire whips around the frames of two of the cots at the back as he moved. He tossed the cots into the row beside me, crashing them against two other cots then seized two more and flung them into the pile.

"I'm going to kill her," he snarled, sending a blast of fire into the space he cleared, scorching the wall and floor. "I'm going to God damn kill her."

He reached his clearing and jerked around — the angel glow in his eyes cutting through Faerie's glow making it clear he'd turned to face us. Fire poured from his hands, pooling around his feet, and his aura blazed angry and red, only partially visible through his flames. "I should have burned you again."

I shuddered and I couldn't tell if he was going to burn me now just to release the rage consuming him or not.

I didn't have a lot of experience with angels — they didn't run in the same kind of circles I did — but I'd never seen one so angry before. I wasn't sure I'd ever seen *anyone* this angry before. He was literally on fire, his power raging out of control.

Bane pressed the ice glyph tattooed on his chest and hissed a quick word. His brilliant white aura flared, blinding me for a second, before the demonic magic infecting him shot ragged black and red spikes through him. A frozen wind gusted into the room and ice swept around Cassius, extinguishing his fire and encasing him up to his thighs.

"Just take a breath." Bane sagged onto the end of the cot across from me and rubbed his face, the demonic magic's light still slicing through him even though he'd finished casting his spell and didn't need to keep pushing power into it to maintain it.

Cassius released another blast at the floor, melting the ice, and dropped to his knees into the puddle, his chest heaving and his fire dancing over his skin, still powerful and yet a fraction of what it had been before. The angry red light in his aura grew clearer now that his fire had weakened, writhing against whatever hold he'd managed to regain of his power and straining to burst free and turn him into a fireball again.

This was more than just frustration, and while Amiah's recklessness had triggered it, it spoke to something deeper, something broken within him. And maybe if I could see more than just his aura, I'd be able to say what was wrong with his power. If he'd let me touch him and use my magic, I wouldn't need to use my eyes to *see*. But even if he let me touch him, I still wouldn't be able to fix it, and I didn't want to touch anyone right now.

Everyone was struggling to keep their urges controlled, and their only ideal outlet was Amiah. Their willpower was already strained. Without a doubt they were all going to find their release, adding to it would only make it harder for them to stay away from her and just jack off in private.

"It's like she wants to hurt herself," Cassius said, sucking in a heavy breath and pulling back more of his fire, which only made the light in his aura blaze stronger.

"You saw her face when you burned Hawk," Bane replied. "It's not that she wants to hurt herself, but I doubt she'd have been able to stand it to see Hawk in that kind of pain again."

I hadn't seen her full expression, but then I hadn't been able to look away from her eyes. Her angel glow had been so weak, proving how little magic she'd had left and how exhausted she was, and her eyes had ensnared me in their vast blue depths, holding me captive with her strength and determination and pain.

No one had ever looked at me the way she had.

Even with my power raging through her, heightening her desire for me — for all of us — she looked at me as if she could see me, my truth, my soul, not just my body or my power, like I was important, precious, and she'd do whatever it took to carry me through the pain... through anything.

I knew it was just her physician's need to get me through the agony, that if it had been anyone else, she'd have given them the same look, but it had still stolen my breath.

I'd never been more than a body, an obsession, a craving to women and a few men. Which had suited me just fine before. Incubi didn't fall in love, didn't have that soul to soul connection that other species had because we couldn't sustain ourselves on one person. It was like a genetic failsafe. Having a single lover ended in the lover's death — by being drained of too much life force — or the incubus's — by starving himself.

But now—

God, it went against everything I was and I still ached for that look again, that acceptance, that being seen.

"How am I supposed to protect her through all this when I also have to protect her from herself?" Fire sparked from Cassius's arms then vanished back into his writhing aura. "She's my responsibility. She's not a field agent. She never wanted to be in the field because of her magic."

"You're not the only one trying to protect her," Titus said, his red-gold aura blazing almost as brightly as Cassius's and a ghostly wolf's head superimposed on top of his. He was losing it too, his beast barely contained. Thankfully the glamour still held, but I wasn't sure how long that would last.

"Hey." Bane barked a bitter laugh. "At least my mother isn't trying to kill her."

"Not sure using the Winter Court's magic to make you sleep together so you can impregnate her is better." The water around Cassius's knees started to steam. "And if we can't figure out how to escape, regardless of whether you can get her pregnant or not, your mother is going to make you have sex in front of the entire Winter Court."

My pulse stuttered in shock.

"You're what?" Titus jerked forward from his spot by the wall, his aura flaring around his hands, his claws extending from his fingers.

I didn't know Amiah well, but I knew having something like that forced on her would break her. I'd known from the moment I'd met her she'd been repressing her sexuality and now desperately wanted to embrace it but didn't know how and was afraid to. Being forced to perform in public would push her into a shell she'd never come out of.

No, she needed to be encouraged without judgment, worshiped until she recognized how beautiful and strong she was, and I wanted to be the one to show her.

Anything long term between us was out of the question. Amiah might fancy a *ménage à trois* but eventually, she'd want something permanent with someone.

That someone wouldn't be me, and I was okay with that.

"I'm not sleeping with Amiah for my mother's entertainment," Bane said, his need for her swelling, radiating against my senses. "I'm not sleeping with her, period."

Well, if he wouldn't. I would. I'd give her whatever she wanted, and not because of the power in her desire — which had been the original reason I'd begged her to return to my tent — but because I selfishly wanted to have that connection with her again, of being seen for who I truly was, however brief, and I wanted her to feel it, too. With my incubus nature, I didn't know if I was capable of giving it to her, but I was damned well going to try. And even if I failed, I'd still be giving her the gift of pleasure, something she deserved.

"Why would your mother think you could get Amiah pregnant?" Titus asked. "You're fae and she's an angel."

"She seems to think the magic of the Winter Court can make it happen," Cassius replied, more fire sparking from his hands and arms.

I would, however, need to be careful of Cassius. He was overprotective of her for good reason, but that was getting in the way of something my magic assured me she desired, all because he wasn't willing to admit he wanted to have sex with her.

"You also didn't need to reinforce the lie that you're married to her by making it look like the Winter Court responds to her," Cassius said, "or whatever it was you did to make the queen and Deaglan think Amiah can control the court's wind."

"Deaglan is here?" Titus's aura exploded, his beast's power blinding me. My instincts screamed to move, to run, his beast was breaking free with a fury that would blindly kill everything in its way.

I heaved onto my side to get off the cot and run — although I had no idea how the hell I was going to run, I wasn't even sure I could stand.

"T," Bane snapped and Titus growled and thankfully stayed where he was. "Hold it together. Everyone just God damn hold it together. Yes, the bastard is here, but now isn't the time for revenge."

"Every time is time for revenge," Titus snarled.

If I was smart, I'd also be mindful of Titus.

Given that he and Amiah had just met, his powerful desire for her had to come from his captivity, not because he was in love with her. But I'd seen him release part of his beast to rescue her from Balwyrdan, and I didn't want to be on the wrong end of that ferocious rage.

"Sure. And you'll just release your beast in the middle of the Winter Court. That'll go well," Bane snapped. "He has that demon-vampire hybrid with him. The rest of his assassination team is probably here as well. If they don't capture you, my mother will use the Winter Court's magic to imprison you, and then you'll be her bitch."

"*And* you'll endanger Amiah," Cassius said.

Titus's beast surged again, forcing me to squint to even catch a glimpse of him, and he jerked toward the door. I didn't know if he was going to go after Deaglan right now or to Amiah to protect her, but he slammed his fist into the wall instead. "I *will* kill him."

"And I'll help," Bane said, "but our priority is keeping you out of the hands of anyone in any of the courts."

"And protecting Amiah," Cassius insisted, the steam around him thickening and the water starting to boil. "You have power over the Winter Court. Can you use that to help us?"

At least Bane, who was already sleeping with her, would understand what I was doing. But even he'd been acting strange since we got here. Yes, Amiah wasn't in any condition for sex and her appearance was shocking and heartbreaking and enraging, but for someone who wanted to sleep with her again, he sure was giving her the cold shoulder. He'd looked like he'd been walking to his death when he'd gone into the bedroom to help her shower.

"I barely have power," Bane said, the demonic magic snapping through his aura, making him gasp. He was going to have to do something about that soon. It hadn't been good when I'd used my magic to get his resonance yesterday and it had gotten worse since then. The demonic magic that wasn't supposed to be in him grew every time he used his magic, be it a spell in one of the glyphs tattooed on his body or a spell woven with raw power with his sorcerer's ability.

"You made the wind gust when Amiah refused your mother," Cassius said.

"I didn't." Bane rubbed his face. "That was all Amiah."

"So you are mates," Titus said, his aura writhing as his beast strained to get free. "It's the only way she'd be able to control the wind."

"For the last fucking time, we're not mates, she's not mine, and she's not a dragon. She doesn't adhere to five-hundred-year-old dragon social norms. She can have whoever's scent she wants on her, whenever she wants it. Hell, if it so strikes her fancy, she could fuck all of us all at the same time or the whole fucking court and still not *belong* to anyone."

Fire rushed over Cassius's arms as his need for release pounded through him. "Amiah wouldn't *fuck* all of us."

"Fine." Bane rolled his eyes at him. "*Make love*. She's her own woman. If you want a sexual relationship with her grow a pair and tell her."

"But the court recognizes her," Titus said.

"We're not mates and we'll never be mates. I will

never make the marriage vow. Ever." The demonic magic flared again, sending painful angry spikes through Bane's aura, and he tried to bite back a groan — he was probably successful at hiding it from the others since they couldn't see the magic inside him. "I have no fucking clue why the Winter Court responded to her. Maybe it's the leash spell, maybe it's my mother's desperate desire to get her pregnant, maybe it just God damned likes her."

Like they all did.

Like I did.

Any of them would be a better long-term relationship than me, but none of them at the moment were going to give her what she craved... what she needed.

Well, until they figured themselves out, I'd give it to her. Discretely of course. There was no point in making the situation more complicated since we were all stuck together until we could get out of Faerie. But I wasn't going to let Amiah go without when it took nothing from me to give it to her.

AMIAH

CASSIUS HAD SLAMMED THE DOOR BEHIND HIM AND I'D cried into my pillow until I'd finally passed out. I must have slept for only a few hours because when I woke, still curled in a ball, my body was still burning like a painful smoldering ember and my power was still low.

For a second, I had no idea where I was, only that I wasn't in my apartment at Operations. I couldn't hear the familiar soft rumble of traffic on the street outside... although maybe it was very early in the morning. The Quarter was often quiet those few hours before dawn...

Then my thoughts tripped and the horror of the last few days flooded me. My pulse pounded and I fought to catch my breath. I'd been taken. Again. Helpless. Again.

I swore—

I clenched my jaw, fighting the storm of emotions threatening to drown me. If I didn't think about it, I'd be fine. Fine. That was the way it had worked the last time. *Stay in control. Don't be foolish and put yourself in dangerous situations again—*

Except I hadn't *put* myself in that situation. I hadn't chosen to get caught up in all of this, and yet, even if my magic hadn't locked onto Titus, I would have still rushed to save him the moment I saw him fall from the sky.

My stomach rumbled and clenched, reminding me that I'd drained my magic and hadn't eaten anything in over twenty-four hours — the few grapes I had when I'd woken not counting — which meant I might have been asleep for more than just a few hours. Without proper sustenance, it was harder to restore my power.

If I was going to heal properly, I needed to get up and find something to eat.

But I didn't want to move. I was afraid if I moved, I'd find out just how much I still hurt. I'd never experienced that kind of pain before. Not even the pain when Sebastian had tried to remove or change the leash spell had compared to the blaze of Hawk's power erupting in my cells.

My nerves were still raw, even after getting a little sleep. Just the miniscule slide of my skin against the soft comforter hurt, and I didn't know if this was something I could heal with my magic or not. I'd never had a patient who'd been flooded with an excess of sexual magic.

Except, if I was going to pull myself together and regain control — *please, any control* — I needed to restore my magic. There was nothing I could do for my soul or my fear, but in the very least, I needed to finish mending my broken bones.

With a groan — I didn't care if anyone including Cassius heard me, I wasn't going to fight to keep it in — I uncurled and sat up. My nerves lit up with agony and I panted, praying if I just kept breathing the sensation would pass.

I could do this. I was strong.

My throat tightened.

I didn't need Cassius to help me. Even if the smart thing would be to call out for help and have someone bring me food.

When had I become that person? The one who ignored practical logic and did something foolish just—

Tears burned my eyes.

Just to stay in control.

Because my control had been taken from me. Again.

Not going to think about it.

I stood on shaky legs and staggered to the door before realizing there might not be any food in the suite. Which meant I was going to have to at least ask Sebastian for help if I wanted to eat.

Jeez. I was going to have to call out and alert everyone to my condition and then deal with Cassius again.

Couldn't I just do one thing on my own? I needed to be able to do something by myself for myself. I couldn't stand being helpless and pathetic and weak, the angel who'd been foolishly captured by that human and now brutally beaten by that fae. I didn't want to accept that that was who I was.

With a trembling hand, I opened the door. The living room turned dining room was still a dining room, the table still set with plates of uneaten food and glasses of undrunk wine. The light emanating from the walls and ceiling was low — guess the guys were in the other room sleeping — but I could see well enough with my night vision. I shuffled to the closest place setting where Deaglan had sat and reached for the fork. He hadn't touched his food, and while it would be cold, at least it would still be food.

"Don't," Titus said, his gruff voice coming from the back of the room, making me jump a little and setting my nerves on fire. "The food could be enspelled."

He sat in the corner with his knees pulled up to his bare chest, his claws dug into the floor, his breath too fast, and his body tense. His gaze, a muddy brown because of the glamour that changed his appearance and not the striking gold that had first stolen my breath, locked on me, filled with a ferocious desperate intensity. His beast was straining to rise to the surface.

"You should shift," I said, holding the edge of the table to keep my balance and shuffling toward him. He hadn't fully shifted and released his beast since I'd met him, and before that, he'd only shifted once in the last five hundred years. And what with the influx of Hawk's magic that had to have been influencing all of us not just me, his beast was probably going crazy.

"I don't want to risk it." He squeezed his eyes shut. "Shifting could break the glamour and with Deaglan in court—"

My throat tightened, my heart aching for him. My captivity had been nothing compared to his, a blink of an eye. I didn't know if Deaglan had hurt Titus as much as Balwyrdan had hurt me — and I wasn't going to think about that, not now, not ever — but not being able to release his beast for five hundred years was bad enough. And I doubted Titus had gotten the physical contact that as a shifter he needed to help calm his soul.

"Let me help you."

"Your magic can't heal this," he said.

"No. But maybe I can help steady your soul. May I?"

"My beast is raging. I could hurt you."

"You won't." I didn't know if that was true or not, but it didn't matter. He needed help and I could give it to him. That was at least something I could do, something I could control. *Please, I need to be in control.* "Why fight this alone when you don't have to?"

I sagged to the floor beside him and he stiffened. I hadn't thought it possible that he could get tenser.

Then he rumbled, a rough, desperate sound and wrapped an arm around me, carefully drawing me against him. "Thank you."

I pressed my hands and cheek against his massive bare chest, giving him as much flesh-to-flesh contact as I could manage. His pulse raced and he trembled, the movement making my skin burn, but I gritted my teeth and took slow steady breaths, trying to will him to relax.

There was a chance he wouldn't be able to, that his beast was too enraged at being held back that physical contact, especially with someone who wasn't his mate — or the same species — wouldn't be able to steady him.

I didn't know what I'd do if that was the case. We were stuck in the Winter Court, hiding him from all of Faerie, and he was the last dragon. The only thing I could do was give him physical contact.

But then he took in a slow, shuddering breath, and his pulse began to slow and his trembling eased.

Thank goodness.

I'd done something. I wasn't helpless, not like when—

I leaned into him, my own soul aching for this contact. I needed it as much as he did, needed to feel his life force warm and thrumming against my senses, needed the distraction. I'd gone almost two months without this kind of contact, contact I hadn't thought I'd needed until I'd mistakenly believed I'd met my soul mate. His shifter nature had made him more physically affectionate than an angel even though we'd only ever been friends and I hadn't realized how much I wanted to be held until it was gone.

I bit back a bitter huff. I hadn't realized a lot of things. Like what a nightmare a soul bond would be, how my mating brand would trap my soul to someone's, possibly a complete stranger's. I'd be helpless to resist, I'd be desperate if something happened to him, and, whether I wanted to or not, I'd fall in love with him.

My pulse picked up and Titus took my hand, rubbing gentle circles in my palm with his thumb calming me — I wasn't even sure he was aware he was doing it.

"I missed this," he said.

"Me, too."

He tensed again. "You have someone?"

"Had. A shifter friend." And I'd been such a fool over him. "I hadn't realized how much I needed his touch until it was gone."

"*His* touch?" Titus asked.

"His. Someone's. He found his mate and that connection, that contact I'd become used to was suddenly gone and I..." I didn't know how to explain the loss of something so small and simple. Couldn't I have just asked someone for a hug? Even if other angels were naturally standoffish, I could have asked a non-angel. But I didn't know how to explain why I, an angel, wanted it. I wasn't supposed to need it, not as deeply as I did.

"You felt lost," he said, "empty, even though you weren't mates."

"Yes." Empty and alone and heartbroken. Although my heartache had more to do with the death of a dream, the childish fantasy that my soul bond was an amazing, beautiful gift.

"I lost my mate the last time the Heart awakened." He tipped his head back against the wall and closed his eyes. "She wasn't my soul's mate, but we'd been happy."

For a second I saw his true rugged appearance and not the glamour, his wide cheeks, slightly crooked nose, and hard square jaw dusted with pale golden-red stubble. He wasn't as breathtaking as Sebastian or Hawk or as classically handsome as Cassius, but there was something stunning and beautifully primal about him. A ferociousness. The promise of a powerful passion that tugged at my heart... and reminded me of Marcus, the man who wasn't my destiny.

The lonely ache I'd been trying to ignore since Essie Shaw had walked into my life squeezed around my heart. "I'm so sorry."

"I lost everyone. I think I would have killed myself if it hadn't been for Seireadan and—" His thumb stopped moving and his grip on my hand tightened. "And Deaglan. I think they would have gotten me through the worst of it if Faerie hadn't called me to hibernate."

"You and Deaglan were friends?" No wonder he hadn't trusted Sebastian when we'd first found him.

"We'd grown up together. Been friends for almost eighty years before—" His hand holding mine started to tremble. "I was such an idiot. Seireadan gifted me with a spell to find him wherever he was, saying that when I woke, he'd be strong enough to sever or block my connection to the Heart. Deaglan gave me chains."

Both magically with the leash spell and physically. I pressed my free hand over the scar on his wrist, a match to the one on his other wrist and around his neck. The glamour hid them, but I knew they were there and that he'd forever bear the horrible proof of his captivity, a constant reminder of Deaglan's betrayal.

"I got those trying to free myself from his shackles." He set his hand over mine, holding it against his wrist, his heartbreaking tremor growing stronger. "I fought every day."

Of course he did. Because he was strong. Not just physically but mentally. I'd barely fought, either time. I hadn't even realized that first time that I'd needed to fight until it was too late.

"I wish I had." Tears stung my eyes. God, I'd been so naive and weak.

I still was. I always would be.

"I didn't even fight the first time when it was just a human holding me. I could have released my wings and flown away." I should have released my wings. "He never had me chained when I was healing the sick for his profit. But I couldn't leave them."

I blinked, fighting back my tears. I'd been young and

curious about the mortal realm and had found that human in the middle of nowhere, dying from a particularly aggressive strain of influenza. He'd left his village to find someone to help fight the illness killing his people and I'd willingly drained my magic and saved them.

Then he'd asked me to help the next village down the road and by the time I realized he was demanding money, choosing who lived and who died, it was too late. He was already chaining me up at night to a trunk filled with rocks too heavy for me to move and I was too weak to resist my compulsion to heal the never-ending line of sick and injured people to escape.

"So many of them were children with parents desperate to try anything, *pay* anything to save them." And my power had trapped me.

I slid my hand out from under Titus's and stared at my palms. Pale light — that only I could see because it was still weak — radiated from them, proof that I had some power available to heal someone, that if someone was in dire need, I'd have no choice, I'd have to try to save them.

"It's who you are," he said, cupping my hands between his and reestablishing that point of flesh-to-flesh contact. "You risked Hawk killing you to save him from more pain."

"Because I'm weak. I can't bear to see someone in pain if I can prevent it and I can barely control my magic. I'd have never been held captive if it hadn't been for my power, if I had an ounce of self-control. I knew that human was going to drain me to death, knew the only way to survive was to hold back my healing magic." From those desperate, sick children.

"If Cassius hadn't found me—" I fought to push the memories back, but I couldn't force them out of my mind and couldn't make myself stop talking. Perhaps it was because I'd kept it bottled up for so long that the minute a crack had formed it was breaking free, or perhaps it was because Titus knew the fear of being held prisoner. No one else could relate, certainly not Cassius.

"I knew eventually he was going to hit me more than just a few times, he was going to stop being careful about leaving bruises that others could see, he was going to—" My breath picked up. "He was going to rape me."

I squeezed my eyes shut. I wouldn't cry.

I. Would. Not. Cry.

My months with that human had been nothing compared to my few hours with Balwyrdan. I'd thought I'd known fear, but I hadn't had a clue what true fear was.

A tremor swept through me and Titus's arm around my shoulders tightened.

Don't think about it. Just don't think about it.

But I couldn't get my body to stop shaking and the memory of Balwyrdan's fist slamming into my face rushed into my mind. His first punch had completely stunned me with shock and pain, my brain unable to fully register what had happened. The next strike had frozen me with fear.

Don't think about it.

He would have killed me if Cassius and the others hadn't rescued me. He would have drawn out my pain until I wished I was dead, then given me to his men for their entertainment, then—

Stop thinking!

Terror clenched my heart and tightened my throat. "If I'd stayed in Sebastian's apartment, if I hadn't gone up to the roof— If I—"

"You couldn't have known Balwyrdan would be there," Titus replied, releasing my hands to draw me tighter against his body, my trembling growing so strong my teeth chattered.

"But I swore." A tear broke free. "I swore to be smarter, to be more careful, to stay in control." Another tear raced after the first. "I swore never again."

Stop thinking.

Please. Stop thinking.

But the panic and desperation that I'd been determined to ignore had broken free. I couldn't think of anything else. He would have killed me. He would have hurt me until I begged him to kill me and then kept going.

I shouldn't have just lain there. I should have fought back, fought through the pain and shock, should have stopped him from kidnapping me in the first place, or avoided it, or something. I should have done something! Anything. Again. Always.

I swore. "I swore."

And my vows were useless.

It didn't matter what I wanted. I hadn't been strong enough to escape Balwyrdan or even that human. There was no way I'd be strong enough to avoid the fate of my mating brand. I'd never be strong.

Why couldn't I be strong? All I wanted was to be strong. Titus had survived five hundred years in captivity. Five hundred! He'd fought to free himself every day. Probably every hour.

I didn't even have a sliver of his strength because I'd done nothing.

Not a damned thing.

"I didn't even try." I didn't want to be weak. I was so tired of being weak. "Why didn't I do something?"

"But you did do something."

I barked a bitter laugh. "Yeah, I cried and cowered."

Titus hooked his finger under my chin and lifted my gaze. A glimmer of gold shone in his glamoured eyes, his expression filled with sorrow and rage and heartbreak. "You survived. You held out until we came for you."

"Is that all I'm capable of?" *God. Please.* "I just wanted to be strong."

"You are." Titus pulled me into his lap and hugged me to his chest, wrapping his body around me. "There are more kinds of strength than just physical and you're one of the strongest people I've ever met. You faced Hawk's magic without blinking an eye even though you had to have known it would hurt. You didn't cower when I threatened to kill you when we first met and then offered to keep healing me, and you sure as hell didn't cower when Balwyrdan had you. I saw the look in your eyes. If there'd been an opportunity to fight him you would have taken it."

I pressed my face against Titus's broad chest and clung to him, sobbing. "Then why couldn't I stop him?"

Why couldn't I?

Why?

"Because he controlled the leash spell," Titus said, pressing his lips to the top of my head. "You knew that. You knew your best move was to hold on, and you did."

And that was the horrible truth. The truth I didn't want to admit because it meant it didn't matter how strong I was or how prepared, or in control. Balwyrdan could have taken Titus or Cassius or any of the guys — with the possible exception of Sebastian — and none of us would have stood a chance against him and his control of the leash spell. None of us would have been able to run away, not from the rooftop or in the abandoned reception hall. None of us would have been able to do anything.

I wanted to scream at the injustice of it, to tear into my pain and terror and helplessness, defy it, defeat it, rip it to God damned pieces.

But all I could do was cry, hacking angry sobs of frustration and grief. Balwyrdan had stolen all those years of determination, of trying to prove to myself that I was no longer the angel Cassius had rescued. He'd shattered my illusion that if I was just strong enough and smart enough and in control enough everything would be fine. I could *do* something, take action, control my fate. But I could have been as strong as Titus, and Balwyrdan still would have taken and hurt me.

It wasn't fair. It wasn't God damned fair.

But then life wasn't fair. And I cried for the loss of another dream, the dream that if I'd just prepared, I could keep myself safe against everything. I cried because I hadn't cried after Cassius had first rescued me or when I realized the horror of the mating brand. I cried because it felt so good to be wrapped in Titus's arms and because that terrified me and because I'd been keeping so many people at arm's length, afraid they'd see how out-of-control I was.

And I cried because fate was a wild raging storm I couldn't control. No matter what I wanted or how hard I tried.

TITUS

I HELD AMIAH AS SHE CLUNG TO ME AND CRIED heartrending sobs, her face pressed against my chest, her small hands clutching my shoulders. It made both me and my beast furious that she thought her inability to do something when there had been nothing anyone could have done against Balwyrdan meant she was weak. Physically, sure. She was delicate and fragile. She didn't stand a chance in a fight, but her willpower and her soul—

Her soul was so damned fierce, her determination powerful, as powerful as any dragon I'd met. More so because she was so fragile. She gave life, pulled it from her very essence and handed it away at her own expense despite her fear. She hadn't cared that my beast could have hurt her. She'd sat beside me and offered everything she had to help ease its turmoil, and it yearned to go back in time and rip Balwyrdan to pieces before Cassius had set him on fire. How dare Balwyrdan make her afraid, make her doubt herself and her worth. How dare that human! My beast wanted to find that human who was probably already dead — probably at Cassius's hands — and give Amiah the justice she deserved.

And it was furious that Cassius was the one to have given her that. It should have been me. Always me.

It didn't matter that I hadn't known her back then. My beast didn't care that its desire wasn't logical. It wanted to protect her. *I* wanted to protect her.

Because she's mine.

I bit back a snarl.

Not. Mine.

Not yet.

Seireadan was right. She didn't belong to anyone. Except I couldn't convince my beast of that, and with her crying in my arms, taking comfort in my body, it was more certain now than ever that she was mine. Even the raging need that had consumed me when Hawk's power had been out of control had eased because she didn't need to have sex, she needed soul to soul comfort, needed to be steadied and reassured.

Yes, I still wanted her. I'd gotten off in the shower — Seireadan and Cassius thankfully letting me go first — and couldn't think of anyone else but her. I'd tried to focus on her injuries, how she was in no condition for sex. I imagined her in bed with Seireadan and then Hawk, but nothing worked. My thoughts kept turning her into the stunning woman I'd first met, determined, and filled with life and kindness. My beast didn't just want a woman because I'd been locked away for half a millennium, my beast wanted *her* and her alone, and it would kill anyone who hurt her. And right now, with her delicate body shaking in my arms, her tears trailing down my chest, I agreed.

Mine.

I would fight for her, and I would go through anyone who stood between us.

Which wasn't healthy. I didn't really know her. We'd only just met. I couldn't possibly be feeling the things I was feeling for her, not to mention she already had complicated relationships with all the other guys, especially Seireadan. He might have said he didn't want her, but my beast found that hard to believe. Who would willingly give her up? Once I'd proven myself to her and she was mine, the only way I'd leave her would be if someone killed me. No, Seireadan would go back to her once he realized what a fool he was, and I needed to figure out how to control my beast and not kill him until I could convince Seireadan she was mine.

For a long time, I just held her as she cried, my soul thrumming at her nearness, and my beast coiled tight within me ready to protect her, possessively satisfied that she felt safe enough in my arms to release her hold on her emotions in front of me.

I didn't know how long she cried, but eventually, her tears subsided, and with a heavy sigh, she sat back and wiped her eyes, sending panic clenching around my heart.

She was done. She didn't need me anymore. I had to accept that. But I didn't want to. I wanted more. I wanted it all with her.

Mine.

"I'm sorry," she said, looking up at me, her eyes rimmed with red and her shockingly blue gaze capturing me as if she didn't already possess me.

My pulse stalled and my beast strained against my control not to break free and shift, but to kiss her, show her how much I desired her.

But the part of me that was man and not beast knew her emotions were still a confused mess. Making a move could scare her and make her push me away, and then my beast would really lose its shit.

"I was supposed to be steadying your soul," she said, "and here you are letting me cry on you."

"It doesn't have to be one or the other." I fought the urge to tighten my grip around her and instead freed a strand of blond hair stuck to her damp cheek and tucked it behind her ear. "You needed my touch and I needed yours."

I still do.

"I should—" She glanced back at the bedroom and another tear trickled down her cheek. "I don't want to leave."

"Then don't."

"Sitting on the floor like this can't be comfortable."

"It doesn't bother me." *I have you.*

"I—" She pressed her hand over my heart — I wasn't sure she was aware she was doing it — and returned her gaze to mine.

My whole essence stalled trapped in the gravity of her soul. *Stay. Please.*

"I wish the Winter Court had windows," she said, sagging back against my chest.

Oh, yes.

"I really need to see the sky. Please tell me there's more to the court than just that square of sky in the healing pools."

"So much more," I said, tightening my embrace. "The Winter Court has a lot of storms, but when the queen is happy, the sky is stunning." *Like your eyes.* "Clear and crisp, the sun reflecting off the ice and snow making it brighter than the brightest day in the Court of Light."

And I wanted to show her all of it.

I'd lost my mind. I swore that if I ever escaped from Deaglan, I'd never return to Faerie, but now I wanted to soar through the Winter Court's ice canyons, ride the thermals at the edge of the Lusaline Desert in the Summer Court, and lie in a meadow of sweet-smelling primrose with her, watching the clouds drift by in the Spring Court. I wanted to show her all the things I'd loved about Faerie before the Heart had awakened and my kin were slaughtered and I was imprisoned.

My beast tensed. The Heart was awake again. Just my very presence put Amiah in danger.

She shifted, snuggling closer, and instantly eased my beast. It would protect her, no matter what, whatever it took. Always. Mine.

"Are all the courts affected by their rulers' moods?" she asked, closing her eyes, relaxing even more into me, the tension in her body starting to melt away.

"Yes, their will shapes their court by harnessing the wild magic of Faerie. Without a monarch, there is no court, and without a strong monarch, the court is in chaos." Of course, a weak monarch usually didn't survive long. If the monarch was weak, Faerie would attack the court's high fae, trying to pull its magic out of them, killing them until it found a fae strong enough to withstand it. That fae became the court's new ruler.

Except being strong only protected a high fae in a court and the moment Seireadan stepped into the Wilds, Faerie would try to claim its magic back until we reached the safety of my ancestral home.

"Is that why the queen is so determined to make Sebastian her heir?" she asked, her word slurring with sleep. "She thinks Padraigin isn't strong enough because the court's wind doesn't blow for her."

"If the Winter Court doesn't respond to her, then she won't be able to control its magic when she ascends to the throne." I shuddered. The Autumn Court had nearly been decimated when its ancient queen had lost her will to live and was consumed by Faerie's magic. Her son hadn't been strong enough and the screams of the court's high fae had filled the Wilds all day and night for days. "But I'm surprised that it doesn't. She's not a sorcerer like Seireadan, but her water magic has always been strong."

"I don't think Sebastian wants to be king," she murmured. "He shouldn't be trapped by that. No one should."

"No. No one should. Ever." Not my best friend, and not my angel. Never again.

It didn't matter how irrational it was, my beast had decided. It would give everything to protect her, be it against a monster like Balwyrdan or the full power of the Winter Court and its queen.

Mine. Always and forever.

And the sooner she figured that out and accepted that, the safer Seireadan and the others would be from me.

AMIAH

I WOKE COMPLETELY ALONE IN THE ENORMOUS BED AND feeling better, lighter, like a massive weight had been lifted from my chest. Last night hadn't healed all my emotional wounds, but it had helped release a pressure that I hadn't realized had been building inside me.

A part of me, however, was sad Titus hadn't stayed when he'd tucked me in. It had felt so good being held by him, his life force soothing, the warmth of his body relaxing. I'd felt safe, if still raw and shaky from my breakdown. I wasn't even embarrassed that I'd cried in his arms. I'd needed to cry in someone's and he, out of all of the guys, could at least relate to what I'd gone through. That, and he'd needed a physical connection as much as I had, his soul had been in as much turmoil as mine.

But if he'd joined me in bed, I might have given in to my desire for a deeper physical connection — not to mention my craving to lose myself and my worries in the sensations of sexual intercourse. That would have made things complicated between us, between me and Cassius, heck, between me and all of the guys... well, maybe not between me and Hawk. As an incubus, he didn't have the same emotional connections other species had.

Besides, even if my not-yet-fully-formed mating brand hadn't awakened, there was still a chance Titus was my soul mate and having sex could awaken our bond, and I wasn't going to risk it. Maybe when Sebastian removed my brand...

Except what about Cassius? Did I love Cassius? There was something between us, but I could also feel something between me and Titus... and between me and Sebastian... and me and Hawk.

It had to be lust.

Yep, that was it. I was confusing honest, long-term emotions with lust because I'd finally broken my vow of celibacy, now knew what I'd been missing, and wanted to make up for lost time.

I couldn't possibly be in love with four men, three of whom I barely knew.

Except Essie was.

Because fate had forced that upon her with her mating brands.

A whisper of pain raced along the ghostly lines of my brand, shooting from the middle of my thigh up over my hip and around my back to my ribcage.

It was a fate I was going to avoid.

I wanted to be with someone because I wanted to be with them. Not because my brand made me.

The pain subsided into an ache that was a little too warm for comfort, making me keenly aware that it was there, that my destiny was coming, and coming soon. It

hadn't been this warm the last time I'd felt it... which had
been the last time I hadn't been in pain.

My thoughts stuttered at that.

I wasn't in pain.

Somehow all of my broken bones had healed while
I'd slept and I couldn't have unconsciously used my
magic. My power didn't work that way. I needed to
concentrate to heal anyone including myself, and I was at
full, my magic warm and overflowing around my hands.

How was I healed?

Just crying in Titus's arms wouldn't have healed my
body like it had helped to mend a part of my soul, and
surely Sebastian would have said something if the Winter
Court could heal someone like this.

Someone knocked briskly on the bedroom door and
cracked it open.

"You need to get up," Cassius said. "You've been
asleep for almost twelve hours and you need to eat
something."

My stomach grumbled, reminding me that I hadn't
eaten in far too long. "I'm awake."

"Are you decent? Would you like to freshen up first?"
Meaning, he was going to help me to the bathroom
whether I wanted him to or not.

"I'm fine." I sat up as he opened the door wider — not
waiting for me to confirm my state of decency — and I
scrambled to make sure my robe was pulled closed after
falling open while I'd slept.

Behind him, the living room was back to being a
living room. Titus sat squished in an armchair still only
wearing the loose pants and showing off the broad

expanse of a chest still beautifully muscular even with the glamour disguising him. Our gazes locked for a second and relief flooded me. He looked more relaxed than I'd ever seen him, more in harmony with both aspects of his nature, and a part of me was thrilled that I'd helped steady his soul even though I wasn't his mate or a dragon.

"You're hardly fine," Cassius said, his expression completely frozen and shutdown. "You still have some broken ribs and a broken nose—" He frowned. "Why does your nose look fine?"

Because somehow I was fine.

Hawk groaned. He sat in the other armchair — strangely enough wearing a shirt — with his head tipped back and his complexion gray. He looked like he had a hangover. Of course, given the amount of magic that had flooded him, I wasn't surprised. I might have taken on a huge amount of his power but he'd still had too much in his system. Not enough to kill him, but certainly enough to make him feel terrible for a good while even with his enhanced healing—

Wait a minute.

I'd taken a huge amount of his magic.

"Oh, my goodness! You did an energy transfer because I forced you to release your power through a kiss." That explained why I was completely healed.

Incubi and succubi consumed life force from the people they seduced, but they could also give it back. That influx of magic helped heal a person. I just hadn't realized so much of it could help someone rapidly heal like an incubus.

"Nope," Hawk moaned. "That's just a myth. We can't transfer energy into someone to heal them."

"Except I know you can." One of Essie's mates had done it to save her life and then swore me to secrecy—

Oh, no.

I shouldn't have said anything in front of the other guys. I was just so surprised Hawk had done it. I'd been told incubi and succubi didn't want it getting out that they could do energy transfers. It was dangerous for them. It wasn't like how I healed someone. I had magic and when it ran out, I was just drained and exhausted. An incubus gave someone their life force. If they ran out of power, they died.

"No point in lying about it," Sebastian said from his spot on the couch, a flash of pain tightening his expression for a second. Something was still wrong with him, but I had no idea what. "It's the only way to explain how her nose is no longer broken and her power is still at full."

"And now Sparky and T know about it." Hawk glowered at him. "Thanks for that."

"If you'd known you could do that—" Cassius started.

"I hadn't realized I was doing *that*." Hawk turned his glower on me. "And don't you dare think about telling any of your healing angel friends or writing a paper about me. I'm not going to become anyone's lab rat."

"Never," I said. I couldn't believe I'd slipped up so badly. I'd just been caught completely off guard by it. "And don't you dare do it again. I was told doing a transfer like that is dangerous for you."

"At least the idiot who let it out of the bag told you

everything." Hawk rubbed his face. "It's potentially deadly to us, especially if we can't get a recharge in time. I think the only reason I wasn't immediately incapacitated was because I was already ODing on too much energy."

Titus sat forward, his attention still locked on me. He hadn't looked away from me since the door had opened. "So Amiah is healed. That means we can leave."

"No," Cassius replied, surprising me. "I don't want the Winter Queen knowing what Amiah's magic is. Your unusual energy transfer aside, angels are the only species with healing magic and only a few have it. Our original reasons for drawing this out still stands. I don't want Amiah becoming any more of a target than she already is."

"Are you crazy?" Hawk asked. "The longer we stay here the longer we're *all* in danger. I'm sure none of you want a repeat of last night... this morning...? God, I don't even know what time it is in here."

"It's the middle of the afternoon and man, I hate that I'm agreeing with him again, but Cassius is right." Sebastian gave me an apologetic look. "Best not to give my mother another reason to search for you after we leave."

Except that meant they were all unnecessarily putting themselves in danger to protect me.

"If that's the only reason we're putting off leaving, then we should leave." I pushed back the comforter, stood, and headed to the door. Not a hint of pain — with the exception of my aching brand. That energy transfer had been a lot more powerful than the one Essie's mate had done. Of course, I'd paid for it with excruciating pain, and even if it wasn't potentially deadly for Hawk, I didn't want to repeat that. "There are four of you and one of me. It doesn't make sense for us to stay."

"It makes perfect sense," Titus said.

"Yeah, if something happens to you and I get hurt, I'm not kissing that asshole," Sebastian said, jerking his thumb at Hawk.

"You know I like it when you play hard to get." Hawk half-heartedly waggled his eyebrows at Sebastian before his expression returned to I-feel-terrible. "If we stay, we still need to figure out a way for me to eat. That should be reason enough for us to get the hell out of here."

"After last night, you should be good for a few days." Cassius stepped aside, giving me way too much room to pass, making my heart squeeze.

I hadn't expected him to just get over me risking my life by taking Hawk's power, but a part of me had hoped he'd understood why I'd done it. He, out of all of the guys, knew how my magic worked, knew how I had a compulsion that was hard to ignore — and impossible to ignore when my magic locked onto someone. It had been hard enough to tell him to burn Hawk the first time. I couldn't have watched him do it again.

Someone knocked on the door and Sebastian, Titus, and even Hawk stood, joining Cassius, instantly ready for a fight.

"Amiah, look weak," Cassius said, stepping between me and the door.

I crossed my arms and tried to make myself look as small as possible. I didn't know if that made me look weak or not, but I didn't have a lot of experience pretending to be weak. All of my pretending had been to try to look stronger than I felt.

"Enter," Sebastian called and two ice maids each carrying an enormous silver platter covered with a large lid, and a third with a tray holding a silver pitcher and glasses hurried inside. They were followed by two more maids with a table made entirely of ice. "Set the table and food by the door and don't bother with the chairs."

"Yes, your highness," they said in unison. They quickly obeyed while the five other maids holding chairs waited in the hall with the two ice guards then curtsied and left.

"Told you we wouldn't need to wait long for something to arrive." Sebastian strode to the table and lifted one of the lids.

Inside were three plates with large servings of... I wasn't sure what. It looked like a roasted small bird of some kind, on a pile of something purple and grain-like, with green, blue, and red chunks of something else.

I headed around the couch to get a plate, but Titus grabbed my wrist, stopping me. "Wait until Seireadan checks it for spells."

"It looks okay," Sebastian said. "Just sit and I'll bring you a plate."

"Gee, thanks," Hawk replied.

Sebastian snorted. "I was talking to Amiah. You don't need a plate."

"But—" Hawk batted his eyelashes. "I can still enjoy the taste and I healed all her broken bones."

"And I'm perfectly capable of getting my own plate," I said.

"He just about killed you and I'm already standing here," Sebastian insisted.

"That's not fair," Hawk groaned as he stood. "She *made* me almost kill her."

"You should still be getting her a plate," Titus said, tugging on my wrist and urging me to sit on the couch.

"Come on, guys. Can't you see I'm dying here?" But Hawk was already at the table, pouring himself a drink. "And jeez, you should have let them bring in chairs so you could sit at the table."

"Sure, and that would be five more of my mother's constructs getting a look at Amiah and wondering if she looks healthy or not," Sebastian said, picking up two plates and two sets of cutlery and returning to the couch.

He set a plate on the coffee table in front of me then sat on the couch as far away from me as possible.

Him too?

But of course, he'd made it clear that he wasn't going to risk Cassius's wrath by having any more contact with me.

"So we're going to be fucking idiots and stay," Hawk said, sitting back in his chair with his drink. His gaze lifted, met mine for a second, and the hellfire in his eyes flickered. My pulse fluttered, surprisingly not in fear at the memory of his power roaring through me, but in anticipation of it sliding sensually into my body and heating my desire again.

A whisper of a smile tugged at his lips and he gave me a slight nod. I wasn't sure what that meant, and Titus sat on the floor at my feet, drawing my attention away from Hawk, before I could figure it out.

The big dragon leaned close, pressing his bare biceps and shoulder against my leg and giving me flesh-to-flesh contact. I wasn't sure if it was for him or me, and I didn't care. Just this simple touch felt good, steadying. With him, I could handle this... whatever *this* was going to be.

"We're also going to keep making trips to the healing pools to keep up the ruse," Sebastian said.

"The plan is still good." Cassius took Titus's chair and dug into his food. "I want a little more time to get a sense of the Winter Court's security and then we'll use the party as a cover for our escape. We just need to time it right."

The party where everyone was supposed to watch Sebastian and me conceive an heir to the Winter Court's throne. I set my plate in my lap and with a trembling hand poked a blue chunk with my fork. "I don't care what the timing is, so long as we leave before I have to have sex in public."

"That's a given," Sebastian said as Titus wrapped his large hand around my ankle, adding another point of contact and easing my shaking.

"Okay, so the first order of business is to lengthen the leash spell and adjust its effects on Amiah, then you and Sebastian should go to the pools," Cassius said, not even glancing my way. "T, you and I will wander back to the ballroom and its receiving rooms."

"You should take Hawk." Sebastian turned his attention to Titus. "You should stay here. I don't think you should be wandering around with Deaglan in court."

Titus tensed and his grip around my ankle tightened. "I'll go with you and Amiah to the pools."

"That's not—" Sebastian started but Hawk interrupted him.

"It's going to take a lot of magic to change the leash spell. If something happens, you might not be able to protect her." Hawk's gaze slid to mine again and this time his expression was clear. He was worried for me.

Sebastian narrowed his eyes and something subtle passed between him and Hawk. Hawk knew something that Sebastian didn't want the rest of us to know, and while I wanted to respect his privacy, if it endangered any of the guys—

"Sebastian—"

"It's fine," he said. "You don't need to worry. We've got you covered." He shot me a 'don't you dare' glance and shoveled a forkful of the purple stuff into his mouth.

I opened mine to protest then snapped it shut. I had secrets I didn't want the others to know too, and without a doubt if I forced Sebastian to reveal his, he'd reveal mine.

"So we're decided." Cassius cleaned his plate and set it on the coffee table. "Hawk, when you're ready?"

"I'm always ready," Hawk replied, flashing me a wicked smile even though he still looked hungover.

Cassius pinched the bridge of his nose and headed to the door. "I really hate working with demons."

"That's not fair," Hawk said, joining him at the door and slinging an arm over his shoulders. "You don't really know me."

"You're an incubus." Cassius shoved Hawk's arm off him and opened the door. "That's more than I need to know."

"Oh, come on, hot stuff. Don't tell me you're not even

curious." Hawk shot me another smile and followed Cassius into the hall, closing the door behind him.

"He's going to get himself killed," Sebastian said, and I took a tentative bite of the purple stuff. It was pretty good with the consistency of rice and an earthy, fresh basil kind of taste.

"Says the man who used to give him just as much grief," I replied. Had it only been a few days since Sebastian had been teasing us— teasing me? It had made me so frustrated and now I wanted that Sebastian back... because now I wanted to take him up on his flirtations and have sex with him again.

"And then I saw how powerful he is," Sebastian said. "I'm never poking that bear again."

"He wouldn't do anything to you." I tried the roasted bird. It tasted like chicken, thank goodness. "That's not who he is."

"Yeah, you keep on thinking that, princess," Sebastian said, taking another mouthful of the purple stuff.

Princess? Was he implying I didn't do anything for myself? "I'm hardly a princess. None of you are letting me do anything for myself. Besides—" I said with a chuckle, trying to keep the mood light, "I'm not a princess. I'm a future queen."

I took a bit of the purple stuff and Sebastian stiffened. "Not even if you fuck me in public. You're not my wife and you never will be."

The purple stuff turned to a lumpy, tasteless paste in my mouth, his words irrationally stinging... just like he'd intended them to. Except I didn't know why they'd hurt.

It had to be because he'd rejected me. That was all.

Not because I wanted any kind of a relationship with him. He wasn't my type. He clearly wasn't my soul mate. Why was that so hard to remember?

And yet I couldn't push aside my hurt feelings. He'd put me in my place and he'd been mean about it.

Well, fine.

A whisper of a cool wind caressed my cheeks.

"That wasn't what I meant and you know it." I met his pale, almost colorless blue gaze, daring him to say something else mean.

Something sad and angry slid across his expression. "You're right. I'm sorry." He ran a hand over his spiky white and silver hair. "I'm angry at my mother and Enowen, not you."

"Enowen?" There was that name again. Both his mother and Deaglan had mentioned her.

"No one important." He let out a heavy sigh and set his half-finished plate on the coffee table. "Let's get this leash spell stretched and adjust its side effects."

Except I was pretty sure she was very important. I'd never seen him react that way to anything.

AMIAH

LENGTHENING THE LEASH SPELL AND ADJUSTING IT SO I didn't suffocate if Sebastian got too far away from me was as painful as before. I would have thought after experiencing the agony of Hawk's power burning through me, changing the leash spell would have seemed like a skinned knee in comparison. But no, it was still like major surgery without an analgesic or sedative, and I didn't even bother trying to fight my tears.

Titus wrapped me in a firm embrace the moment Sebastian withdrew his hand from over my heart, and I trembled in his arms trying to get my breath back, while Sebastian sagged forward, his head between his knees.

"Fucking hell," he gasped. "I'll be really glad when I can get rid of this spell."

Which I knew was going to hurt as well. But at least it would be the last time.

I shuddered.

Would removing my mating brand hurt like that? Working with the leash spell always felt like Sebastian was tearing into my essence, and the leash spell wasn't a deep connection, it didn't feel rooted in my soul like my mating brand did.

I pushed that fear aside. I would deal with that when I had to. We had to get out of Faerie first and possibly deal with Faerie's awakening Heart.

But that thought only made my pulse race faster. I was running out of time and too much was happening for Sebastian to be bothered with my brand.

"Let's get to the pools so I can get my magic back," Sebastian said.

"I'll go get changed." Titus pressed his lips to the top of my head, released me, and headed to the servants' room.

Sebastian glanced up at me and his eyes widened at what he saw. "You can get through this one more time."

"That's not what I'm worried about." I brushed my hand over my hip before I realized what I was doing then tried to hide the movement by standing. The sudden action so soon after Sebastian had adjusted the leash spell made the room spin.

"Hey." Sebastian stood as well and grabbed my shoulders, steadying me, his expression soft with concern. "I haven't forgotten."

My pulse stalled and time froze. For a second I thought I glimpsed the real Sebastian, the man who hid behind sharp words and bravado, who'd fled his home, hid his identity, and swore never to return, and who'd been a generous lover and a fierce protector.

Then he rolled his eyes at me and his expression turned mocking, reminding me that he flirted — and probably slept with — every woman he could, and that now that he'd had me, he wasn't having me again. "Trust me. You're on the list right after escaping my mother. Cassius seriously needs to get laid."

"Gee, thanks." But I wasn't going to argue with him that I still didn't know how I felt about Cassius. If that's what motivated Sebastian to get rid of my brand, I'd take it.

"Now." He stepped back, his full-body glow dimming for a second revealing that gray complexion that concerned me so much, and held out his arms. "Let me carry you so you look weak and my mother doesn't pay us another visit."

"Are you sure? You look pale."

He quirked a hint of a smile. "I told you. I'm winter fae. I'm supposed to look pale."

"And I told you that's not what I meant." Not when I'd first said it to him in his bathroom two days ago and not now.

"Yeah, well. I'm good enough to carry you to the pools and I really don't want my mother to get more concerned about our marriage. That could make her add something magical to our public display and make it harder for us to avoid it."

"Good point." I shuddered at the thought, and let Sebastian pick me up.

Titus returned wearing a plain white thigh-length tunic that matched his pants. His gaze landed on me in Sebastian's arms and his eyes narrowed. For a second it looked like his pupils had slitted, his beast straining to get free, but he turned his back on us and marched out the door before I could get a good look at him.

Sebastian followed him and we headed down the hall with the ice guards a few steps behind, but when we turned the corner, an ice maid holding a small silver tray stood in front of the large intricately carved door blocking our way.

"You have a message, your highness." She curtsied as we approached and held out the tray with a small black coin on it that at one second looked like it glowed and the next didn't.

"Who's it from?" Sebastian asked, setting me on my feet but not reaching for the coin.

"I wasn't told," the maid replied, still holding her curtsey.

"Deag—" Titus glanced back at the guards then cleared his throat. "His Majesty of the Shadow Court?"

"It's not his magical signature," Sebastian said.

"He could be hiding it." Titus inched protectively close behind me but didn't touch me.

"He could, but there's only one way to find out." Sebastian tapped the coin with his finger. Light burst from it and his full-body fae glow flared bright for a second. His eyelids fluttered shut, his head tipped back, and he tensed. Then the light vanished and he opened his eyes. "I have to meet someone."

"Who?" Titus asked.

Sebastian turned to face us with a strange — was that happy? — expression, but his gaze jumped past my shoulder and his expression returned to grim. "Help *my wife* in the pool. I won't be gone long."

Titus tensed and also glanced back again at the ice guards looming half a dozen feet behind us. "It's not safe for you to be alone."

"I'll be fine. I have my mother's constructs to protect me." He stepped closer, capturing me between him and Titus and making my thoughts jump to being caught between them while wearing a lot less clothing.

I tried to push the inappropriate thought aside, but Sebastian hooked a finger under my chin and brushed his lips against mine.

I knew it was just an act for his mother's guards and maid, but that whisper of a caress from his lips stole my breath and heat rushed between my thighs. Just a touch and I was lost, as if the desire I'd had when all this had started had never been extinguished, just muted by my pain. I ached for him, ached for his mouth to return to mine, ached for it to go lower like it had the other night.

"You should stay," I murmured. *Stop worrying about Cassius's wrath and make me feel amazing again.* "T's right. It's too dangerous for you to be by yourself." My thoughts stuttered. "And what about the spell... connecting... you know." He could have made a mistake and not lengthened the leash spell or weakened its deadly effects. We hadn't had time to test it.

"It'll be okay. Trust me," he whispered back, "you don't need to worry about that and you want me to make this meeting. I'm hoping it'll be good news for you."

"Good news?"

He slid his hand over my left hip and met my gaze, his message clear. He was meeting someone about my brand. I could be free.

Oh, my goodness, I could be free!

"Can we trust this person?"

"That's what I'm going to find out." Sebastian stepped back and raised his gaze to Titus's. "I'll meet you back here."

"Stay safe," Titus said, his voice gruff.

Sebastian commanded the guards and the maid to not enter the healing grotto then hurried back down the hall with one of the ice guards following him.

With a growl, Titus pushed open the heavy door and ushered me inside, as the remaining guard closed it behind us.

The grotto's warm humid air wrapped around me and I sagged onto the bench by the door and stared up at the small square of bright blue sky in the skylight.

I was going to be free.

My mating brand was going to be removed and I'd be able to pursue a relationship with anyone I wanted. I wouldn't have to look to Sebastian or Hawk to relieve my desire... although Hawk would certainly be a good choice to help explore everything I'd learned about in anticipation of meeting my mate.

Free.

If whoever Sebastian was meeting could be trusted.

Fear and anticipation twisted in my gut.

Please let them be trustworthy. Please.

I didn't know why Sebastian wasn't removing my brand himself. He'd said he was the only one who could. Except when he'd said that we'd been in the mortal realm where he was likely one of the most powerful beings around. Here in Faerie there could be someone else better able to remove it. *Oh, please.*

My mixed emotions twisted tighter and swelled into my chest—

No, not my emotions, the leash spell. Sebastian had reached the end of its range, gone beyond, and now the weight of the spell squeezed around my lungs, tight and a little painful, but not agonizing like it had been before.

"Are you okay?" Titus asked, crouching in front of me.

I pressed my hand over my heart and strained to draw in a full breath. I could, but it was still hard. "Well, the spell hasn't removed all the air around me, so that's an improvement."

"Not sure by how much," he said, holding out his hands to me.

I took them and he closed his fingers completely covering mine.

"I'm not suffocating," I said. "I'll have to consider that a win."

"Can you walk or would you like me to carry you?"

"I'm fine here. I don't need to go into a pool." So there was no point going any farther from the door.

"Carry it is." He tugged me to my feet and picked me up. "I want to show you something before Seireadan returns."

"What?" I asked as I leaned into his embrace and savored the feel of his body and his essence brushing against my senses.

"You'll see." He strode to the back of the grotto to a hidden set of stairs carved into the side of the wall and took them up to a small landing mostly hidden by winter greenery. At the back stood a simple narrow ice door.

With ease, Titus held me with one arm and opened the door, and — turning sideways to get his broad shoulders through — stepped out onto an ice and rock balcony set into the side of a mountain. Cold crisp winter air swept across my face and teased down the neck of my robe and vast blue sky stretched out before me, stealing my breath at its vast openness.

I didn't care that it was too cold for just the thin robe I was wearing. I barely noticed the goose bumps rushing over my skin. There was just so much space. It was so open, so free, so beautiful and steadying. I'd known not being able to look out a window had been crushing my soul as much as everything else that had happened, but I hadn't realized just how much I needed to see open sky.

The balcony was about twenty feet by twenty feet with an intricate ice railing at its edge. About thirty feet to the left was an identical balcony with an identical plain ice door, and ahead, lay a sprawling mountain range of snow topped peaks. Far off in the distance a flock of white birds, the sunlight catching in their feathers, soared and dipped, riding the thermals.

"This is amazing." The spot between my shoulder blades where my wings appeared ached and I yearned to release them and join the birds — something I'd never desired before. But then, I'd never been so unsteady and stuck underground before. Even when that human had held me, I'd been able to see the sky.

"I wanted you to see this," Titus said, his voice gruff.

"It's beautiful. Will you let me down?"

"It's a little cold."

"I don't care." I needed to stretch out my arms, feel the air rushing around me and breathe it in.

He set me down. The balcony floor was smooth and cool under my bare feet, but not stinging cold like ice, and I crossed to the edge and leaned against the railing. The wind picked up and I stretched out my arms and turned my face into it, letting it sweep my loose hair back from my face and tug at my robe as I drew in a deep breath. Even with the leash spell squeezing around my lungs, it was easier to breathe.

Space. Sky. Free. So free.

"There are ice canyons over there." Titus drew close behind me, this time close enough that his chest brushed against my back, and pointed to a deep V in the mountain range. "It's so deep sunlight never reaches the bottom."

I leaned into him and he wrapped his arms around my waist, holding me tight. The warmth from his body radiated into my skin and seeped into my muscles. God, this felt so good.

"It has tiny blue flowers that pulse with the power of the Winter Court and tinkle like little bells when the wind blows just right or if you gust them with your wings. And at the very end is an enormous frozen waterfall, hundreds of feet high, with ice passages riddled throughout."

"It sounds amazing."

This was amazing, having the open sky I'd desperately needed and the physical contact I wasn't supposed to need. I could feel Titus's life, his energy, pulsing with power against my magical senses. He was healthy, well, even mostly content with his beast. For the moment, they were almost properly aligned, almost completely merged into one whole ferocious soul, filled with strength and power and certainty.

"It is." His voice softened and he pressed his lips to the top of my head.

That was the second time in a few minutes that he'd done that small, soft intimate act.

It sent a shiver of need whispering through me, and he curled more of his body around me probably thinking I was cold. I didn't correct him. I felt so safe and strong with him embracing me like this. And while I knew this kind of contact didn't necessarily mean anything coming from a shifter, that it could just be his nature making him more intimate than an angel, I also knew it *could* mean something, something I could explore once my brand was gone.

"You should see it all," he said. "You should make the flowers chime and play tag flying through the waterfall."

The wind changed directions and showered us with a flurry of ice crystals that caught the sunlight and sparkled like diamonds. I held out my hand to catch some on my palm, but instead of landing and melting, they sparkled and danced less than an inch from my skin held aloft by a miniature whirlwind.

"You should watch the sunrise from the top of the Silver Mountain on a clear day, and lie on the Calmarine Ice Plains at midnight looking at the opalescent glimmer of the Winter Court's protective boundary."

He cupped my cheek with his large hand and gently

urged me to face him. His pupils were fully slitted with a hint of gold shimmering behind the plain brown of the glamour. His beast had fully risen to the surface with his emotions. But it wasn't rage fueling the ferocious aspect of his nature, it was desire.

Its intensity stole my breath. Marcus had never looked at me like that. I'd only glimpsed a fraction of his powerful emotions because I hadn't been his soul mate. I'd known the look he'd give his true mate would have been intense, consuming, and the longer I'd waited for him to look at me like that and for my brand to awaken, the more I yearned for it. Would it have looked like this?

I wasn't sure anyone could match Titus's ferocity. He was more powerful, wilder, and more primal than a wolf. Perhaps this was how he'd looked at his mate before she'd been killed, the one who hadn't been his soul mate. He'd been without sex for a long time, and Hawk's loss of control had to be straining Titus's willpower.

That was it. And yet, I still yearned to kiss him, give him that connection that he hadn't had in such a long time.

Except if I kissed him would my brand light up? Would we be bound together for the rest of our lives?

With him looking at me like that, his yearning inflaming my own, it was so hard to remember that I didn't want a connection forced on me, that I wanted to fall in love like everyone else. I wanted to *choose* my happiness.

His gaze dipped to my lips and my pulse stuttered.

I ached for him to kiss me.

And that terrified me.

Something skittered down the mountain behind us, and Titus jerked around as an ice man in the same kind of ice armor as the queen's guards — although only as big as Titus and not bigger like her guards — half-slid half-jumped from the cliff face above the door. He landed on the balcony between us and the door with a dark light emanating from inside his semi-translucent body. Above him, still clinging to the jagged rock and ice were dozens more identical ice men.

"You're supposed to still be in the grotto," the man said, drawing an ice sword that without a doubt was as hard and sharp as steel.

AMIAH

I backed up and hit the railing, my heart pounding in a chest still tight with the pressure of the adjusted leash spell. Another gust of wind showered us with ice crystals, and three more ice men landed in front of the door.

They now blocked us from our only means of escape, and while I could release my wings and fly, I wasn't strong enough to take Titus with me. Sure, he could also shift and fly, but that might break the glamour hiding him and leave Sebastian, Cassius, and Hawk still in the Winter Court. And the queen would be furious to know Sebastian had been hiding the last dragon and the only connection to the most powerful magic in all of Faerie right under her nose.

"Tell me where the dragon is and I'll let you run away from court instead of killing you," the ice man said.

Titus stepped in front of me and flexed his hands, extending his fingers into wolf-like claws. "Step away from the door and I won't kill *you*."

"This is just a construct, wolf," the ice man said. "Destroying it won't hurt me."

"Sure it will," Titus snarled back. "The harder I have to work to protect Amiah, the more I'm going to rip into you when I find you."

"And how do you plan to do that?" another ice man asked in the same voice as the first as he dropped from the mountain face and joined the line in front of the door.

"Prince Seireadan will be able to find you."

"Prince Seireadan will be dead just as soon as I finish with you," the first man replied.

My pulse stalled. Sebastian was low on magic and he hadn't had a chance to go into a pool to restore it. Had the message about removing my mating brand been a trick, a way to separate us? And how soon would the ice men attack him? How many could he fight off by himself in his condition?

"You can either join him or just become a widow," the man said. "Tell me where to find the dragon."

"I don't know what you're talking about," I said.

Another gust of wind, suddenly frigid and making me shiver, showered us with more ice crystals.

"You and your bodyguard aren't from this realm. There's no point in sacrificing yourself by lying." The man took a step forward and Titus tensed. "Tell me and you can run off with him."

"Now who's lying," Titus growled. "You can't let her live. The court responds to her. You kill his highness and she becomes heir."

The dark light inside the ice man flared. "You're awfully knowledgeable of court ways for an outsider."

"His highness warned me of the dangers of court politics," Titus said.

"You *will* tell me where the dragon is."

The ice man swung at Titus's head with a powerful two-handed strike, but Titus lunged in, blocked the man's attack, and tore his claws through the man's arm. The man didn't even utter a sound as his arm shattered and Titus tossed him into one of the other ice men who was blocking the door, knocking them both back.

The rest of the ice men in the line leaped at Titus who batted one into another and twisted to avoid getting impaled by a third. Two ice men dropped from the rockface above and grabbed Titus's right arm before he could get in a good swipe at either of them, and two more grabbed his left.

"Fly." Titus wrenched the men on his right arm off balance and jerked his hand free. "Get to the door at the next balcony and warn Seireadan." He grabbed one of the men on his left arm and tossed him over the railing, but another ice man lunged in, plunging his sword into Titus's gut.

Blood seeped into his white tunic and splattered on his pants, but the wound wasn't serious enough for my magic to lock onto him. With a roar, he swung the man still on his left arm into the man who'd stabbed him, sending them tumbling into two more men.

Another ice man slashed at Titus's arm, but he yanked a third man into his way and the sword dug deep into that man's shoulder. Except the man didn't react to getting cut, just stumbled because the sword was caught in his body.

"Fly," Titus snarled. "I can handle them."

My pulse beat faster, and the wind sweeping around the balcony grew stronger. I didn't want to leave him, but if I stayed, I'd just get in the way, and I needed to leave before my compulsion to heal forced me to stay. Someone needed to warn Sebastian.

Another man sliced at Titus. He twisted just enough so the blade slipped past his side, and raked his claws through the man's face. The man's nose and cheek shattered and with a loud crack, a fissure sliced through his head and chest. He collapsed, bursting apart as he hit the floor, his pieces skittering across its smooth surface in all directions.

I pushed a trickle of power into my back and released my wings with a flash of white angelic magic, but an ice man leaped from the cliff onto me, pinning me against the railing.

"Tell me where the dragon is," he demanded.

"No." I pushed him off, but another man fell onto me before I could launch myself into the sky.

"Tell me."

I shoved at the new guy and the wind snapped, knocking him over the railing. But the first man grabbed my wing before I could fly away, and painfully twisted it.

Tears sprung to my eyes and I heaved against his grip, but he wrenched hard, shooting agony into my back.

"Don't make this harder on yourself."

The wind — it had to be the Winter Court's wind — gusted around me, tugged at my hair and robe, and jostled the man holding my wings. His grip loosened and I pulled my wings back into my body, but more men grabbed me. Something sharp bit into my thigh and I was yanked to my knees before I could figure out what had happened.

Somewhere, beyond the crush of ice bodies, Titus roared.

My breath caught with the fear that he was mortally wounded, but my magic still didn't lock onto him, and two of the ice men holding me down were yanked away.

Ice shards showered me, and Titus seized another ice man, threw him over the railing then shattered two more.

"Come on." Titus threw me over his shoulder, bolted the three steps to the left side of the balcony, hopped onto the railing without losing momentum, and jumped to the other balcony in one great leap.

We landed with a heavy thump and Titus set me on my feet but didn't let go. His gaze, strangely brown and gold at the same time and filled with rage and fear, captured me. Then he grabbed the back of my head and smashed his lips against mine in a ferocious kiss that stole all breath and thought. Time froze and there was only Titus, his strong arms holding me close against his hard body, his warmth, his life, and his mouth igniting a sudden desperate desire.

Oh, wow.

His kiss was filled with a wild, passionate need as if he didn't have the words and could only show me how he felt, how much he wanted me. It sent heat swelling through my body, radiating from his lips and rushing to my toes in a giant, breathtaking wave.

Oh, no.

He jerked away, gasping, and shoved me toward the door. "Run. I'm right behind you."

The kiss had only lasted a second and yet my senses were reeling from it. I was warm... was I too warm? It didn't feel as if the heat radiated from my brand. Did that mean he wasn't my soul mate?

The ice men scurried up and across the sheer cliff face from the grotto's balcony and dove toward us.

Titus shoved me again. "Run. Find the others. Warn Seireadan."

I scrambled to the door and wrenched it open as Titus roared and an ice man shattered on the floor behind me, its shards stinging the backs of my bare calves.

Another ice man dropped from the cliff face above me, trying to cut me off, but the Winter Court's wind surged, frozen and sharp, and blew him over the side of the balcony.

I ran inside before someone else could reach me and Titus slammed the door shut between us.

"What are you doing?" He was supposed to be behind me.

"Find Seireadan," he said through the door.

"T—"

"Seireadan," he roared and something heavy crunched on the other side of the door. "We can't trust the queen's constructs. He's by himself."

And magically weakened.

Right.

Titus was hurt but he was a fast healer. He could

handle the ice men. *Please let him be able to handle the ice men.*

I raced across the wide empty room to the only other door. I had no idea what the room was supposed to be, there wasn't any furniture or decorations, only a pale light emanating from the walls and ceiling and none of that mattered. I had to find Sebastian.

I just had no idea how.

I was pretty sure I wasn't even on the same floor as the grotto so I couldn't just go down two halls back to our suite and hope Cassius and Hawk were there. I'd have to find some stairs and preferably someone to show me the way.

Except could I trust anyone? I didn't know who controlled those ice men, and while they hadn't looked like the ice people I'd already encountered who belonged to the Winter Queen — who I doubted would try to kill me after going to so much trouble to make Sebastian sleep with me — that didn't mean they would help me or that all the other ice people I met were safe.

I threw open the door and stared into a wide, white hall that stretched left and right. It looked like all the other halls I'd been in and I had no idea which direction to go.

Left or right.

Left.

Right.

Behind me, the door to the balcony jerked open then slammed shut. My heart leaped into my throat.

Titus is fine. He's a fighter. Sebastian isn't, not without his magic.

I bolted right, praying I would find...

I had no idea what. I needed to find someone I could trust. But who?

The hall ended in an L intersection and I careened around the corner and slammed into a hard body.

The sense of cold lifelessness shivered across my senses and I looked up into black eyes with smoldering red hellfire.

Deaglan's demon-vampire.

My stomach bottomed out and fear rushed frozen through my chest. I jerked back, the court's wind sweeping around me, as Deaglan strode out an open door between me and the demon-vampire.

They both still wore black leather, the demon-vampire's clothing the same as before, but this time Deaglan wore a leather jerkin with a dozen silver buckles and no shirt underneath, leaving his sculpted, muscular arms bare.

"Ah, the future queen of the Winter Court." His lips curled back in a wicked sneer and a dangerous gleam lit in his eyes. Shadows billowed under his skin, gathering like a storm, and his gaze slowly trailed down my body, hesitating on my cleavage and making fear churn in my gut.

I stumbled back a few more steps, getting out of arm's reach, my thoughts whirling. I needed to get away from him, needed to get to Sebastian before the ice men did—

Was Deaglan controlling the ice men?

I didn't know what kind of magic he possessed, and even if he didn't control the ice men that didn't mean he hadn't told someone else to.

The demon-vampire rested a hand on the scabbard of his katana sheathed at his hip, his emotionless gaze locked on me, and Deaglan took a step toward me.

I stumbled back another step. My foot slipped on something wet on the floor and I staggered into the wall to keep my balance, my gaze dipping down to the thin red streak in the floor.

Blood. I'd stepped in blood.

My thoughts stuttered and I realized warmth trickled down the side of my right thigh and the back of both of my calves. Somehow I'd been hurt and with all the adrenaline pumping through me hadn't realized it.

"You seem to have gotten hurt and misplaced your husband," Deaglan said, his voice dark, sounding too much like Balwyrdan's when he'd taken and beaten me. "Not even a bodyguard to keep an eye on you."

My pulse roared in my ears and I started to tremble. I was going to get taken again, hurt again. Worse. I could see it in his eyes.

"My hybrid says you don't know where the dragon is, that Seireadan took his half of my broken leash spell."

"That's true." There was no point in denying that I knew about Titus. The demon-vampire had already seen me with him, I could only pray that Deaglan wouldn't figure out that Titus was Titus.

"He also says the Spring Court's seneschal couldn't break you."

I glanced at the demon-vampire. His hellfire still smoldered, small red pinpricks, but a hunger now also burned in his eyes and his mouth had parted slightly, his fangs partially extended.

"Is Rin right?" Deaglan took another step forward, forcing me back again. "How much can you take?"

None. No more.

The Winter Court's wind gusted around me, ruffling Deaglan's hair, and making Rin's sash and long ponytail sweep out behind him.

"So Seireadan really didn't control the wind back in your room," he said.

Never again.

"I thought Seireadan had disguised my leash spell and that's what was binding you together, but it really does look like he married you." Deaglan's sneer deepened. "I'm going to enjoy the look on his face when he realizes I broke you."

No. Never. I wouldn't be taken again. I had to run back to Titus. It didn't matter if he was still fighting the ice men or if Deaglan saw him. I didn't know how to fight and I didn't have magic I could use to defend myself, not against Deaglan let alone both him and his demon-vampire.

"I broke in his other betrothed," Deaglan purred.

Except vampires, even ones a few hundred years old, had enhanced speed, and I doubted someone like Deaglan would put a baby vampire on a three-man assassination team and send him after the most valuable being in all the realms.

Which meant running wasn't an option.

And I didn't want to run. I was furious that running was my only choice, furious that I was so scared, furious at that human for making me doubt myself for over a hundred years, and furious at Balwyrdan for terrifying and hurting me.

"Rin says you never lost that look in your eyes," Deaglan sneered.

God, I wished I knew how to fight, was strong, had some kind of power. If I couldn't run away, the best I could hope for was to stall him until Titus found me and then pray he was strong enough to get Deaglan to back down — and that Deaglan wouldn't recognize him.

"Yeah, that look." Deaglan glanced at the demon-vampire. "Do you think I can wipe it from her face? Want to bet her blood?"

The demon-vampire's expression didn't change, and Deaglan huffed.

"Stop trying to hide your hunger," Deaglan said. "You can have her once I break her."

"As my lord wishes," the demon-vampire said, his voice so soft I could barely hear it and without a hint of emotion.

No.

Not going to happen.

Never again.

The court's wind grew colder and more bitter, reminding me I wasn't entirely helpless. It had thrown ice men off the balcony to protect me. Could I create a storm like the Winter Queen had in her throne room? Could I actually stand my ground?

Deaglan took another step forward, his horrible gaze raking up my body again. "Now where should I begin? Here?"

He reached for my neck and the wind snapped

around me, knocking his hand away. My power surged into my back with a sudden spike of fear and adrenaline, and my wings released. "No."

Never again. Deaglan didn't control the leash spell like Balwyrdan. I might not be able to get him to leave me alone, but I *could* hold my own until Titus came. I wouldn't cower any longer. I would fight with whatever I had, even if that was with a magic I didn't know how to control and a bluff that I wasn't afraid of him.

I pushed my power into my hands, forcing them to light up even though I was the only one injured. Deaglan didn't know what magic I possessed, and I prayed he'd assume I had offensive magic. "You don't want to threaten the future queen of the Winter court."

"Oh, I don't?" Deaglan asked with a chuckle and the shadows under his skin swelled, bleeding across the floor and over the walls. "But I'm more powerful than you. I'm the *king* of the Shadow Court."

I clenched my hands, fighting to hide my trembling, and glared at him. I just had to buy time until Titus arrived. That was all.

Except the shadows devoured the light from the walls, and thick, sticky tendrils twisted around my ankles and dug into my flesh.

I wrenched against the shadows, jerking my legs and flapping my wings, but they twisted up my calves and past my knees, creeping painfully higher, drawing closer to the crux between my thighs.

"You really thought you could challenge a king?" Deaglan asked, drawing close and reaching for my robe's belt.

I slapped his hand away but more shadows captured my wrists and yanked them up.

No, please.

Panic seized my lungs and the court's wind exploded into a whirling frigid storm, shoving Deaglan back and sweeping shards of ice through his shadows and tearing them apart. The icy gale pounded into him, slicing his cheeks and bare arms, and toppled him into the demon-vampire then knocked both of them over and shoved them thirty feet down the hall.

He jerked to his feet with murder in his eyes and the court wind knocked him down again. "I'm the king of the Shadow Court," he snarled at me.

"But you're not *in* the Shadow court." I stretched my wings, brushing the tips against the walls on either side of me, knowing the glow in my eyes blazed with my fear and determination and rage, while praying I looked as angry as I felt.

I knew it was foolish to embarrass him like that, knew the next time he came after me — and from the look in his eyes there'd be a next time — I might not have the power of the Winter Court protecting me, but God, no more!

I was done feeling like a victim. I needed to fight back, even just this once, and the Winter Court was giving me that chance. Right now, against this monster who'd held Titus in captivity for five hundred years, I was going to vent my years of fear and anger. I was taking my power back.

SEBASTIAN

I raced down the hall, desperate to get to Amiah and Titus. It had been a long time since the Winter Court had spoken to me — it hadn't even spoken to me when I'd first entered it again — but its rage had exploded with fiery agony in my chest while I'd been in the middle of my meeting with Karthick.

Someone was threatening Amiah and the court was pissed. Except the court didn't even have to compel me to go to her. Amiah hadn't deserved anything that had happened to her and she didn't deserve any more. Sure, technically it had been her fault for getting caught up in this mess, but if she hadn't rushed to heal Titus, he would have died and I'd never have gotten my friend back. In the short time I'd known her, she'd only really asked for two things for herself: for me to get rid of her mating brand and for me to show her the pleasures of sex. And a part of me feared I'd failed her on both accounts.

I'd yet to remove her brand and at the first sign of danger from Cassius, I'd pushed her away, and as a result had put a stop to her sexual awakening — something she'd already waited far too long to explore.

I'd bolted from the Winter Forest, not bothering to go out the way I'd come in and pick up my mother's ice guard. I didn't want to have to explain to it what was going on and there was a chance it would stop me if it thought I was running into danger.

The court led me to the level above the healing grotto, its fury and fear building, gusting frozen around me so strongly I almost missed the spike of heat and flash of light in my wrist from my shadow fae alert glyph.

Shit.

I really hoped it wasn't Deaglan who was nearby, but given that he'd made a point of visiting me, I had a bad feeling it was.

God. He'd looked at Amiah with the same predatory hunger with which he'd looked at Enowen—

No, more. His look in our suite yesterday hadn't just been a desire for sex but pain as well. In the three hundred years since he'd tried to assassinate me, it seemed he'd developed a taste for sadism, and not the kind that would stop with a safe word.

I raced around a corner, afraid of what I'd find as a massive blast of frigid wind parted around me, tugging at my tunic and pants. At the far end of the hall Deaglan fell onto his demon-vampire hybrid already on the floor, and thirty feet beyond them stood a furious, spectacular angel.

"I'm the king of the Shadow Court," Deaglan snarled.

"But you're not *in* the Shadow court." Amiah stretched out her wings. Her angel glow blazed from her eyes and her power filled her palms with a bluff I hadn't thought she was capable of. The Winter Court's wind gusted around her. It rippled through her robe — which was on the verge of falling open and exposing everything — and swept her long blond locks around her head.

She was breathtaking. An enraged goddess, worshiped by the Winter Court. Its wind defended her and its essence called to me to protect her. Even Deaglan, with his eyes ever-so-slightly too wide, saw it.

He'd assumed— Hell, *I'd* assumed because she wasn't fae, the court wouldn't race to fulfill her will like it used to do for me. But it had never behaved this ferociously for me even when I'd fully accepted that I was one day going to be the king. It only behaved like that for my mother and she had to force it to her will. I doubted Amiah even knew she could force the court to do anything.

Fucking hell. Had I actually married Amiah and not realized it? I hadn't thought that was possible. We hadn't done the ceremony and bonded our souls together.

And if I hadn't married her, was I going to remain a fool and continue to push away this determined, amazing, powerful woman?

She'd said while we were having sex that she was certain I wasn't her soul mate, but seeing the Winter Court fully embrace her made me seriously doubt her words. Maybe we *were* meant to be together. Just because her brand hadn't awoken when we'd had sex didn't mean it wouldn't. An angelic mating brand could form at any time, before sex, during sex, after lots and lots of sex. Maybe the Winter Court's connection had just awakened before her brand had.

Jeez, what the hell was wrong with me?

I didn't want a wife. And I certainly didn't want that wife to be Amiah. She drove me crazy. Besides, she was meant for Cassius — that much was obvious, even if both of them were too blind to figure it out — and I was pretty sure Cassius wasn't the sharing type. He was far too uptight for that... although his brother who was also pretty uptight was soul bound to a woman with three other mates and he hadn't had problems sharing...

The Winter Court's wind snapped around me and shoved me forward a few steps, reminding me why it had summoned me.

It would continue to protect Amiah, but if Deaglan really wanted to put up a fight, he could, and that could get nasty even without his hybrid to back him up.

"I see you've found my wife." I plastered on my over-confident asshole expression and strode closer, catching a glimpse of the fear and relief barely hidden behind the rage in Amiah's eyes. "Spectacular, isn't she?"

Deaglan glared at me and stood as the hybrid rose behind him, an expressionless deadly shadow among the Shadow King's other deadly shadows.

"And here I'd thought she was a kitten," Deaglan said, wiping his thumb through a trickle of blood that was slowly oozing down his cheek, "with little kitten claws trying to stand up against the Winter Queen by refusing to fuck you."

"You honestly think I'd marry a kitten?"

"You were going to," Deaglan replied, "and I never would have thought you had it in you to take a wild cat to bed, especially one certain to draw blood." Dark desire lit up his eyes at that and I clenched my jaw, fighting the urge to punch him in the face.

No way in hell was he getting anywhere near Amiah's bed. Ever.

"But you surprised me," he said. "You're not that same starry-eyed fae I grew up with. You've changed."

"Being poisoned by your best friend and your betrothed and left in the Wilds for Faerie to rip its magic out of you will do that to a fae." I'd barely survived and only because Karthick had found me. Another hour and the only thing left for Faerie to have ripped out would have been my essence and soul.

"I couldn't let you live. You were going to figure out I had Titus chained up in my court if that fool Enowen didn't tell you first." Deaglan's eyes narrowed. "And of course the first thing the beast did when he broke free was go running to you."

"Because I promised to sever his connection to the Heart."

"And he was stupid enough to believe that?" Deaglan huffed a dark laugh. "Don't pretend you don't want the power too. You crave it just as much as I do, as every high fae does."

"I don't want it. I don't even want the Winter Court." Yes, I missed Faerie, missed the feel of the court's magic always at the edge of my senses, missed breathing air always crackling with a power that fed my soul, but that was it. In the mortal realm, I wasn't chained to a role I was born into and didn't choose, and I had all the same power and wealth but none of the duties and a hell of a lot less of the danger. I could do as I pleased, love how I pleased, and leave as I pleased. No one to answer to and no responsibilities.

"Well that's good," he said, "because the Winter Court won't be yours. When your mother finally decides to fade, the court will pick your wife to rule, not you, and then you'll have no way of breaking her."

"A king shouldn't break his queen." The thought of breaking Amiah's will made my stomach churn. She didn't deserve to be broken, no woman did, she deserved to be built up, cherished, worshiped.

God, how amazing would she be if she released her fears and embraced all of who she was.

"I doubt you could, even if you wanted to. Word from the Spring Court is that Balwyrdan couldn't break her." Deaglan chuckled the sound dark and grating. "Such a difference from Enowen. She broke without me even trying. I had her crawling through shadow thorns to suck my cock on the first day. Just dangled a throne in front of that kitten and she jumped at it."

Just one punch. Right in that smug smile.

Except I wouldn't be able to stop at one punch and I didn't have enough power right now to stand up against him and his hybrid, especially since the Winter Court didn't respond to me like it did Amiah.

"Poor Seireadan," Deaglan mocked, "I bet your angel is too high and mighty to suck cock."

My cock tightened at the thought, even as my brain decided she probably wouldn't. Miss Prim-and-Proper probably thought it beneath her to wrap her soft lips around a cock. And if she wasn't interested, I wasn't going to make her. Sex was only good if it was good for everyone.

Deaglan turned to Amiah. "You'd never kneel for Seireadan, would you?"

"You think having him in my mouth and knowing that with my lips I bring him pleasure and with my teeth I bring him pain isn't a position of power?" she asked with a dangerous glint in her eyes that made me even harder. "Then please, by all means, bring your cock closer."

Fuck me. Did she just say that?

"No?" she asked.

Deaglan glared at her, and that dangerous glint tugged at her lips, making her look downright wicked. God, I'd had that in my bed and I'd pushed her away.

What the hell was wrong with me?

"Then excuse us, your majesty of the Shadow Court," she said, her tone brusque, a clear dismissal. "I'd like a word with my husband."

Deaglan raised his chin and she matched him, everything about her screaming strength and defiance. The Winter Court gusted, shoving him back a step and bumping him into his hybrid as if telling him where to go, and Amiah raised a delicate blond eyebrow, not backing down from his challenge. She had the full force of the Winter Court protecting her. Did he really want to turn this into a fight?

"You're going to wish you'd just let me fuck you in private," he spat at Amiah before storming past me with his hybrid close at his heels.

He marched around the corner and Amiah pulled in

her wings and rushed to me, cupping my face with her palms and sending a warm thread of magic into me, checking my condition, and making my pulse pound with a fucked-up mix of fear for her wellbeing and desire for her body.

"Are you okay?" She gazed into my eyes, searching for an answer her magic was already giving her.

I was fine. Or at least I was as fine as I was going to get given that I'd just had the shit scared out of me seeing her facing off against Deaglan, and was infected with demonic magic that I couldn't get out of my system.

"The court told me you were in danger. Are you all right?" I asked. Her robe at her right thigh was ripped and stained with blood, and she looked like she was running on fear and adrenaline. "You're bleeding."

"And Titus could be worse." She turned to rush down the hall in the opposite direction Deaglan had gone when Titus barreled around the corner at the far end.

His eyes were wild, his pupils slitted, and he radiated dangerous ferocious power, his beast's fury barely contained. Blood stained his white tunic and pants. A lot of blood. Dozens of cuts, some deep, crisscrossed his arms, and blood oozed from a nasty gash above his right eye. His gaze landed on Amiah and his expression grew darker.

With a growl, he pounced on her, yanking her to his chest and baring his teeth at me.

Oh shit. His beast wasn't straining to get free, it was free. It just had enough sense not to shift and break the glamour.

"T, I'm okay," she said, somehow not panicking at

Titus's sudden attack or trying to pull free. She pressed her palms to his cheeks just like she'd done to me a moment ago, and her eyelids fluttered shut. "We need to get you back to our rooms so I can stop your bleeding."

"I'm fine," he said. "I'll heal. I'm taking you back to our rooms then killing whoever threatened you." He shoved past me and headed in the same direction Deaglan had.

"Let's go the other way." I reached for his arm to stop him, but he jumped on me, seizing the front of my tunic, wrenching me off my feet, and shoving me against the wall.

"I'm glad your safe," he snarled. "Don't get in my way."

Fuck. What the hell was wrong with him? I'd never seen him like this before, never seen him with this little control over his beast. But he'd spent five hundred years unable to calm his beast with physical contact or shifting. I should be more surprised that he'd managed to control his beast for as long as he had already.

"Deaglan went that way," I said, straining to resist the urge to struggle. If it looked like I was fighting, his beast would strike and I didn't want to have to hurt him to defend myself — that could get Amiah hurt. "I don't want to run into him again."

"Is he responsible?" Titus asked.

"I don't even know what happened," I replied.

"This isn't a conversation we should be having in the hall." Amiah tried to push out of Titus's hold but he released me and added his other arm to his embrace, making it impossible for her to escape.

"You're right." He marched — thankfully — back the way he'd come, and I hurried to catch up with his stride.

Amiah met my gaze over his shoulder and a whisper of court wind fluttered through her hair. She was worried and upset and still too wide-eyed from her encounter with Deaglan and whatever else had happened.

Jeez. Whatever it had been, it had scared the hell out of her and sent Titus into beast mode.

We needed to get the hell out of court and fast... just as soon as I took Amiah to Karthick and got her brand removed.

Titus took a set of servants' stairs down to the next floor, and I followed, trailing my fingers along the hall wall, asking the court to summon Cassius and Hawk back to our rooms.

I prayed my summons would go through the court itself and not my mother, but given how bad the situation looked, I didn't care if my mother knew I was calling Cassius and Hawk back or not. We needed to regroup, and someone needed to tell me what the hell was going on.

We reached the door to our suite as Cassius and Hawk came barreling down the hall.

"What's wrong?" Cassius asked, fire snapping over his hands. "We just got the urgent sense that we had to return here." His gaze landed on Amiah in Titus's arms, both of them now covered in Titus's blood, and his eyes narrowed.

"Jesus," Hawk hissed.

Titus wrenched open the door — I was surprised he didn't yank it off its hinges — and stormed inside.

"Watch Amiah," he snarled to no one in particular as he set her on her feet. "I'm hunting the bastard who tried to kill her."

"Who?" Cassius grabbed Titus's wrist and the dragon tossed Cassius to the far end of the room.

Cassius landed with an *oomph*, tumbled across the floor, and hit the wall.

"T, stop. You need healing. You're still losing blood," Amiah said.

"And you need a plan," Hawk added.

"Kill him," Titus's beast growled.

Cassius rose, fire blazing up his forearms, and stalked back toward him. "That's not a plan."

"I know!" Titus roared back. "My beast doesn't care."

"So take a breath." Amiah rose on her toes, leaned into him, and tangled her hands in his hair. She pressed her forehead against his — as best as she could with their height difference — and gave him the firm physical contact that should have helped calm his beast, but his breath picked up instead of slowing and his canines extended.

"He tried to kill you. They piled on top of you and I thought—" His fingers shifted into claws and hints of red and gold scales swept over the back of his arms.

Ah, shit. He was losing it.

"I won't let him threaten you again." He shoved her, knocking her into Cassius's flaming arms and making the angel yank his fire back under his skin, and jerked to the door.

Fucking hell. I couldn't let him storm around court, not with him barely holding onto his human form.

God damn it. This was going to hurt.

I pressed my hand to my shoulder, awakening the power I had stored in my sleep glyph, and slapped my other hand over his heart. The spell activated and the demonic magic surged, screaming through my veins, a black acid consuming me from the inside out.

Titus growled and swatted me across the room — thank God he didn't use his claws — and I slammed into the wall. Pain snapped through my chest and the back of my head, and I sagged to the floor as my sleep spell took hold and Titus dropped to his knees.

"Seireadan, please. I have to protect—" His eyes rolled back and he collapsed.

"What the fuck just happened?" Hawk asked, hurrying to close the suite's door.

"We were attacked." Amiah rushed to my side and captured my head between her hands again. She forced me to look at her, staring into my eyes looking for... I had no idea what. With the demonic magic consuming me, I could barely think straight.

Then the gentle warmth of her power swelled into me, stronger than the fire of the demonic magic, soothing the pain in my head and chest. For a second it felt as if she was calming the demonic magic as well, but it was really just easing off because I was no longer using my magic.

"Someone sent ice men after me. They wanted to know where the last dragon was and they wanted both me and Sebastian dead." The light in her eyes flared and her hands on my cheeks started to tremble.

I pressed my hands over hers, trying to reassure her

with my touch. Which was stupid because she was an angel, not a shifter, and didn't respond to touch like they did.

And yet her trembling eased and a primal need heated inside me. I'd give her more than my hands if it wiped away that look in her eyes.

Fucking hell.

Wasn't I supposed to be helping her and Cassius realize they were in love with each other?

If I didn't get my shit together, I was going to do something stupid. And I'd sworn I'd never do something stupid for a woman again.

Except Amiah wasn't just any woman. If the Winter Court's response to her meant anything, she was supposed to be my queen. Something she'd never want, and I'd do whatever it took to ensure she'd never be permanently bound to me.

AMIAH

A STRANGE LOOK PASSED OVER SEBASTIAN'S FACE. HIS GAZE dipped to my lips as if he wanted to kiss me, making me ache for more than just his hands on mine, then he gently shifted his grip to my wrists and nudged me away, reminding me that Titus was still hurt. I was hurt. Someone had tried to kill me. Deaglan had almost—

If Sebastian hadn't shown up, Deaglan could have seriously hurt me.

My pulse picked up and a whisper of wind fluttered around me, reminding me of how much power I currently had at my command.

God, I'd wanted to hurt Deaglan, wanted to take out my frustration over everything on him. I finally had the power to defend myself. I'd knocked him and his demon-vampire off their feet and I'd seen fear in their eyes.

A shuddering mix of desire and revulsion swept through me. I was supposed to heal people, not hurt them.

"We were afraid you were in danger," I said as matter-of-a-factly as I could.

Maybe if I embraced my cool professionalism I'd stop thinking about how afraid and angry I was. Really. Whoever attacked me and Titus was still out there, still wanted me and Sebastian dead.

Except I couldn't do it, couldn't rein in my emotions and my hands were trembling again.

I turned to Titus and placed my palms on his back over his heart and released a small trickle of magic to assess his condition. Most of his lacerations were already on their way to sealing shut, and it wouldn't take a lot to heal everything.

"I was trying to find you when I ran into Deaglan."

"Deaglan?" Cassius jerked a step toward me, glanced at the smoke curling from his hands, and stopped, shoving them into his armpits as if he needed the reminder not to touch me. "Did he hurt you? Is any of that blood yours? Where the hell were you, Bane?"

My heart skipped a beat and I glanced at him. *Please don't tell him. Please.*

"I was making contact with someone who might be able to get me some protection against the Wilds," he lied. "And she looked a lot less bloody before Titus picked her up."

"Most of it's Titus's," I confirmed. Because he'd protected me, risked his life so I could get away... and kissed me.

God, that kiss! It had been amazing and shocking and added to the whirling mix of emotions that I had no right indulging in because he was hurt and we were in danger.

And while I was pretty sure my mating brand hadn't awakened, I couldn't check with everyone watching me.

I pushed a little more power into him, letting it ooze through his veins to the worst of his injuries, warm and gentle. It would take a little longer to heal him this way, but doing it too quickly would hurt him and that could wake him from Sebastian's sleep spell, something I was sure Sebastian didn't want to cast again. Two of his ribs had been cracked and he'd gotten a minor concussion from Titus's strike. The next time could be worse. Titus could use his claws.

"Tell me about the ice men," Sebastian said.

I finished with Titus and sat back on my heels. My fear and anger and God, all my emotions surged, and I forced my gaze to slide over Cassius and Hawk, trying to visually assess them as a way of distracting myself.

"They all looked and sounded the same," I said. *Focus on the guys. Just them, their health, nothing else.* "And they had this strange black glow inside them."

My power flared, warming my palms, and somehow my magic connected with them even though I wasn't touching them. Which was supposed to be impossible. Yes, my magic locked onto someone when they were dying, but it didn't connect with them and tell me their injuries, just compelled me to go to them. I always needed physical contact to properly assess and heal someone. Except I'd connected with Mavis when Balwyrdan had murdered her, and now I was connecting with the guys.

"Did you recognize them?" Cassius asked.

"No. But I've barely been outside of this room." And I

was trapped again in this windowless suite with people outside wanting to kill me. I was sure others would have felt safe with only one way in and out, but it felt like the walls were drawing closer and closer together, now more than ever, and I had nowhere to run.

Focus on how weird it is that you connected with Cassius and Hawk without touching them.

My trembling increased.

Focus.

"Titus took me up to the balcony so I could see the sky," I forced out. "The ice men knew we were in the grotto and knew you'd been called away," I said to Sebastian.

God, I wanted to go back to that balcony and stare at that vast open expanse of blue. Maybe then I'd be able to figure out what I was feeling, why my magic could connect with them and tell me they were fine, how I'd so badly wanted to hurt Deaglan, and why I couldn't stop being afraid. I was so tired of being afraid.

"How many people could have known you weren't in the grotto?" Hawk asked.

"Depending on who it is and how powerful they are they could have placed a scrying spell outside the grotto doors." Sebastian ran a hand over his spikey white and silver hair. "But that would mean they've got some serious power. It would take a lot to hide something like that from me."

Hawk's eyes narrowed.

"Even in my weakened condition," Sebastian said, meeting his gaze. "I need to check out the grotto and the balcony and then maybe poke around court. If at all possible, I'd like to avoid being caught off guard when we leave." The muscles in his jaw flexed. "Especially with Deaglan around."

My chest tightened at his words, partly in fear but mostly in anger for myself, Titus, and Sebastian. Sebastian's mother had said he'd just needed time to get over that silly business with Enowen, but from the sound of it, the situation had been anything but silly. I already knew Deaglan had confessed to seducing her, but I hadn't realized Sebastian was going to marry her and then they'd tried to kill him. It made me angry to think of how horrible that must have been.

The court wind gusted around me, blowing my hair back from my face.

"I won't let him touch you," Sebastian promised, mistaking the wind's reaction for just fear.

"None of us will," Hawk added.

"Cassius," Sebastian said as he stood, "will you have my back? Your power is more deadly than Hawk's and from the look of Titus, those ice men weren't an easy fight."

Cassius glanced at me and the smoke billowing around him thickened. Was he actually considering staying instead of going out and hunting down whoever had attacked me? I wasn't sure if I should be surprised that he wanted to stay or be worried that he thought I was in so much danger he felt he needed to.

"The Winter Court won't let anyone past that door who wants to hurt her," Sebastian said.

The light in Cassius's eyes flared. "Because your mother is so desperate for you to have an heir?"

"No, because it likes her. It knocked Deaglan on his ass to protect her."

Cassius opened his mouth and Sebastian raised a hand, silencing him.

"And I have no idea why, so don't bother asking." But something flickered across Sebastian's expression. He might not know for sure, but he was definitely working on a theory.

I started to rise and Sebastian held out his hand, offering to steady me. Without thought, I accepted his offer, savoring the feel of his cool skin against mine and remembering his fingers roaming my body, bringing me pleasure.

Funny how just a few days ago I'd adamantly refused his help even though I'd nearly drained myself saving Titus's life. Now I embraced the simple gesture, craved it, and didn't care if it made me look weak. He'd already seen me at my worst. They all had. I couldn't look weaker if I tried, and I selfishly wanted to feel his touch again.

A hint of a wicked smile tugged at Sebastian's lips, his victory at getting me to accept his help lighting his eyes, then his gaze jumped past me to Cassius, and he slid his hand out from mine. "Let's get Titus in a bed first," he said.

Cassius and Hawk carried Titus and laid him on a cot in the servant's room. Then Cassius and Sebastian left to try to find whoever had attacked me, while Hawk left to quickly check the hall for any extra spells.

I went to the bathroom to heal and clean my wounds, grabbed a small cloth from a shelf between the tub and the shower, and held it under the sink's tap — having managed to figure out earlier that holding something under the tap made the water run.

A stunned, pale, wide-eyed version of myself stared back at me in the mirror above the sink. My hair was a wild, wind-blown mess, and my robe was on the verge of falling open, revealing a shocking amount of cleavage and an indecent display of inner thighs.

And I didn't want to think about the kind of show I could have given the guys when I'd rushed to help Sebastian and Titus. Had they seen it all? How had I not noticed that the guys might have gotten a view of everything?

Because I was in shock and desperate not to think about the attack, not about Deaglan, Titus, or the ice men.

I hadn't even been able to fly away. Those ice men had grabbed me and would have killed me if Titus hadn't pulled them off me.

My pulse pounded.

Deaglan would have hurt me worse than Balwyrdan and then given me to his demon-vampire to feed.

Don't think about it. Just don't think about it.

I pushed my magic away from my hands and into my body, something I should have done long before now. The cut in my thigh was deep and so was one of the cuts on my calves, and I concentrated on flooding those injuries with power and sealing the wounds shut.

But I couldn't stop thinking about Deaglan, about how scared I was, how much I'd wanted to hurt him, wanted to fight back, and how satisfied I'd been when the

Winter Court had cut him with ice shards and knocked him and his demon-vampire to the floor.

My magic might force me to heal anyone and everyone regardless of who they were, but that didn't mean I'd lost my angelic desire for justice. Yes, my desire for order and goodness and justice wasn't nearly as strong as most angels. Compared to Cassius it was almost non-existent. But it was still there, and Deaglan deserved more than just being knocked down for imprisoning Titus and trying to kill Sebastian.

A shiver swept down my spine and I hugged myself.

Except when I left the Winter Court, I didn't know if I'd be able to keep its magic, and I wouldn't be able to use it fully, not to hurt Deaglan the way I wanted. My healing magic would kick in and force me to heal him.

I bit back a scream. It wasn't fair.

And I was sick and tired of thinking that.

But I had no idea how to come to terms with that. I'd never be able to defend myself, let alone those I cared about. I'd always be dependent on someone else. All I could do was be around to pick up the pieces afterward, and even then, I could only heal the physical injuries.

"Hey," Hawk said, his seductive tenor sliding across my senses and drawing a very different kind of shudder.

My pulse stuttered and my gaze jumped to him.

He leaned in the doorway, his posture casual, confident, and radiating raw sexual energy. He was breathtaking. The hellfire in his unusual blue-gray eyes flickered, little more than embers but enough to show he wasn't holding back his power, and his complexion was back to normal — his magic finally having dealt with his hangover. I ached for him to step closer, to touch me, kiss me, and direct all his heated sensual magic toward me again.

"You okay?" he asked.

Please touch me, make me forget. Make me forget who I am.

Except I couldn't force out the words.

God, I was such a coward.

"I only got a few lacerations and I've already healed them." I tugged my robe closed, set my foot on the closed toilet lid, and wiped at the blood on my calf, but I couldn't get my hands to stop shaking.

"Not what I was talking about."

It wasn't. I knew that. He wanted to know how I was feeling. But I didn't want to talk about it, and for some reason, I couldn't say what I really wanted to say.

"There isn't anything I can do about it," I said, moving back to the sink, putting the cloth under the tap, and activating the stream of water.

"So you're just going to ignore it?" Hawk stepped up behind me, close but not touching, not even his hands on my arms.

Heat radiated from his body — his body temperature, like all demons, naturally higher than humans or other supers — and it seeped through my thin robe, bringing with it a seductive whisper of sensual magic, promising me everything I desired if I'd just speak up.

"Yes," I breathed, but I didn't know if I was answering his question or asking him to have sex with me.

With his magic and his body, he could make me forget everything: the look in Deaglan's eyes, the look in Balwyrdan's eyes, and the fury building inside me that I needed someone's help to find justice. His caress and kiss, his body against mine, and the thrum of his life force against my senses could take me away, free me, even if it was for just a moment.

What was I so afraid of? I'd already asked him to satisfy me before. He'd already seen me at my absolute worst and still wanted to sleep with me.

So what if he sees you like Cassius does, weak and helpless? So what if you're just using him?

I met his gaze in the mirror, my pulse pounding with the irrational fear that he'd reject me. He was an incubus. He survived on sex and he'd already made it clear he wasn't afraid of Cassius.

"Make love to me." *Please. Make me forget.* I said the words in a rush, knowing if I didn't blurt it out, I never would.

AMIAH

THE HELLFIRE IN HAWK'S EYES FLARED AND I HELD MY breath, anticipating his rejection, but he didn't even hesitate, didn't have to think about my request. He drew closer, brushed my hair aside, and pressed a tender kiss to the divot behind my ear. A soft tendril of seductive magic unfurled from his lips and curled down my neck, sending a shiver of need racing to my core.

"Anytime. Anywhere," he murmured against my suddenly sensitive skin.

Thank goodness.

I released a shuddering breath and leaned into him, savoring the feel of his strong body supporting me and the hard proof of his desire pressed against the small of my back.

Just focus on the sensations, not the loss of control.

"Tell me what you like," he murmured against my skin.

"I don't know." My eyes fluttered closed and I tipped my head back, offering him better access to my neck. I certainly liked it when he kissed my neck and when he let his power slide into me.

"You don't know?" He hooked his index fingers into the neck of my robe and slowly followed the fabric over my collarbone, his knuckles grazing my skin, inching closer and closer to my nipples.

I liked that too.

"Or you don't want to admit it?" he asked.

Which was also the truth.

"I—" My breath picked up with a mix of desire and fear. I didn't want to think, not about what I did or didn't like or anything else. I didn't *know* what I liked. I knew from all the things I'd researched what intrigued me but I'd barely experienced any of them. I couldn't say for certain if it felt good or not until I tried it. And now my mind was spinning, worrying about wanting him and about being inexperienced.

"I won't laugh at you or judge you."

"I—" Embarrassment heated my cheeks.

Stop thinking. Just answer his question and get back to not thinking.

"Hey." He hooked a finger under my chin and urged me to look at him. "Whatever it is, I'm into it."

"It's—" *Jeez, just tell him. He'll figure it out soon enough anyway.* I squeezed my eyes shut, unable to meet his gaze while I made my confession. "Sebastian was my first."

"That's okay," he said. "I just didn't realize you were that young."

"I'm not. I'm over a hundred. I was—" My throat tightened. I was a naive fool thinking my mating brand was wonderful and beautiful and not realizing it was a life sentence. "I'd made a vow. I'd thought I was waiting for someone."

"For Sebastian?" he asked, surprised.

"No."

"Fuck." He tensed, my one word chilling his seductive magic leaving me aching and cold. "I pushed you over the edge to do something you didn't want to do, didn't I? That's why you freaked out after you two had sex."

He started to step back, but I grabbed his hand, still tauntingly close to my nipple, and captured it against my chest, not allowing him to step away. "It's okay."

Please, don't reject me.

"No, it's not."

I caught his gaze in the mirror again and tried to will him to understand how desperately I needed to forget, to not think, to just *feel*. "I didn't have intercourse with Sebastian because of your power. You just gave me the push I needed."

"But then I—"

"Made me orgasm again with your hand and promised me more later?" The muscles in my core trembled at the memory of his fingers sliding into me. I wanted to go back to that moment and chase after him instead of running up to the roof. Everything would have been different if I'd just taken him up on his offer for the both of us to go into Sebastian's bedroom and finish what had been started.

"I didn't realize— You wanted it so badly your desire hurt."

It hurt now. Couldn't he feel it?

Make me forget. Make me feel good.

"I thought you'd just gone without for too long," he said.

"I had." My whole life. "Hawk, I'm done waiting and holding back. I was done before I'd decided to sleep with Sebastian. I want to have sex with you. I want to feel good with someone, connect with someone."

The hellfire in his eyes flared and he offered me a soft, sad smile. "You know I can't do a relationship."

"Which is why you're perfect," I said. A bitter huff escaped my lips before I could stop it. "It was why Sebastian was perfect until he decided it was too dangerous to risk upsetting Cassius." Although it probably hadn't helped that I'd run from his bed right after having intercourse.

"So that's his problem." Hawk wrapped his free hand around my waist and drew me tight against his chest. "The idiot."

His sensual magic unfurled again between my thighs, and I throbbed with the need that hadn't even gotten close to being satisfied with that one moment with Sebastian. Hawk had merely teased me with that gentle orgasm when I'd woken in bed with him, and since then I'd had his power and the Winter Court's aphrodisiac swelling inside me. I needed a release, from my desire and worry and fear, from everything.

And Hawk was the perfect man to give it to me.

"Just to be clear," I said, my voice breathy, "I'm using you."

He drew his hand free from my grip and teased his thumb over my nipple. It was a barely-there brush over the thin fabric of my robe but it shot hot, sultry desire straight to my core and made his hellfire blaze stronger. "Yeah, because I get absolutely nothing out of this."

His hand traveled down my body to the belt holding my robe together, his touch light and slow, building the ache inside me, so different from the sex I'd had with Sebastian.

That had been wild, unrestrained, both of us desperate and aching for release. This was just as intense and made my pulse race just as quickly, but Hawk was taking his time to build a throbbing tension inside me. He was in complete control, his hands and mouth and magic in command of my desire, and that should have made me panic. If he was in control, I wasn't. But for some reason, knowing I didn't have to be in control relaxed me. I could just let go, just feel and not worry. I didn't know why I trusted Hawk, but I did, and I knew he was going to make me forget everything and feel good. He already was.

He undid the knot on my belt. My robe slid open, exposing the curls at the crux between my thighs, my still almost invisible sleeping mating brand curling over my left hip, and even more cleavage — the robe catching on my taut nipples instead of falling completely open.

With a low hum of pleasure, his gaze stroked down my body's reflection in the mirror, filled with a heated need that made the muscles in my core clench.

God, he could make me come with just a look. I wanted him to make me come with a look. In his eyes, just for this moment, I wasn't the weak angel who couldn't defend herself. I was beautiful, perfect, and desired. It was the same look Sebastian had given me when he'd first undressed me and I wondered if this was how all men looked at a woman before they made love to her. It had to be, because I wasn't special and neither man loved me.

I pushed that thought aside. I didn't care if Hawk looked at every woman like this. Every woman *deserved* to be looked at like this. And right now I was going to wrap the feeling around my heart and pretend the look was for me and me alone.

The hellfire in Hawk's eyes sparked and his expression grew hotter. His gaze, along with his hand, stroked slowly, sensually back up my body, inflaming my sensitive skin and making my breath pick up. He brushed aside the edge of my robe and kneaded my breast while his other slid over my brand, his fingers tracing the seam between my thigh and torso, heading toward my inner thigh.

My breath caught, but I had no idea if it was at the intensity of his look, his teasing touch, or the chance that he'd noticed my brand.

"So beautiful," he murmured, releasing my breast to slide the robe off my shoulders and let the silky fabric pool at our feet,

His lips pressed back against my neck as his fingers dipped into my curls and brushed my already slick folds with a whisper of a touch that made my desire twist tighter.

Oh, yes. This was what I wanted.

"Lace your fingers behind my neck, give me your lips, and let me make you feel good."

I obeyed, sliding my fingers through his soft sandy

blond hair at the nape of his neck and turning my head just enough to kiss him.

The kiss was slow, sensual, and released a bone-melting curl of power inside me, stronger than before. It swelled around my heart, making my breath pick up again, which pushed my breast against his palm. Then it sank lower, filling me with sultry, breathtaking need.

I moaned, aching for more, for his finger to find my clit, for his hand on my breast to tighten. I knew he wanted me. His erection pressed hard against me, and his breath had gotten faster too. But he continued to tease me, his touch light, his slick fingers close but never hitting the right spot, building my need until I was squirming against him, every nerve throbbing in anticipation.

Oh, yes. My fear had vanished. All thoughts had vanished. There was only his touch, the heat and strength of his body, and the thrum of his life force pulsing against my senses. Each caress twisted my desire tighter, drawing me closer and closer to climax.

Then he brushed my clit. I gasped and my muscles clamped tight, the wave of an orgasm starting to form, but his power swelled. It yanked me back to teeter once again on the edge, trembling and ready — God more than ready — my need tight, promising a shattering release that I'd only just caught a glimmer of.

"Not yet," he said against my lips, brushing my clit again, making me shudder, still at the edge, desperate for release and yet loving the pressure continuing to build inside me.

"I didn't know you could stop an orgasm like that," I

breathed. Of course, I hadn't thought I'd ever have sex with an incubus, so I hadn't spent a lot of time researching their sexual powers.

"I usually don't. I think it's cruel, but that was too fast. You deserve more than just a little flick." He pushed two fingers inside me and pressed his thumb against my clit.

"Oh, wow," I moaned, my eyelids fluttering shut at the feel of him slowly invading me. "Pretty sure you've already given me more than just a flick."

"Yeah, but this is better." His grip on my breast tightened and he rubbed his thumb over that sensitive bundle of nerves, picking up speed as his fingers, pumping in and out of me, picked up speed as well.

My breath grew ragged and my need twisted tighter and tighter until I couldn't stand it any longer.

I crashed over the edge again, crying out, my muscles clamping around his fingers. My orgasm hit me hard. I didn't even need more of his magic for stars to flash behind my lids. It roared through me, a giant wave of sensation that scattered my thoughts and made my knees weak.

Hawk held me tight, his fingers buried inside me as I rode the wave, staying put until I was completely satiated, then he picked me up, took me into the bedroom, and laid me on the bed.

I squirmed, savoring the bliss radiating through me and the feel of the soft covers against my hyper-sensitive skin. This was exactly what I needed. I felt so good, so sexy. God, I wanted more. I wanted to feel like this all the time.

He smiled at me, a breathtaking grin of pure joy, and

shrugged out of his tunic, showing me the gorgeous expanse of his muscular chest.

My pulse stuttered. "*Now* you're getting undressed? I can barely move."

His smile turned wicked, sending an aftershock of my climax trembling through me and making my eyes roll back in pleasure.

"I'd be a piss poor incubus if you only got one orgasm." He pushed his pants off his narrow hips, freeing his erection, and my pulse stalled completely. I hadn't imagined his size when I'd seen him in the healing grotto... and it was much more impressive fully engorged.

With a groan, he settled on the bed beside me. He captured my lips in a deep kiss, stealing all breath and thought and worry that I wouldn't be up for more, and added fuel to a desire that hadn't even been close to going out from my first orgasm. I kissed him back, tangled my fingers in his hair, and rubbed my thumbs against the base of his horns.

His breath quickened and his erection pressed against my hip, hot against my mating brand. He kneaded and pinched my nipples back into aching peaks before nudging my legs apart with his knee, settling one leg between my thighs, and teasing his fingers through my folds.

Oh, wow. I arched into his hand, moaning into his mouth, aching for him to fill me, bring me to the edge of pleasure and send me soaring again.

His sensual magic trickled from his lips into my cells, and he moved his other knee between my thighs, his erection pressed against my mound.

My pulse pounded, anticipation making my muscle clench.

But instead of entering me, he grabbed my hips and rolled, pulling me up to straddle him.

"I *gave* you pleasure in the bathroom," he said. "Now I want you to *take* it, be in control."

I stared at him stunned for a second. I didn't know how. I mean academically I *knew* how, but there was a difference between reading and doing. And yet the only way to know was to try.

I dropped my gaze to his erection nestled against my curls, thick and hard with a drop of pre-ejaculate glistening on his tip, and my pulse picked up. He was larger than Sebastian and Sebastian had been a tight fit.

"You're good and wet, and I promise I won't let it hurt." He set his hands on my hips, urging me to rise up. "Just take it slow."

I can do this. God, I want to do this, need to do it.

I rose and he wrapped his fingers around his shaft, running his hand down its length and leaving a glistening slick substance.

"Did you just—?"

"Add a little extra lube just in case," he said, aligning himself with my opening. "You really don't know much about incubi, do you?" He raised his hips just enough to press his tip against me and brushed his thumb over my clit.

I shuddered, and he released a soft heat inside me and gently urged me down to slowly impale myself on his shaft, his magic turning the pain of stretching to accommodate him into a heart-racing pleasure. Each fraction of an inch slid against already heightened nerve endings, rebuilding my desire along with a growing awareness of his life force, something I hadn't noticed with Sebastian, although at the time I'd likely been too distracted. It was as if having him inside me heightened my senses, making my pulse throb in time with his.

I was panting with need by the time I'd reached his base, every nerve in my core thrumming— No every cell in my whole body thrumming. God, this felt so good.

Hawk's grip on my hips tightened and his breath hitched. "Holy hell."

I tensed. "Good hell?"

"Oh, yeah, gorgeous," he purred, as his hellfire blazed and his seductive magic swelled inside me. "Fuck yeah. Now let's figure out what feels good for you, what angle, what pace, what motion."

He urged me into a slow rocking motion, his hands resting lightly on my hips just to steady me and giving me full control. For a moment it was hard to concentrate on anything but the feel of him inside me, his sultry magic sliding through me, and his life force heightening all of it. It felt amazing just as it was, then I accidentally shifted and caught a sliver of what it *could* feel like, what it was *supposed* to feel like.

"Oh," I breathed, the sudden brush of amazing sensation making me tremble.

"Exactly." Hawk's face lit up with masculine satisfaction, and he shifted my angle bringing me back to the position that flooded me with sensation.

The feelings swelled from my core and entwined with Hawk's power, filling me with pulsing, aching bliss. He raised his hips in time with my rocking, and I tipped my head back and closed my eyes, giving in to all of it, letting my body's natural instinct take over. It was overwhelming and amazing and so much more than I'd ever expected.

My desire surged into an urgency, making my heart pound and my breath ragged. I clung to Hawk's wrists to keep my balance, moaning and panting, holding on for dear life as the promise of an amazing climax surged inside me.

"Oh, Amiah," he groaned, and I glanced down at him.

His gaze captured mine and for a second there was a softness to the desire burning in his eyes, an awe... that I couldn't possibly have seen because I wasn't anything he hadn't already experienced before.

Then he rubbed his thumb over my clit with strong fast circles, ratcheting up the sensations beyond what I thought possible until every muscle in my body contracted with a full-body orgasm. Hawk sat up and captured my mouth, muffling my scream of pleasure and groaning his own, as bliss tore through every cell in my body. I was on fire again from Hawk's magic, but this time it felt amazing, crashing through me over and over again, sending me spinning, my essence thrumming.

Oh.

Oh my.

There weren't words to explain how I felt.

I was totally and utterly ruined for other men.

Sebastian had been amazing and now so had Hawk, and I doubted every man could make me feel like this.

AMIAH

"Hey, Amiah," Hawk murmured, brushing hair out of my face, his fingers sending rippling aftershocks rushing through me.

I cracked open my eyes and realized I lay on Hawk's chest with his arms wrapped around me. He was still inside me and I could feel the throb of his rapid pulse against my cheek and between my thighs.

"When did we lie back?"

"When you passed out," he said.

"I passed out?"

"Also common with my magic," he said with a chuckle. "Way back when, it used to be a defense mechanism so we could escape after feeding."

"And the magical formation of lubricant?"

"So we can get the best possible meal with anyone." He slid a hand down to cup my rear, his implication clear he meant anal sex which sent more shivering aftershocks rushing through me as well as a whisper of renewed desire.

Oh my! I guess that interested me as well, especially if it went with the suggested *ménage à trois*.

But right now it didn't interest me enough to move and leave Hawk's embrace.

No, right here and now is perfect. My naked body was pressed against his with his life force strong and sure, steadying my soul.

Hawk moaned and drew his hand away from my rear. "I really want to stay here, make you come again, but Sebastian and Cassius are coming closer. Or at least two people with the same frustrated sexual energy, and I suspect you're not ready to tell them about this."

My throat tightened. He was right. I shouldn't feel bad about having consensual sex with Hawk, and yet I wasn't ready to deal with everything that came with everyone knowing that I'd slept with him—

No, that wasn't true. It wasn't everyone, it was just Cassius. I wasn't ready to deal with his overbearing protectiveness when he learned what I'd done.

"Hawk, I—"

He shifted me to his side, sliding out of me but still holding me tight, and met my gaze. The hellfire in his eyes flickered in a mesmerizing dance, making my heart race. "It doesn't bother me if you don't want them to know about this—" He flashed me a wicked smile. "About us."

"Us?" That one word filled me with such hope. It implied there was more to our... arrangement than just this one time. With him, I could explore my desires without fear of my soul bond awakening or him wanting a committed relationship.

"Of course." He captured my lips with a breathtaking kiss. "For as long as you want me. Even after this mess is over."

"Pretty sure you have more experienced lovers you can turn to once we get back to the mortal realm."

"Silly angel." He rolled his eyes at me. "That doesn't mean I still can't give you what you desire until you meet someone you want to settle down with."

"But I'm—"

"Gorgeous, amazing, determined, strong?"

"Inexperienced."

"We can fix that." The hellfire in his eyes flared and a curl of sensual magic swelled inside me. "We've already started. Get over your worry. I said I'd make love to you anytime and anywhere and I meant it." He kissed me again just as passionately as before, his embrace tightening and his erection pressing hard against my thigh.

Oh, yes. No—

Wait a minute...

He pulled back with a groan. "If you don't want Sebastian and Cassius to see me coming out of your bedroom, I have to go."

"Yes... of course..." I said, trying to focus my scattered thoughts.

He pulled his pants back on — the loose fabric doing nothing to hide his erection — and grabbed his tunic. With another strange, soft look, very much like the look he'd had when he'd said my name during sex, he left.

I stared at the ceiling, my lips tingling from his kiss, my body aching to have him fill me again, and only a slight heat radiating from my mating brand. Hawk wasn't my soul mate, and sex with him had been amazing. God, what would it be like to have both Hawk and Sebastian? I wasn't sure I'd be able to handle that.

And given how Sebastian was keeping his distance, that wasn't going to happen at all.

I got out of bed and — on wobbly legs that brought a smile to my face... because I'd had sex with Hawk! — took a quick shower.

I was putting on a new robe, frustrated that the only thing for me to wear were robes when the guys got pants and tunics, when I heard them talking in the living room.

"I don't like that we don't have a clue who was behind the attack," Cassius said as I opened the bedroom door.

His gaze jumped to me and the light in his eyes flared, the intensity in his look stealing my breath. He was tense, the tendons in his neck standing up, but there wasn't a hint of smoke curling around him which meant he was trying to hold it all in.

Sebastian's attention also jumped to me, and for a second the look in his eyes was just as intense as Cassius's with an expression I couldn't read, then he yanked his gaze away and dropped onto the couch, stretching out to take up all the seats like a spoiled house cat. "I don't like it either, but it is what it is."

"Not acceptable," Cassius growled.

"What's not acceptable?" Hawk asked, coming out of the guy's bedroom with wet hair and wearing just his pants.

Water dripped from his jaw-length locks and trailed over a sculpted pec.

My pulse stalled— goodness, everything stalled and

the memory of what we'd just done flooded me, heating my face.

"Pull it back, incubus," Cassius snapped. "She deserves to be a part of figuring out what we're doing, not enthralled by your magic."

Hawk winked at me and shot Cassius a wicked smile. "Don't be jealous, Sparky, there's more than enough of me to go around."

"I don't want to sleep with you." Cassius pinched the bridge of his nose and the muscles in his jaw twitched. "Can you be serious for just a moment? Someone tried to kill Amiah and they're still out there."

"Someone is trying to kill both me *and* Sebastian," I corrected, taking the other chair and wishing Sebastian had ordered more food. Even though it had only been a few hours since I last eaten, I hadn't gotten nearly enough. A snack would be lovely. Ideally something that wasn't purple or bright blue.

Hawk's expression flashed from playful to serious. "You've got no clue who made the attempt?"

"No," Sebastian replied, "so we need to come up with a plan that involves leaving soon. I still need to conclude my business and get magical protection from the Wilds so I'm not incapacitated, but once that's done, even if my mother hasn't announced her party, we have to go."

"Will the Wilds kill you?" Cassius asked.

"No, but—"

"Then getting protection isn't worth risking Amiah's life by sticking around," Cassius said.

"Yes, it is. But I want to be ready to run the moment I've got it." Sebastian shot me a quick look and his gaze dipped to my left hip, making me suddenly hyperaware of the heat radiating from my brand. This wasn't about getting protection. This was about freeing me from my fate, a fate that I might have been able to ignore in all the pain and chaos, but one that was still coming my way.

I could be free before the day was done.

Free.

My pulse pounded and I tried to keep my expression calm.

"Why don't I wake Titus and we'll figure out a plan first," Hawk said.

"Don't." Sebastian jerked up. "Not until we know what we're doing. We need to give him something he can focus his rage on or he won't be able to control his beast."

"We need a contingency plan for if he loses control." Cassius paced to the front door and turned to come back.

"If he fully loses it, he'll shift and we'll be fucked," Sebastian said. "My mother will lock the court up so tightly no one will be able to get out."

"Hawk, are you strong enough to carry him by yourself?" Cassius asked.

"Yeah, but he'll seriously slow me down." Hawk slid into one of the chairs, oozing heart-stopping sensuality and I fought to not stare at him.

Moments ago I'd had all that sensuality, all that desire, focused on me and it had felt amazing... and not what I was supposed to be thinking about.

Jeez.

Except if I wasn't thinking about sex with Hawk, I was thinking about the heat in my brand.

I wrenched my attention to Cassius who had paced to

the back wall and was making another pass to the front door.

"I'll try to keep his beast calm, but I don't know if I can keep it at bay." I turned my attention to Sebastian. "I couldn't do it before and you had to cast your sleep spell on him."

"The sleep spell and carrying him is the best option," Cassius said. "I don't want you endangering yourself by getting close if his beast takes over and he loses it."

"Hey, maybe we'll get lucky and we won't have to worry about it," Hawk said, but from his expression, he didn't believe that we would.

"Yeah," Sebastian huffed, "because we've had the best luck so far."

"It is what it is, we'll deal with it," Cassius said. "Okay—"

Someone knocked on the door to the hall.

Cassius stiffened and glared at it.

"If they mean Amiah danger, they won't be able to get in," Sebastian said as he stood, his body tense.

"How sure are you?" Hawk asked, also standing.

The door opened, revealing an ice maid carrying a large silver platter with a jug of something pale yellow, and a plate with fruit, cheese, rolls, and cold cuts. All of it looked very mundane and mortal, just like what I'd been wishing for. Behind her followed another maid with a platter of glasses, plates, and cutlery.

"More food?" Cassius demanded. "Really? Didn't we just eat a few hours ago?"

"Hey." Sebastian raised his hands in defense. "I didn't request it."

The ice maids set the platters on the coffee table, curtsied, and scurried out.

Hawk's eyes narrowed. "So your mother sent it?"

"Guess so," Sebastian said, giving me a strange look then turning his attention to the food. "It's safe."

I filled up a plate with food and dug in, unable to stop thinking about being free and the achy heat building in my hip... because it wasn't building, that was just my imagination because my attention was focused on it.

As I ate, the guys talked about what they'd learned while Sebastian and I had been visiting the healing grotto, what the security was like, and what our first and second choice exits out of the Winter Court were. The biggest problem was the ice guards. Sebastian didn't know if we'd be able to lose them — something that would have been easier to do during the party — so we were going to have to make a run for it and pray we could get out before the Winter Queen noticed her guards were damaged and backup arrived.

"It'll be tight, but if we make our move by the silver sitting room, they shouldn't be expecting anything and we'll have time to get out," Sebastian said.

"That's still four long halls from our closest way out," Cassius replied. "We should do it closer to the exit."

"Any closer and they'll get suspicious and then it won't be a matter of catching them off guard, we'll have to actually fight them," Sebastian said. "We might have a reason to go to the silver sitting room, but not farther."

"Fine." Cassius rubbed his face. "Go deal with whatever it is you have to deal with and let's go."

Sebastian glanced at me, making my pulse pick up, as I bit into a sweet roll with white frosting on top.

Soon. Soon. But—

Was he going to tell Cassius the truth? How was he going to get us out of the suite without anyone else knowing?

A heavy knot formed in my stomach. He wasn't. I was going to have to accept that. It'd be safer if all the guys came with us. They'd know the truth, but at least I'd be free. Free to choose my destiny, be in control of my life, and to fall in love like everyone else.

Soon.

"Yeah, about that..." Sebastian said.

The light in Cassius's eyes flared. "Bane?" he said, his voice dark with warning.

"Remember when we went searching for evidence of whoever attacked Amiah and Titus and no one attacked us?"

"No," Cassius said. "Whatever you want. No."

"It'll be fine. I promise," Sebastian insisted.

"Hey man," Hawk said, "even I think this is a bad idea and you haven't even said anything yet."

"How about we hear him out." I set the rest of my roll on my plate and licked frosting from my index finger, trying to look calm and not reveal the panic racing inside me. This was it. Sebastian needed to tell Cassius I had to go with him and he was going to have to explain why.

I could do this. I could handle it if it meant I was free.

I could. Really.

Hawk's hellfire flared and his lips quirked, sending a

shiver of desire racing through me, while the muscles in Cassius's jaw flexed.

Hunh?

Then realization hit me. They, along with Sebastian, were watching me suck the frosting from my finger.

Really? All of them? Hawk's power must still have been influencing them.

I jerked my finger away from my mouth and clutched my hands in my lap, determined to hide my trembling.

Sebastian raised an eyebrow at me, a hint of his wicked smile tugging at the corner of his lips. "The deal to get protection from the Wilds is that I introduce Amiah to Karthick, and we come alone."

My thoughts stuttered. He'd lied.

Smoke erupted from Cassius's hands. "No."

"I'll protect her," Sebastian huffed. "And so will the court."

Was it really safe for us to leave the suite alone? Someone was trying to kill both of us.

And yet I couldn't deny the desperate hope twisting inside me that I could be free and no one would ever know.

"Absolutely not." Fire snapped up Cassius's forearms and with a growl, he yanked both it and his smoke back under his skin.

I sat forward, my pulse racing, praying this lie would actually work — which was completely out of character for me. It didn't even bother me that Sebastian was lying even if it wasn't logical to go knowingly into danger. But the voice inside me screamed that I had to be free, above everything else, that I couldn't wait any longer, and it was stronger than my need to be honest and any common sense I still had left.

If my brand was gone, I could allow myself to look at Cassius as more than just a friend. I could look at anyone I wanted. I could have a committed relationship if that was what I desired.

I glanced at Hawk.

Or I could wait. But it would finally be my choice.

"How important is it for you to be protected from the Wilds?" I asked.

"He said it wouldn't kill him," Cassius growled.

But Sebastian had also said when we'd been facing off against Deaglan and his demon-vampire that when he'd been left to die in the Wilds Faerie had ripped its magic out of him. There were a lot of painful degrees between healthy and dead, and this sounded like something I couldn't heal.

"If my mother chases after us, you don't want to be carrying both Titus and me," Sebastian replied, never looking away from Cassius even though he was answering my question. "I swear, I'll keep her safe."

Cassius's eyes narrowed.

I had to put a stop to this. Yes, I should be smart and not go, or I should confess to Cassius the truth. But that would become another fight and there might not be another chance anytime soon to have my brand removed.

"It's not your decision to make," I said, setting my plate on the coffee table and standing. "Sebastian needs this protection. All I have to do is go, protected by the court, Sebastian, and his mother's constructs."

"There are people trying to kill you." Cassius grabbed my wrist and I glared at him, my heart pounding.

"And unless they're listening in on us right now, they don't know exactly what we're doing." I dropped my gaze to his hand then back up to his eyes and raised my chin, daring him to keep holding me. "We can't afford to have both Titus and Sebastian out of commission. That would mean you and Hawk would be carrying them and I'd be the only one with free hands. Do you expect me to fight the Winter Queen's men by myself?"

The light in Cassius's eyes flared. "Amiah—"

"Let me go." I tried not to sound like I was begging even though everything within me was. I had to do this, had to be free, and I was this close to doing it without Cassius's judgment.

And really! This was my life, my choice. He had a right to express his feelings, but not to tell me what to do, even if I was always going to be the weak pathetic angel he'd rescued all those years ago.

"Fine." Cassius jerked away and fire crackled over his hands.

"Great. Now that we have your permission," Sebastian said, his tone dripping with sarcasm as he stood and strode to the door. "If we're in trouble, the Winter Court will tell you, just like it told you to meet us back here after the first attack."

"That doesn't make me feel better," Cassius said.

Hawk sat forward and brushed his index finger against mine, just a whisper of flesh against flesh that sent a shiver of desire racing through me. His hellfire flared and a hint of that soft strange smile swept across his expression again then vanished, the moment so quick I wasn't sure I'd actually seen it.

"We won't be long." Sebastian opened the door, revealing the two large ice guards standing at attention in the hall.

I hurried out, Sebastian right beside me, and we headed down the hall — the ice guards falling into step a dozen feet behind us.

"Thank you," I said, keeping my voice low.

"Doing it for myself, remember? Sparky needs to get laid."

AMIAH

SEBASTIAN LED ME DOWN LONG, WHITE, SHIMMERING HALL after long, white, shimmering hall without a window in sight until we reached an enormous arch with two towering statues of the Winter Queen standing guard on either side. Each statue held a massive sword, its point on the ground and its pommel reaching her waist, and each wore an intricate crown larger and more detailed than what I'd seen her wearing in the throne room when we'd first arrived.

Beyond lay a thirty-foot stretch of perfect untouched snow, glittering in the late afternoon sunshine, along with a vast expanse of cloudless sky framed by snowy mountain peaks and a forest made of both deciduous and evergreen trees as well as shimmering ice trees mimicking their live counterparts.

I hesitated at the threshold as a frozen wind ruffled through my robe, reminding me that was all I wore and that I didn't have shoes. This was the first time I'd actually felt the cold in the Winter Court, and walking in the snow was going to be painful. I'd have to monitor my feet carefully to watch for frostbite. But I could heal that and it was worth the use of my magic to be free.

Soon. Soon.

Except before I could grit my teeth and step into the snow, Sebastian swept me into his arms.

I tensed, habit making me ready to argue that I could make it without his help, but shoved aside the urge to say anything. It was safer for my feet if he carried me. He knew that, I knew that, and him holding me didn't mean anything... no matter how much I loved the feel of his arms around me.

It was just touch I wanted, and not specifically his. That was all.

Still, I relaxed into his embrace, savoring the feel of being pressed against his muscular chest, his arms wrapped around me, and the heat radiating from his body — which was odd since he was usually on the cool end of the body-temperature spectrum.

"We really need to get you some real clothes," he said, striding toward the forest, his footsteps crunching in the snow.

"Ideally before we leave," I replied.

"Yeah," he said, his voice gruff. "Although no clothes might speed things up between you and Cassius."

Given how Cassius had reacted to me in the healing grotto I wasn't so sure about that. He'd tried his hardest not to look at me or touch me, and I, unlike Sebastian, wasn't going to assume that was because he wanted me.

Behind us, the ice guards took up position at the archway and stared at us as Sebastian drew farther away.

"They aren't following us." And I hadn't heard Sebastian order them to stay behind like he had every time we'd gone into the healing grotto.

"They can't. The Winter Forest is sacred. The court only allows a select few to enter." Sebastian's grip tightened and his pulse under my ear beat a little faster. "But the Winter Court likes you, so it was safe to assume you'd be on the approved entry list."

"Except you didn't know the court liked me until after you had your first meeting with Karthick. What would have happened if I wasn't?" I asked, shivering as the cold seeped into my skin and making me even more aware of the warmth in my not-yet-awakened brand.

"You would have hit a magical barrier. Which would have been awkward with me holding you. But you are and this is the most discreet place for this meeting."

He stepped into the shade of the trees, making my heart sink a little bit as branches partially obscured most of the sky, and headed down a path, its edges marked with little snowbanks. Sunlight streamed through the trees' naked limbs and shimmered in ice branches and the air grew heavier and colder. It chilled the inside of my nose and throat as I inhaled and released as a glittering mist when I exhaled.

Sebastian's pulse slowed back to normal and he drew in a deep breath. The light radiating from his skin swelled and beat in time with his heart, and the rhythm of his life force thrummed against my senses. "God, I missed this."

"The forest?" This was the first time I'd seen him at

ease in the Winter Court and it broke my heart to think he'd been forced away from his home for centuries.

I might have left the Realm of Celestial Light, but I could return whenever I wanted. There wasn't much for me in my native realm, my parents had passed away just before the war and my sister worked in Tokyo with her earth magic, calming earthquakes, but Sebastian had said he'd never wanted to return. He clearly didn't want the life that waited for him in Faerie and it was obvious that if he returned, he wouldn't be able to avoid it. Case in point, everything that had happened since we'd arrived.

"I miss the magic," Sebastian replied, his voice wistful, then he chuckled. "Poor Hawk needed a shield against all of it and I'm pretty sure I wasn't able to completely block it out for him."

"Because he's magically sensitive?"

"And not from Faerie. I'm sensitive too but my essence is a part of Faerie. More so because I'm a sorcerer and can directly connect with it. The mortal realm is like walking around at high altitude for me. I can survive, but the air is thin." He drew in another deep breath and released it with a heavy sigh, his breath misting, filled with glittering flecks of... well, I guessed magic even though I wasn't magically sensitive and shouldn't have been able to see it. "But the power is the only thing I miss about this place."

He rounded a corner and the trees opened up, revealing a large clearing with a shimmering ice gazebo in the center. The structure looked like it had been spun from delicate threads of ice, the pillars and roof woven in an intricate design, offering some shade, but also allowing in light — and more importantly letting me see more of the sky again. A dark blue rug and dozens of pillows in various shades of blue surrounded a small metal brazier radiating a glorious warmth, and the moment Sebastian set me on my feet, I dropped onto a pillow close to the brazier and held out my cold hands.

Sebastian sat beside me, within arm's reach but still a proper Cassius-amount of distance away as if he hadn't just carried me here.

I bit back a sigh. He'd made his choice and I had Hawk. I shouldn't be feeling upset that he'd suddenly decided to respect my boundaries... and yet I missed the Sebastian who used to tease me.

"Karthick should be here soon." Sebastian's full-body glow dimmed for a second and his expression hardened. "Then we can get the hell out of here and away from my mother and Deaglan."

Guilt twisted in my stomach. If it hadn't been for me, we would have left already and Sebastian wouldn't be risking his life. "You didn't have to insist on this."

Except if we'd left, I'd still be trapped with no guarantee that Sebastian would be able to find the time to free me before my brand fully formed.

"I don't know if I can remove your brand, but I know Karthick can. This is your best chance." He shrugged and turned his gaze skyward. "And maybe I wanted to return to the forest one last time before I left for good. I hadn't gotten a chance the last time."

I opened my mouth to tell him... I wasn't sure what. That I was sorry he'd been forced to abandon his home, that I was furious on his behalf that his friend and his fiancé had tried to kill him. But heavy footsteps crunched in the snow on the far side of the forest, drawing his attention away from me and I let the moment go.

A squat, bulky man marched out of the trees across from us on the other side of the clearing from where we'd entered. He wore heavy brown pants with the legs tucked into black boots that laced up to his knees, and a dark green shirt, the sleeves rolled up to his elbows revealing thick, muscular forearms. A bandolier with dozens of small pouches was slung across his broad chest and he wore a pale green knitted scarf, the only indication he noticed the cold.

"It's been a long time since the Winter Forest has had heat," he said, his voice low and gravelly. "Winter fae don't usually notice the cold even in the forest."

"The Forest doesn't usually allow a being from the Realm of Celestial Light to enter," Sebastian replied as the man sat a few feet away from me, putting me in the center between him and Sebastian. "And you knew it would, Karthick."

Karthick shrugged and held out his hands to the brazier like I did. "The Winter Forest was always going to welcome your wife, Seireadan."

Sebastian rolled his eyes at Karthick. "You know very well she's not and never will be."

Karthick turned a bright green gaze on me. "Because you belong to another."

"No." *Not yet. Never.*

Flecks of gold danced in his eyes, mesmerizing me, drawing me in, as if he could hold me captive, see into my soul, and pull out my secrets... like how I was still attracted to Sebastian and yet desired Hawk... and maybe

Cassius... not to mention how I wanted a repeat of my kiss with Titus—

I jerked my attention away from him. It was just my pent-up sexual frustration making me desire all the guys around me. It wasn't that I desired them specifically. Just men.

And maybe if I told that to myself enough times, I'd believe it.

But even if I did like them, even if they were my soul mates, I didn't want a soul bond, not with any of them. Ever.

"I don't *belong* to anyone." I didn't want something that killed me or made me insane when my other half died, and I didn't want my death to mean someone else died or went insane. Neither option was acceptable. I couldn't believe I'd been foolish enough to think it had been, to have thought it was beautiful.

My pulse picked up, fear chilling me so deeply I barely felt the brazier's warmth, only the heat from my brand. The moment my soul bond awakened I'd be trapped. They'd be trapped. *Please. This might be my only chance.*

"Seireadan says you can remove it," I forced out, my voice frustratingly small, exposing my fears.

"If I do, you'll never be able to form a soul bond with anyone," he said. "You'll always feel as if a piece of your soul is missing."

A small part of me felt like a piece of my soul was already missing, but it wasn't enough for me to wish for a bond that made me fall in love with a stranger.

"An angelic mating brand is rare even among angels

and no other species can form a bond like that," he pressed. "Are you absolutely sure? This can't be undone."

I raised my gaze to his and held it. "Everyone says the bond is beautiful, but I've seen the truth. I've seen it crawling on the floor desperate and I've seen it turn caution into recklessness."

My thoughts stuttered at that. I'd already become reckless. I'd done things that defied common sense, tried to do things on my own when it was more practical to ask for help, and had risked my life to save Hawk. I was already becoming the thing I feared, the thing I'd admonished others for.

I had to put a stop to it, regain some self-control — and I owed a certain someone a huge apology. It had been all too easy to make the choices I had to not burden those around me and to protect them even if it meant endangering myself.

"I want to choose who I fall in love with."

"You'll love your soul mate." Karthick's eyes narrowed.

"Because the bond will make me. Please." I'd beg if I had to. I'd do anything to be free of this fate. "I've had my choices taken away from me before. I can't do that again." My throat tightened. "I'll never let anyone have that kind of power over me again. Ever." I didn't know what I'd do if Karthick refused to remove my brand. I'd already lived through someone controlling me, using my natural compulsions against me. I couldn't do it again.

Never again. Never.

Sebastian pressed his hand against my back, the soft touch instantly steadying me, and I glanced at him. He had the same look I'd seen on Cassius's face when he'd rescued me from the faith healer. Concern— No, pity. Because I was weak. And in this case, I was. I couldn't fight or deny that truth. I wasn't strong enough to deal with an unwanted soul bond, and my heart raced at the thought of it forming.

"I've already told you I'll pay her debt," Sebastian said.

I stiffened. "Sebastian, no. It's my price to pay." I squared my shoulders and a gust of frozen wind swept through the gazebo making the fire in the brazier snap and flicker. "What do I owe?"

Karthick's eyes widened and he glanced over my shoulder at Sebastian. "So she does control the wind."

"You're a little late to the party," Sebastian groaned. "She used it to knock Deaglan on his ass, probably would have pummeled him into tomorrow too if I hadn't shown up and put it at ease."

"Yeah, and then he'd have just run a shadow blade through her heart. But boy I would have loved to have seen the look on that bastard's face." Karthick's gaze returned to mine and he held out his hand. "The price hasn't been decided. You'll owe me a favor."

My mouth went dry. What kind of a favor would a fae ask for? Would it be something I'd be able to do or would my natural compulsions prevent me?

I stared at his hand and instinctually my magic connected with him, again without me needing to touch him. It rushed through his body, a whisper of power, connecting with each cell and making my compulsive need to heal surge.

Every joint in his body was painfully inflamed, the

cartilage and bone damaged from advanced osteoarthritis... and the cause was extreme old age. It was astounding he could walk. In fact, it was a miracle he was walking normally. And I wasn't even going to try to wrap my head around the thousands of years he'd been alive. I hadn't even met angels who'd been alive that long.

"You must be in such pain." I raised my hand above his heart but didn't touch him. "May I?"

"I'm not in pain," Karthick said as Sebastian grabbed my arm and pulled it back.

"Remove her brand and she'll heal you."

"It doesn't work that way," I said. The urge to heal Karthick twisted inside me. If he said no it would ease off. His condition wasn't serious so my magic hadn't locked onto him, but I had the power to help him, ease what had to be constant agony. If he'd let me, I'd help. No strings attached.

"It does in Faerie," Sebastian said. "Having a debt with Karthick isn't bad. There are worse fae to be indebted to, but you have something valuable to trade. It's a good deal."

"If I charged for my services you'd be up to your eyeballs in debt," I shot back. I'd already healed Sebastian a number of times, at one point draining myself to save him. "Would you like me to send you a bill?"

He glared back at me. "Go ahead. I'd be able to pay, no problem. Then I'll send you a bill for removing your brand."

"But you're not going to remove my brand, Karthick is." This was not the conversation I wanted to have, and we could argue about it after my brand was removed and we'd escaped the Winter Court. I jerked my attention back to Karthick, who wore an amused smile. "This won't take long."

"Those are her terms," Sebastian insisted. "I can vouch for her power."

"You'll still owe me for pulling you out of the Wilds," Karthick said. "And for protection against it now."

"I'd expect nothing less." Sebastian released my arm and I held my hand back up to Karthick's heart.

He nodded and I pressed my hand to his chest. My power rushed into my palm, glowing around my fingers, eager to take action, but I held it back, only allowing a thick thread to ooze into him, and not the sudden painful rush that it wanted. There was no need for this to be fast. While Sebastian and I didn't have all the time in the world, I could still take a little time so healing Karthick wouldn't be painful. He'd already suffered with pain for too long.

My magic slid through his body, seeping into each cell and clinging to his joints. I closed my eyes and let my power take over, maintaining just enough control to restrict its flow. It wove his swollen, damaged cartilage back together, starting at his feet and moving up.

I savored the feel of my power, thick and sticky like blood around my hands and teasing up my forearms, and yet always flowing out of me into someone else. I felt his body and life force strengthen and my soul sang with joy. I'd done that. I'd stopped his suffering. This was who I was. Always and forever.

With all the recent pain and fear and heartbreak, it

felt as if I'd forgotten that, forgotten who I truly was, *what* I truly was. Life.

My magic surged, a great final swell healing the last of Karthick's arthritis, and dissipated from his body, releasing me.

With a sigh, I sat back and drew in a deep relaxed breath, my pulse steady and sure, my hands still glowing. The compulsion to heal him had vanished, less than half of my power had been used, and my soul felt steadier than it had been in days.

Karthick stared at his hand, his expression shocked, and he slowly curled his fingers into a fist. "I never thought I'd feel this way again."

"If you take care of yourself, you should be pain free for a long time." Perhaps another thousand years.

"Thank you." He cupped my hands between his and met my gaze, a soft warm smile making the gold in his eye sparkle.

"No, thank you. It was nice to just let go." *Accept who I'm supposed to be and not care about anything else.*

He barked a wry laugh. "That wasn't you letting go. I could sense you holding your power back, slowing it down."

"If I'd let go completely, you'd have been healed in a heartbeat and it would have been painful."

His smile melted away, replaced with a grim determination. "I won't be able to do the same for you. This will hurt and there's no way around it."

My throat tightened and my fear returned, his words chilling my joy. "I understand. I figured as much."

I'd already realized this was going to hurt. He was

tearing out a piece of my soul. There wasn't any way it could be painless. But I could do this. I'd be free after this. Free.

"Take a breath and release it," Karthick said as he closed his eyes.

I obeyed, and warm, gentle power swelled over the back of my hand and up my arm. For a moment it was comforting. It billowed into my chest, gathering around my heart, and sank to my hip. But the moment it reached my brand it burst into sharp, stinging bites. First rushing along the complicated lines of the brand that trailed from the middle of my left thigh, over my hip and waist, and curled around my back to my bottom ribs, before surging back to my heart.

I gasped and Karthick's magic snapped, crushing around my heart and searing down my leg. It burned me from the inside out, liquid fire rushing through my veins, consuming me. Then Karthick's eyes opened, his green gaze captured mine, and blazing agony sliced into me.

My muscles seized and I screamed. Darkness swarmed my vision and I strained to stay conscious, strained to draw in each breath. But the pain kept growing, the fire tearing into me, ripping at the long, powerful threads of my bond woven into my soul.

The world lurched and dimmed. Karthick's power shredded my insides. Each breath grew into a battle, a fight against the pressure and pain, and I fought to stay conscious.

I could do this. I had to do this.

Please. God. I had to be free.

I clung to that hope, repeated it over and over again

— *free, free* — desperate to shut my mind away from the pain. But I couldn't shut it out, couldn't do anything but sob as Karthick ripped a ragged tear in my soul... because that was what I wanted.

Then the fire vanished and Sebastian gathered me into his arms before I collapsed onto Karthick. I pressed my face into his tunic and cried, my body shaking with painful tremors.

"Is it done?" he asked.

"Check for yourself," Karthick replied.

Sebastian pressed a cool hand against my knee and his chilly magic whispered through my enflamed skin for a second as he searched for my brand with his magical senses.

"It's gone," he murmured against the top of my head.

"Let me see." I grabbed the hem of my robe with a shaky hand and drew the fabric up high enough to see my upper thigh.

The barely-there shimmering lines that had been on my body for as long as I could remember were gone, and, if I concentrated, so too was the heat and ache.

I was free to love who I wanted, how I wanted, and when I wanted. The terrible destiny that awaited me was gone.

Finally. I was free.

CASSIUS

I PACED THE LIVING ROOM UNABLE TO STAND STILL *AND* keep my fire under control. It was one or the other and my fire was the priority. And no matter how hard I tried to focus on being hard and icy, my internal flames blazed through those thoughts, yanking me back to Amiah and my worry, urging me to go, take action, protect her.

She wasn't safe. I couldn't lose her like I'd lost my brother. She and Bane had been gone for too long — which probably wasn't true. It was hard to tell time in the suite, but I didn't think they'd been gone for more than half an hour.

"He'll keep her safe," Hawk said, thankfully not telling me to calm down.

"I still should have gone with them." I should have forced Bane to let me go. Except Amiah had been right. If both Titus and Bane were incapacitated that left her to defend us or her trying to carry Bane, and neither option was acceptable. We couldn't afford for the Wilds to incapacitate him which meant going ahead with his deal for protection.

"He's just as concerned about her safety as you are." The hellfire in Hawk's eyes flared and the muscles in his jaw flexed. Was he worried too? "He'll protect her."

"She's not his responsibility." And I knew if Bane got a better offer, he wouldn't think twice about betraying her—

Except that was the person I'd thought Bane was. It wasn't the man I'd seen the last couple of days — and if I was being honest, it wasn't the man who'd put his life on the line to help save my brother, Gideon.

Flames sparked over my hands and I heaved them back under my searing skin.

Just because he wasn't the mercenary I'd thought he was, didn't mean he'd be able to keep her safe. The only way I could be sure she wasn't in danger, was if I was protecting her.

"She'll be fine," Hawk insisted, but again it sounded like he was worried and trying to convince himself.

Which was strange. He didn't know Amiah. They'd only met three days ago.

"What's your story, incubus?" I growled.

Jeez. Not the most diplomatic way to ask the question, but I was sure everything I said right now was going to come out angry. And I wasn't even sure what I was asking. I didn't know him, I didn't know why he seemed concerned about Amiah, and I didn't know what Bane and Amiah were walking into.

God damn it. I didn't know anything.

My power surged and I strained to keep it controlled,

wishing that the floor and walls were actually ice and they'd be able to help cool me down.

"What do you mean what's my story?"

"Who are you?" *Should I be worried about any outstanding arrest warrants? Can I trust you and why the hell have I been trusting you?* Because I had been. Which wasn't like me at all. Not without at least doing a basic background check.

But my raging power was making it difficult to stay calm and concentrate. I couldn't lose her. Even if we were only ever friends, I had to keep her safe.

"I'm nobody," Hawk said, his gaze sliding to the hallway door.

"Only somebody who's somebody says they're nobody." My gaze followed his, my fire churning stronger. Was she about to arrive? Could he sense her energy — and did I want him able to sense her energy? Because that would mean Bane was flirting with her and she was enjoying it. "How do you know Bane?"

"We met during the war." He ran a hand through his jaw-length sandy blond hair. "And no, I'm not talking about it."

"That's not an option." I didn't want to talk about the things I'd done in the war either, but demons had no problems lying. Just because he said he was a vet didn't mean he actually was and requiring him to provide details might help me see through his lies. "What was your rank and deployment?"

Hawk gripped the arms of his chair. "You don't get to interrogate me."

"I don't know you and we're stuck in this together. If I

want to ensure Amiah's safety, I have to know what kind of experience you bring to the table." It was a logical argument. Just like when I'd needed to know Amiah's physical condition. It was important to understand the strengths and weaknesses of each one of us.

Hawk was decent in a fight. I didn't know how he handled a sidearm or rifle since — much to my surprise — Bane hadn't had any firearms in his apartment, but Hawk had been deadly with the karambit and its wickedly curved blade, and taken out his fair share of Balwyrdan's mercenaries. I still, however, didn't know how he'd manage if faced with more powerful supers.

The hellfire in Hawk's eyes flared. "And I've just got to take your word that you've the experience to keep her safe."

"I've been keeping her safe for a hundred years," I said before realizing how possessive that made me sound, especially since I'd announced that we weren't in a relationship.

"As a sister," Hawk said, his tone clear he didn't believe me.

"Yes," I forced out. If I corrected him, he'd keep on taunting me, trying to get me to confess I wanted something more with her when that would put her in more danger.

"That doesn't mean you have the experience to protect her."

"You're just trying to get me to tell you what I did during the war." Which, even if I didn't like it, was fair. He didn't know me either. Except he didn't have a responsibility to keep Amiah safe. I glared at him. This wasn't a

conversation I wanted to have. She wasn't his concern...
and I didn't want her to become his concern.

Hawk glared back, his expression serious with no hint
of sexual playfulness. "You tell me yours and I'll tell you
mine."

No.

Except I needed to know who he was.

But would he even tell me the truth?

I jerked away from him and paced to the back of the
living room. God damn it. I was just going to have to hope
he would.

"Fine. I was a lieutenant in special operations before I
was moved to the second division on the front line." I'd
assassinated a dozen of my own kind who'd sided with
Michael in his quest to exterminate humans and supernatural beings before my rage had become a liability to
the team. Then they'd put me up front and I'd let my fire
burn through everything and everyone. All the
misguided humans and supers who hadn't realized
Michael's end goal, all the angels who'd agreed with him,
and all the mindless nephilim he'd created.

My fire surged, racing up my arms, snapping and
crackling, and I strained to pull it back. It had felt so good
just to let go, to let my fire rage.

And it had been terrifying to realize I was a monster
too.

"You're the Salamander," Hawk said, his voice tight,
edged with awe and fear.

"Not anymore." I yanked my fire back under my skin.
Except not being the Salamander was only a fantasy, a

desperate wish that I could regain control of my fire and become just plain Cassius again.

"I was the canary for the forty-third infantry."

Hawk said it so softly, so matter-of-factly that his words almost didn't register. Canary was slang for a magically sensitive soldier in a squad. Because of their sensitivity, they were the first to notice magical traps and attack spells, hence the term. They were the magical canary in the coal mine of the battlefield. But that wasn't what had made my thoughts stutter.

"The forty-third?"

"Yeah."

No wonder he didn't want to talk about his experiences.

The forty-third had been assigned to check out a warehouse with some unusual activity and had come across one of Michael's labs. Except instead of creating unnatural monstrous nephilim for his army, he'd been conducting horrific experiments on human children.

The forty-third had lost two-thirds of its men trying to take the lab and Michael's soldiers had slaughtered half of the children, attempting to destroy the evidence. The remaining children had been so horribly mutilated, physically and mentally, that none of them could have been saved, not even with the help of angelic healing.

"In short Bane, who I'd thought was a faekin glyph witch at the time, and I were assigned the magical cleanup."

"And by cleanup you mean...?"

"Killing children. Michael made us kill children because it was that or let them suffer in agony for days, maybe months, before they died." Hawk's grip on the chair's arms tightened, turning his knuckles white. "He fucked with their DNA and the healing angel who'd been assigned to the mess couldn't save any of them. His magic couldn't reverse whatever Michael had done and we couldn't even pump them up with drugs to ease their suffering. Ever been in a room with over a hundred wailing dying children that you can't sedate?"

So not only had he fought a bloody battle, he'd had to suffer through the aftermath, too.

"Don't doubt my resolve, Salamander. I'll do what I have to. And don't doubt Bane's," Hawk said. "We're not besties — I'm pretty sure Bane doesn't let anyone get that close to him — but I know what kind of man he is."

"Tell me both of you visited a lethe demon at least once since then." If they hadn't had a *lethe* devour the emotions of those memories and soften the edges, the two of them could break down the moment Amiah needed them the most.

"It's none of your business, but we have," he said. "That and a little more than years later it just feels like a bad dream or a horror movie, not something I actually did... unless some asshole makes me think about it."

Hawk's attention jerked to the door before I could reply and it opened, revealing Bane and Amiah. They entered and my heart skipped a beat at the sight of her.

She was pale, her eyes rimmed with red as if she'd been crying, but she had a soft smile that made my breath hitch.

I took a step toward her, drawn to the gentle warmth in her expression before I realized what I was doing and my fire burst over my hands, my affection and desire for her making it blaze stronger.

Hawk sat forward, clearly drawn to her as well, the hellfire in his eyes flaring.

"Are you okay?" I asked, the urge to move closer twisting in my chest.

Instead, I forced myself back a step and heaved at my power.

Icy cold. Frozen. Hard. Just be frozen.

My priority was and always would be to keep her safe, and that included being safe from me.

"We're okay," she said, her smile disappearing behind her usual mask of cool, determined professionalism. "Has Titus woken?"

"Nope," Hawk replied, standing. "It hasn't even been an hour since the sleep spell was cast. Are we finally good to get the fuck out of here?"

"Oh yeah." Bane grabbed a roll from the tray of food on the coffee table with a trembling hand, and I realized he was shaken. He was trying to hide it, but whatever had happened during their meeting, it had set him on edge. "An appropriate change of clothes for Amiah should arrive in a minute or two and then we're good."

"Who wants to help me wake Titus?" Amiah asked, heading to the door of the bedroom with the cots. "I think if I do it, he's less likely to attack, but I'm not going to wake him by myself."

My chest tightened at the thought of her getting close to Titus. He'd tossed me across the room as if I'd weighed nothing, and there was no guarantee that his beast's fury would be gone when he woke. But she'd also gone forehead to forehead with him in an attempt to calm him down and the worst he'd done was shove her into my arms. Out of all of us, she was the one most likely to get the best response from him.

And even as I came to that conclusion, my fire burned hotter with my need to protect her. I couldn't fail her like I'd failed Dominic. Except I also couldn't lock her away to keep her safe, as much as a part of me really wanted to do. Someone had already locked her up and it had killed me to see her like that and to watch her struggle to regain her strength and confidence.

No, the best I could do was watch her back like a good friend.

Except I wanted so much more than that.

Flames snapped around my hands.

But more was too dangerous. I was an uncontrolled inferno, and I put her in more danger than anyone else.

TITUS

My angel's soft voice shivered across my senses and my beast roared inside me, straining to break free and take control. She was in danger, someone had tried to kill her, and everything within me screamed to protect her with my very life if I had to.

Except somehow, I'd given her the first key to unlocking Faerie's Heart, something I hadn't thought was possible without killing the original keyholder, and she was in even more danger. Deaglan would eventually figure out she had it and come after her.

He'd been overjoyed when the first key had become empowered, ready to unlock the spell containing the Heart, and the compulsion to go to it had seized me. And he'd been completely pissed when I grabbed it before he could and it had somehow helped me break his leash spell, allowing me to escape.

I'd hoped to never tell anyone about the first key, not even Seireadan — it was safer for everyone that way —

and then I'd somehow gone and given it to Amiah by kissing her.

It was as if some strange instinct had taken over, some knowledge that the key would be safer with her, or perhaps the key had possessed me. I'd smashed my lips against her, my need for her overwhelming, and the key had rushed out of me into her.

My beast heaved and clawed inside me. Protect her. Kiss her. Again.

It had felt so good, so right, and had been too quick. I'd wanted to explore her mouth, her body, show her how much I wanted her, how she was mine and always would be. But I'd only had a few seconds and the need to give her the key to keep it out of Deaglan's hands had been overwhelming. If I'd died, the key would have fallen from my body and anyone could have picked it up, and I had no idea if having one of the keys would allow someone who wasn't a dragon to find the others. It didn't matter that it put her in more danger. I'd had to do it.

"Titus."

Yes.

Call on me. Need me. Let me protect you. Always.

"Titus." Her essence warmed my cheeks and entwined with my beast's raging power.

My pulse picked up and my beast's claws dug into my soul. Whoever had tried to kill her was still out there and still a threat.

Kill. Protect. Mine. I would go through anyone who stood in my way to keep her safe. Not just my beast, but all of me.

Mine.

And the other guys had tried to stop me—

No, they'd tried to make my beast see reason. But it had no reason. It was pure, primal instinct, and seeing those ice men pile on top of her and thinking it had lost her had sent it into a desperate, ferocious rage. Hell, *all* of me, both man and beast, had panicked.

If she'd died—

If I'd lost her—

I couldn't. Please. *Mine. Always.*

I had to go. Now. Kill. Protect.

I jerked awake and stared into her shockingly blue gaze, captured, mesmerized, drowning. For a second, there was only her, leaning over me, her hands against my cheeks, and the warmth of her soul steadying mine. My beast reveled in the closeness, ached for more contact, ached for more flesh.

Then panic seized me, my fear taking over. I grabbed her around the waist as I sat up, and pulled her protectively tight to my body. The other guys standing a few feet away near the doorway to the living room all jerked forward.

I snarled, flashing my canines to show how serious I was even though I logically knew they didn't endanger her. If Seireadan hadn't stopped me, I would have raged through the Winter Court, revealing my true nature, and put Amiah at greater risk.

And my beast didn't give a shit about that.

"You put me to sleep," I growled.

"Because you weren't thinking straight," Amiah said,

shifting to get more comfortable against my side but not trying to pull away, which made my beast extremely happy. But that also made Cassius's glower deepen, the hellfire in Hawk's eyes flare, and Seireadan frown.

Mine.

I resisted the urge to hold her tighter, but couldn't keep back my snarl.

Jeez. Not mine. Not yet.

And really, I *knew* I hadn't been thinking straight, my beast's desire for blood had been too strong. Seireadan had probably saved my life, and I'd thanked him by bashing him into a wall.

Something my beast didn't give a shit about. He'd gotten in the way.

I gritted my teeth. Losing control wouldn't help Amiah, and neither would alienating the other guys. My beast might want to be the only one protecting her, but it was better if I had help.

"Are you all right?" I asked Seireadan.

He shrugged. "Nothing Amiah couldn't fix," he said, which made my beast heave against my control.

She'd touched him, comforted him, given life from her body to heal him.

Because that was her magic. It didn't mean anything.

I bit back another growl. I had to get ahold of myself. I hadn't proven myself to her yet and I couldn't just claim her. Seireadan had been right. She didn't adhere to five-hundred-year-old dragon social norms. I had to figure out how angels claimed their soul's mate—

No...

Those weren't the words I'd meant. It couldn't have

been. She wasn't my soul's mate. She wasn't even a dragon. Sure, my beast had decided she was mine, but that didn't mean she was *mine* mine. My beast was confused. *I* was confused. That was it. My soul was in turmoil from my captivity, my beast enraged because I'd been unable to release it.

"I have to get out of here." I needed to think, needed to tell my beast to shut the fuck up. Yes, I wanted her as my mate, because she was amazing and strong and her soul sang to mine, but—

Fuck.

Amiah cupped my cheeks again and pressed her forehead to mine, instantly sending soft warmth into my soul and steadying me.

If she was my soul's mate it was going to be even harder to keep my beast controlled while she worked out her relationships with the other guys.

And what if she didn't choose me? What if she picked Seireadan? They'd already had sex and the Winter Court responded to her. No matter what Seireadan said, they were practically mated already.

"I have to leave." I met her gaze. *Please pick me. I want you and I don't want to hurt them.*

"We're going to. We have a new plan and we're leaving soon," she said.

Thank goodness. If we could get to the Wilds, I could release my beast and the emotions threatening to crush me.

"Can you stay in control?" she asked.

No. "Yes."

"You better," Cassius snapped. "I won't let you

endanger Amiah by pulling that shit you did earlier. For better or worse, we're a team right now. If we're going to survive this, we need each other."

Someone knocked — presumably on the door to the hall — and everyone jerked to face the door out of the bedroom.

"Must be Amiah's change of clothes." Seireadan stepped into the doorway to the living room and froze then dipped into a deep bow. "Your maj— Mother."

My beast dug into my soul and I tightened my grip on Amiah. The queen might not want Amiah dead, but that didn't mean she wasn't going to hurt her.

"Shit," Hawk hissed, stepping up behind Seireadan.

Cassius joined him, the three of them creating a wall with their bodies in the doorway.

"A little snowflake told me your wife is in better health," the queen said, her tone sickeningly sweet. "I've come to see the miraculous recovery for myself."

"Your little snowflake is mistaken," Seireadan replied. "The pools couldn't possibly have healed her injuries this soon."

"Unless you've been lying about how hurt she was." A gust of wind swept through the door. "Tell me, Seireadan. Have you been lying to me?"

"No, Mother." Seireadan dipped into another bow.

"No?" The wind picked up, then snapped, forming a barely visible rope. It wrapped around Seireadan's neck and yanked him stumbling into the living room and out of sight.

Cassius and Hawk stepped forward to fill in the doorway and Amiah tugged against my hold.

"Let me go," she whispered.

"It's not safe," I hissed back. I didn't know what she was going to do, but there was no way in hell I was letting the Winter Queen see her. "She won't hurt him too badly, but she might hurt you."

"Except she's still going to hurt him," Amiah said, but she stopped trying to break free of my grasp as if coming to the same conclusion I had: there wasn't anything she could do.

"Do you honestly think you can protect her?" the Winter Queen asked. "That if you waited long enough, I'd forget that she *chose* to fuck you in public?"

The room's temperature dropped and ice crackled over the floor in a thick uneven coating, sweeping past Hawk and Cassius's feet and inching toward my cot.

Something thumped and Seireadan groaned. Hawk jerked forward a step, but Cassius grabbed his arm, stopping him.

"You will conceive an heir and everyone in court will bear witness."

"I'm still concerned for her condition," Seireadan gasped.

"Then fuck her gently," his mother snarled.

"Mother—"

"I'm tired of waiting. The King of the Shadow Court assures me she can take it. So she either puts on a dress and acts like a queen, or I tie her naked to the bed in the ballroom until she does her duty."

"There's no need for th—" Seireadan gagged as if he was being choked and Amiah tensed, her fingers digging into my forearms.

"If any other words except 'yes, Mother' come out of your mouth, I'll let the entire Winter Court fuck her first to remind you that you've been self-indulgent enough. A monarch never marries for love."

Amiah froze, her eyes flashing wide with fear, and my beast snarled. It strained to be free even knowing it would put Amiah in more danger if it attacked the Winter Queen like it wanted.

Seireadan was smart. He wouldn't disobey his mother like that, wouldn't risk Amiah's body like that. Please.

"Yes, Mother," Seireadan said. "I'll show her the delights of the Winter Court and we'll conceive an heir."

The room's temperature flashed back to normal, suddenly too warm in contrast to the queen's cold, and yet Amiah's skin under my hands remained cold and her body trembled.

"That's a good boy," the queen purred. "I'll even supply the good winter wine so you can melt her frigid angelic inhibitions. I expect to see you in the ballroom in ten minutes."

A door slammed shut and fire erupted over Cassius's body. He jerked away from Hawk and stormed to the back of the room where he'd had his other meltdown — the cots still piled out of the way.

"We're leaving. Now." He sucked in desperate deep breaths clearly trying to regain control of his power and failing.

"It's okay," Seireadan gasped as he staggered into the doorway, a large, bleeding welt encircling his neck.

"How is this okay?" Hawk asked, helping Seireadan to the closest cot.

"Let me go." Amiah pushed against my grip and this time I forced my beast to let her go. She hurried to Seireadan's side and sat on the cot beside him.

"I thought you said the court wouldn't let in anyone who would hurt Amiah," Cassius growled, his fire dripping from his hands and sending black smoke billowing to the ceiling.

"The court still bows to my mother's will and clearly it doesn't think conceiving an heir in public will hurt her," Seireadan replied as Amiah reached to place her hands on his neck. But he grabbed her wrists and pulled her hands back before she made contact. "Don't. If you heal me, my mother will know for certain that you have healing magic. Right now she might suspect, but it's more likely that I'd lied about your condition."

Amiah huffed. "Fine. Hawk give—" Her gaze swept over his bare torso then turned to me. "Titus, give me your tunic."

I yanked my top off and tossed it at her then dug my claws into the mattress so I wouldn't pull her back into my arms. If I did, I'd hold on tight and make a break for it. To hell with the other guys or the fact that I probably couldn't get out of the Winter Court alone. "You said we had a plan."

"The new plan isn't going to work," Seireadan said as Amiah wrapped my tunic's sleeve around his neck. "The guards will only take us to the throne room and all of my mother's other constructs will be on the lookout for us. We'd never be able to make it out of court."

"Hold that and apply pressure," Amiah instructed.

Seireadan wrapped his hands around his neck and

offered Amiah a small smile. "No, we're back to the original plan," he said, "slipping away during the party when my mother's concentration isn't focused entirely on her constructs."

"I'm not having sex with you in public." Amiah's breath picked up.

"I won't let it come to that," Seireadan said.

"We'll fight our way out before it comes to that," Cassius added, his fire back under his skin, but his body was so tense the tendons in his neck stood out and he shook with the effort to hold his flames in.

Amiah's gaze jumped to him then slid to me. My beast snarled his agreement. I would kill everyone to protect her. I would sacrifice myself to prevent her suffering.

The light in her beautiful eyes flared and her fear deepened with a horrible realization. "Against all of the queen's constructs? Against the Winter Court itself? It's too dangerous."

That didn't matter so long as she was safe. And I was certain that at least Cassius believed that as well.

"Promise you won't fight. Please." She jerked her attention to Hawk. "Promise you'll enthrall me so it won't hurt, so I'm not thinking."

Hawk dropped to his knees before her and grabbed her hands. "It won't come to that. I swear."

"Promise me anyway," she begged. "If you fight, she could kill you, and Sebastian and I will still have to do it. I can't get through it without you." Her terrified gaze jumped to Seireadan then Cassius then me. "Being humiliated isn't worth your lives. It won't break me if you're all alive, if I know we can still escape."

But my beast wasn't going to listen to her. If it looked like she and Seireadan were going to be forced to have sex, there was no way I'd be able to control it. It wouldn't be able to just stand there and watch, no matter how practical her request. I didn't think any of us could.

HAWK

WE ALL PROMISED AMIAH WE WOULDN'T RISK OUR LIVES BY fighting our way to freedom if she was going to be forced to have sex in public, and without a doubt, we all lied, even the angel.

What shocked me was that Cassius and Titus agreed to go along with Bane's plan instead of grabbing her and running since Cassius was barely holding onto his fire and Titus his beast. But everyone had to admit Bane's plan was the best— or rather the one we were all most likely to survive.

Bane assured us there wouldn't be a lot of guards in the ballroom, and the plan was to split into two groups, mingle with the crowd, and make our way to a narrow hall at the back of the room. The hall led directly to the Winter Forest, where only a select few could enter and hence wouldn't be watched, but just before the way was magically blocked there was a door leading into the catacombs and a hopefully forgotten way out.

All we had to do was survive a little time at the party.

"My mother will want to build up the suspense," Bane said, still holding Titus's tunic to his neck, his pale gaze never leaving Amiah. "She won't make us have sex right away."

"But she will punish us if we're late." Titus stood. His pupils were still slitted and his canines extended even though he'd managed to calm down a bit while we went over the plan. "Did she leave us clothes?"

"They rolled in a rack," Cassius replied. His expression was back to stern and icy, but his aura writhed around him, angry and red as if his expression was just a mask and he still seethed inside.

"Okay." Amiah drew in a steadying breath and squared her shoulders, her fear hardening into determination. "Let's do this."

I gave her fingers a reassuring squeeze and stood, keeping hold of one of her hands as we followed Titus and Bane into the living room.

The servants had left the rack by the door, having scurried in with it after Bane had agreed to his mother's terms and then scurried out. It had three pairs of heavy leather dark blue pants that had laces instead of a zipper for a fly and three red sashes, along with a pair of white leather pants with the same lace-up fly and a white sleeveless leather jerkin with blue and silver embroidery and intricate silver clasps down the front. At the end hung a white gown made of soft gauzy material.

Cassius went through the hangers of the men's clothes, the muscles in his jaw twitching. "We just get pants."

"And a sash," I said brightly, unable to help myself.

Cassius scowled at me. "Not all of us enjoy walking around half naked."

"Well that's a pity." I slid my gaze down his body, letting it show in my eyes that I appreciated his physique even though he was fully dressed. I'd seen him in his briefs in the healing grotto. He had nothing to be ashamed of. His chiseled musculature, honed from his years as a soldier and then as a JP agent and his classic handsome features could attract women just as easily as my good looks. I doubted the man had trouble finding companionship... if he hadn't completely closed himself off from everyone.

"Back off," he said, yanking a pair of pants from a hanger and holding them to his waist to check their size. "I'm not having sex with you."

"Aw, come on." I knew I shouldn't. Cassius had no sexual desire for me. The closest I might get to having sex with Cassius was if he let me join him with a woman and the jury was still out on whether he was open to that. But it was just too easy to push his buttons and it actually relaxed him a little, surprising him into forgetting that he had to keep a tight hold on himself.

"Flirt with Bane," he said, tossing me the pants that were too small for him.

I caught the pants one-handed and batted my eyelashes at Bane who rolled his eyes at me.

"I think we've already established you don't do it for me, pretty boy." Bane headed back to the bedroom with the cots. "I need to clean up before I put on all that white."

"You probably shouldn't be calling Hawk pretty, pretty

boy," Amiah said, sliding her hand from mine, making me ache at her absence.

I'd only had her once, but now I craved her. She'd felt amazing, both physically and magically, and she'd truly been a goddess when she'd thrown her head back and ridden me until she'd orgasmed.

But there'd been something else, something more than just sex. It had whispered within me the moment I was sheathed inside her and had swelled into an amazing, stunning sensation just before she'd climaxed. It was a connection that was deeper than our physical bodies, except she hadn't used any magic. Even if by some twist of fate Amiah was one of the rare angels able to create a soul bond with someone, I still would have sensed and seen the power of a bond forming — Bane's shield on me blocked out a lot, but not everything. But that moment with Amiah... I had no idea what it had been, only that it had felt amazing and absolutely right.

Bane's desire for her flared and he flashed her a wicked smile. "Gee, you think I'm pretty?" Then his eyes widened for a second and his gaze jumped to Cassius before he strode into the bedroom.

Jeez. Both of them were completely fucked up.

Titus huffed, his beast still straining to get free, his desire for Amiah ferocious.

Correction, all of them were fucked up.

Amiah took the dress and went into her bedroom to change, and I reached to yank off my pants where I stood, but my cock was hard and I hesitated.

Crap. I was supposed to have more control than that. Just thinking about a lover shouldn't have been enough to make me hard, not unless I'd wanted it to, and I hadn't been purposely desiring her... except I had been. I'd been thinking about her from the moment I'd left her bedroom, and I wasn't sure I'd ever be able to stop. I wasn't sure if I'd ever get enough of her.

And while I usually didn't care who saw me naked and hard, Cassius was barely holding his shit together. He'd either rightly assume I was hard for Amiah or wrongly assume I was hard for him and both would make him react badly. Thank God the leather pants were heavier than whatever our other pants were made out of and would keep me in.

Titus grabbed the remaining pants and sash, and followed Cassius into our bedroom, while I quickly stepped out of my loose pants and pulled on the leather ones before Cassius realized I wasn't following him.

"Hey. You should change in here," Cassius said, leaning out of the bedroom's doorway as I jerked the heavy leather pants over my ass and started to lace myself in.

"Nah, I'm just about done," I called over my shoulder.

"Don't make things more uncomfortable for Amiah than they already are. She— ah... She..." he stuttered, his desire suddenly spiking, hot and desperate.

I looked up to see what the problem was and my gaze locked on Amiah.

She was breathtaking in the gauzy dress with her long blond hair hanging loose in soft curls and blushing so hard it colored her cheeks and ran all the way down her neck into her cleavage — which with the dress's plunging neckline was a whole lot of cleavage.

I'd thought all the gauzy layers of fabric would have made the dress hard to see through, but it was shockingly sheer and, with its sleeveless faux Grecian cut covered very little. And while it didn't show *all* the goods, it was awfully close and would if she didn't watch how she sat. Especially with the slit up the left side that went all the way to her waist. There were also cut-outs over her abs and at her sides and when she turned to Cassius, I could see that the dress was backless and cut so low it showed a teasing glimpse of the top swell of her amazing ass.

She crossed her bare arms, drawing my attention back to her breasts and the silver and blue embroidery embellishing the bodice. Embroidery also accentuated the hem along the slit and I had no doubt she and Bane would match when they stood side by side.

"You look amazing," I said, drawing her attention back to me.

Her striking blue gaze captured me, stealing my breath, and I was grateful I was more or less tied in or Cassius would know for certain how much I wanted Amiah — and if I were to guess, he would be more upset if I was hard for her than if I was hard for him.

"I'm practically naked, and I still don't have any shoes." She huffed even as her gaze slid over my body just like mine had slid over Cassius's and her desire billowed, teasing through my veins with glorious seductive power. "Not that any shoes that would go with this impractical dress would be practical for fleeing."

"Well, fuck," Bane said, stepping up beside Cassius, adding his desire to the mix. He'd discarded Titus's tunic and washed the blood from his hands and neck. The welt had stopped bleeding, but it was still obvious, a stark contrast to his pale skin. "At least my mother has good taste."

"This is not good taste," she insisted.

"Yeah, you're right. The white virginal bride thing is a little on the nose," he said, making her stiffen and her blush burn brighter, "and inaccurate." He gave her a dismissive shrug and a hint of a sneer, reminding her that he'd been her first and silently telling her he was done with her, even as his desire for her grew.

Her desire vanished and, because I knew to look, I could see the hurt in her eyes before she quickly hid it behind a stern mask of professionalism.

I bit back a nasty retort to defend her. Saying anything would just make Cassius aware that something had gone on between them and she wasn't ready for that. Which Bane clearly knew and had used against her.

When we finally got out of here, I was beating some sense into the asshole. She could have gone to any of us for her first time. She could have gone to Cassius, someone she already knew and trusted. But she'd chosen Bane, trusted him to give her what she needed.

He didn't have the right to use that against her, especially to protect himself. No one should ever be made to feel bad or guilty about sex.

"But it does effectively show off your body." He grabbed his clothes from the rack and headed back to our bedroom. "And for my mother, the point of this is to publicly humiliate us... well, you, which is supposed to upset me."

"It should upset you," Cassius said, following him into the bedroom to change.

"Don't think it doesn't just not for the reason my mother thinks," he replied. "I don't want to fuck Amiah, let alone in public."

Liar.

All of us wanted to have sex with her. Something about her drew us to her and it wasn't just her good looks. There were women out there more beautiful than her, more confident, and not nearly as uptight. Perhaps it was her sexual awakening, her desire to explore all the things she'd been denying herself that called to us on a subconscious level. Or perhaps it was her fierce determination, her strength to carry on when the four of us knew, in part, the horrors she'd been through. Perhaps it was her scarred soul resonating with ours... maybe that was what I'd felt when we'd had sex. The connection with a kindred spirit just as wounded as me.

"Hurry up and get dressed," Titus said as he opened the bedroom door, striking an imposing figure. Wearing just the pants and sash made his massive, muscular chest appear bigger and broader even with the glamour changing his appearance. Where Cassius was honed, and Bane and I with our leaner frames were sculpted, Titus was bulky heavy muscle. Rugged and raw.

His attention instantly jumped to Amiah and his gold-red aura flared as his desire surged.

With a snarl, he stormed toward her, the ghostly image of a wolf's head superimposed over his own, indicating his beast was trying to gain control of his body.

Oh, shit.

I jerked forward, instinct moving me to protect her, but she stepped up to meet him and rested her palms against his massive chest. The wolf's head sank back under his skin, his beast instantly calmed, and he pressed his hands over hers.

"The Winter Queen is going to regret giving you that dress," he said, his voice gruff. "No one will be able to keep their eyes off you."

"I hope that isn't the case. The whole point is to blend in with the crowd and slip away." She leaned into him, making his desire burn hotter but his aura soften, his beast relaxing even more. "You need to shift the moment we're out of the Winter Court and it's safe. I don't care if it destroys the glamour changing your looks, you're not going to be able to keep your beast at bay for much longer."

"I'll manage."

She leveled an unimpressed glare at him. "You've shifted once in the last five hundred years. If you don't let your beast out, you'll permanently damage the connection between you two and then you won't be able to control him. That's not something I can heal."

"I agree," Bane said, striding out of the bedroom looking regal. The white strangely suited him even with his pale skin. It made him more luminescent, to the point where I had to concentrate to see the demonic magic writhing inside him. It also accentuated the black glyphs tattooed on his bare arms and curling up his neck out of the collar of his jerkin. Not only did he look regal, but with that many spells on his body, he also looked dangerous, and I wasn't sure if his mother had realized that or not when she'd selected our clothing. "Now let's get this shit show on the road."

He stepped into the center of the room and offered his arm to Amiah. She strode to him, her expression icy as the dress fluttered behind her. Titus followed her, and I quickly tied my sash around my waist. Cassius hurried out of our bedroom, looking uncomfortable in just his pants, and as a team, we stepped out of the suite.

Two ice guards waited for us and walked a dozen feet behind us as Bane led us down long, white, softly glowing halls.

We heard the ballroom before we reached it. The rumble of many voices mixed with lilting music carried down the hall, growing in volume as we approached the grand entrance. The woman with the gossamer fairy wings who'd yanked us into Faerie waited in the doorway and two more ice guards stood at attention on either side of two, fully open, massive doors. Beyond, was a wide balcony that ringed the room and a two-sided grand staircase.

Bane strode through the door, a slight arrogant smirk pulling at his lips, and led Amiah to the wide ice railing at the balcony's edge. His gaze swept over the large room below, filled with hundreds of people all wearing fancy gowns and suits — as well as a few just in pants like us who carried themselves like fighters and were most likely personal guards.

The room was strangely lit with dancing fae light orbs the brightest biggest ones hovering around the edges of the room and dimming the closer they got to the center, but that only accentuated the beam of shimmering moonlight pouring through the massive skylight high above. It landed like a spotlight on a large bed swathed in red shiny sheets, dusted with glimmering flecks of white reminiscent of scattered rose petals.

The muscles in Amiah's back tightened and her breath picked up.

I gritted my teeth against the urge to pull her into my arms and tell her she wouldn't have to perform in public. I was pretending to be Bane's bodyguard. I couldn't just hold his queen. So I forced my attention to the crowd, looking for potential dangers instead. I might not have been much of a soldier compared to Cassius, but I knew enough to get a good idea of who was a possible threat.

At the back on a large raised throne, in a red gown to match the sheets, sat the Winter Queen with her men on cushions on the floor around her, also in red — pants only as well. Her crown was tall and more imposing than before and a gentle breeze danced around her, ruffling her long loose hair, adding to the sense of power. She was queen and the Winter Court's wind was hers to command. She gazed across the room to the balcony and her lips curled back in a wicked smile.

Between us was the packed ballroom. People danced in the center around the bed while others mingled, talking and eating and drinking. I suspected they'd gotten more than the ten minutes to get party-ready than we did. Their bodyguards — the female guards in leather pants and halters with red sashes — mostly kept to the edges of the room.

A hint of hellfire caught my attention and I focused under the balcony, halfway between the grand entrance and the throne. The demon-vampire stood by a pillar, shirtless and wearing black pants and a black sash, the hellfire in his eyes blazing, his attention locked on us... no, locked on Amiah.

A shiver rushed down my spine. His expression was flat, more closed off than Cassius's when he tried to contain his power, and the hybrid's aura was a strange, barely visible black, unlike any aura I'd ever seen even on a demon or a vampire. I'd only ever seen a hybrid once before and that had been during the fight at Left of Lincoln, which meant this was the King of the Shadow Court's hybrid and that the king and possibly the rest of his assassination team were close by.

"Demon-vampire hybrid, three o'clock," I murmured.

Bane rolled his shoulders, the only indication he heard me. Cassius gave a slight nod and Titus grunted as a hush descended on the crowd.

The woman with the fairy wings fluttered into the air and everyone below stopped what they were doing and looked at the balcony.

"His Royal Highness, Prince of the Realm and Heir to the Throne of the Winter Court, Seireadan and wife," the woman proclaimed.

Murmurs rushed through the crowd and everyone dropped into a low bow or curtsey.

The queen stood and the breeze swept around her, making her dress billow dramatically. "Tonight I celebrate my son's return, his marriage, and the conception of a new heir."

She raised her hands and the crowd released a heartfelt cheer on cue.

"Welcome home, Seireadan."

Another heartfelt cheer. When I'd met Bane, I would have never in a million years have guessed he was a Faerie prince. The only reason I'd known he was full fae was because we'd combined our magic in a desperate attempt to save those children.

The queen gave a dismissive wave, telling the crowd to return to their merrymaking, and glided down the three steps to the ballroom floor. Two of her men followed her as she made her way toward us — parting the dancers instead of weaving through them — while the rest of her men dispersed among the crowd.

Bane led us down one side of the wide stairs. He'd told us we were going to have to meet his mother as a group, but after that, he and I would distract her for a bit, while the others slowly made their way to the narrow archway three-quarters of the way down the left-hand side of the ballroom.

The queen stopped at the bed, of course. It was the grand finale of her night and given that she wanted to remind Amiah of her place, the location to meet us didn't surprise me.

The queen's eyes narrowed as we reached her. "I can't believe you covered your arms in those disgusting spells."

"Mother." Bane dipped into a bow, wisely not responding to the queen's comment and telling her those *disgusting* spells covered more than just his arms.

Amiah curtsied and the rest of us bowed.

Bane gestured to the ballroom. "You've outdone yourself."

"My heir has returned and I'll soon have a grandchild." The queen flicked her finger and the wind gusted through Amiah's skirt, parting the fabric at the slit and making her flash the entire room.

Amiah grabbed the front of her dress, holding it down, but the back still billowed out, giving me, Cassius, and Titus a front row seat to most of her ass and making it clear she wasn't wearing any underwear.

Cassius and Titus both tensed — I did as well — but we all managed to at least look calm. We only had to play this game for twenty minutes. Doing anything else might jeopardize our escape.

"I'm so looking forward to your performance," the queen purred.

"Amiah and I are looking forward to our first child." Bane swept a lock of hair out of Amiah's face, his knuckle caressing her cheek. The touch was surprisingly affectionate but it didn't awaken any desire in Amiah.

"I am too." The queen raked her gaze down Amiah's body and gave her a wicked sneer. Then the wind suddenly vanished and her attention snapped to Bane. "Come, Seireadan, I've heard the Heart has awakened. We need to discuss how you're going to get it."

"Of course, Mother." Bane brushed his lips across Amiah's cheek, another tender motion, and if I hadn't known better, I would have sworn he was in love with her. "Enjoy the party, my love."

"Yes," Amiah murmured. She turned to leave, and Cassius and Titus moved to follow her.

"No, you're with us," the Winter Queen said, her gaze turning heated as she studied Cassius and Titus. "The incubus is more than enough to watch your queen. Do you want him to loosen her up first? He can't use this bed, but I can have another one brought out."

"That won't be necessary," Bane said. "Cas and T, you're with me."

The queen led them away, leaving me with Amiah.

"How long do you think they're going to be discussing the Heart?" Amiah asked.

"I don't know."

"It's probably a good thing," she mused. "Now we'll have inside knowledge of her plans, even if Sebastian isn't going to be the one fulfilling them."

"At least there's that."

They exited through a side door near the throne, and Amiah and I wandered in the opposite direction — and across the room from our escape hall — to a long buffet table set against the wall. I didn't recognize much of the food, but none of it was enspelled, so I made a small plate of what looked like finger food for Amiah in the hopes that holding something would help distract her from her revealing dress, not to mention everything else.

I wasn't sure if it did, but it at least gave her something to do with her hands.

A few minutes later, a man with the icy coloring and stunning looks of a winter high fae approached, bowed, and offered his congratulations. A rotund woman with a shockingly cold body temperature that I could feel standing four feet away from her joined him, along with a few other men and women, all congratulating Amiah and engaging her with small talk.

I divided my attention between watching for Bane and the others to return and looking for potential danger.

The hybrid had disappeared into the crowd while we were talking with the queen, and I'd yet to see any other members of his team.

One of the younger women asked Amiah about how she and Bane had met, and Amiah spun a romantic tale about him coming to her rescue during the war while she was attempting to evacuate children from one of the many war zones that had sprung up all around the world.

It was a complete lie... well, Amiah probably had been part of a team rescuing children. Cassius had said she didn't want to do field work, but that didn't mean she hadn't. I didn't know all of the shit Bane had done during the war, but I doubted their relationship was twenty-five years old. No, they reacted to each other as if they were still pretty much strangers.

By the end of the tale — which thankfully Bane wasn't going to have to repeat because we were leaving — the women were sighing over their romantic prince and the men were puffing out their chests at their heroic prince. Without a doubt, the tale was going to go through the crowd like wildfire and everyone was going to end up in love with Bane. Jeez, if he wanted, he'd probably be able to usurp the throne before the night was done... depending, of course, on how afraid everyone was of the Winter Queen.

Bane and the others emerged from the doorway soon after Amiah's tale, and Cassius caught my attention and pressed his palm to his shoulder two times. We were leaving in ten minutes.

Thank God.

I reached to touch Amiah's arm and get her attention

when a wave of desire swept through me that wasn't from any of the guys or Amiah.

Crap. If it was someone desiring Amiah, we couldn't afford to be caught up in anything that slowed us down or drew attention.

I glanced around, searching for the source. We were at the end of the buffet table, near a narrow dimly lit hall... where the desire came from.

There. A couple about fifteen feet down the hall.

They were mostly hidden in the shadows of a statue, but they stood close, their foreheads touching and her hands cupping his cheeks. Desperate desire, the kind that came with heartbreaking longing, not hot wild need, radiated from both of them.

They were in love and they couldn't be together.

And they weren't a threat.

I started to turn back to Amiah when the couple broke apart and stepped out of the shadows. It was Bane's sister and someone's personal guard, wearing only a pair of dark pants and a sash. He was a pale and gorgeous winter high fae with his long red and silver hair pulled back into a ponytail that reached his waist and he looked really familiar.

Bane's sister turned sharply, making the skirt of her dark dress swish around her and she hurried away deeper down the hall. For a second it looked like something dark oozed through her aura, but then it vanished and my attention slid to the man now heading toward the ballroom.

I brushed Amiah's arm. "My lady." I didn't know if

that was what I was supposed to say to a future queen but it sounded appropriately formal.

She excused herself from the group and drew close to me.

"Ten minutes," I said, keeping my voice low.

"Thank goodness," she breathed. "It's starting to get hard to keep track of my lies about Sebastian."

I chuckled and we turned to head toward the stairs — there was no way we were going to get closer to the throne to cross the room — but Amiah bumped into a werepanther in the queen's red pants as he was turning to head in our direction.

Amiah yelped and lost her balance.

I grabbed her shoulders and caught her as something flashed at the edge of my vision.

A spell?

Close?

Time stuttered and I glanced toward the glimmer. The fae man who Bane's sister was in love with — who, holy shit was one of the queen's men but not wearing red pants! — stepped close and jabbed a knife at Amiah. He kept the blade low, partially hidden by his body, and with everyone's attention on the werepanther almost knocking Amiah over, no one had noticed him.

Thankfully, the blade wasn't enspelled. The glimmer had just been a flash of the fae lights on the metal, but I didn't have time to let Amiah go and stop the man's attack.

On instinct, I drew close and turned her, blocking the blade with my body. I could heal just about anything quickly. Getting stabbed would still hurt but it wasn't a problem.

The blade pierced my side with a slice of pain, sliding through my sash as if the fabric hadn't even been there, and plunged into my flesh all the way to the hilt.

The fae man's eyes flashed wide with surprise and he yanked the blade free and jerked away.

"Hey." I reached to stop him and blinding agony, as painful as Cassius's fire, tore through me.

Oh, God.

I'd been poisoned. That man had tried to kill Amiah with a poison so potent even my rapid healing wasn't going to be enough to save me.

AMIAH

HAWK PAINFULLY CLENCHED MY SHOULDERS AS THE CROWD that had been drawn to my stumble dispersed, and my magic flooded my hands and locked onto him, demanding I save him.

Oh, no.

My pulse stuttered and the court's wind fluttered around me. Everything within me started screaming. *Save him. Save him. Now. Fast.*

He was dying.

Poison.

I knew the source before I'd even realized I'd connected with him. The poison was attacking his cell membranes and was so strong his natural healing wasn't able to eliminate it, let alone hold it back. All it could do was draw out his suffering which would entail massive bleeding from his eyes and nose and organ failure.

Save him. Save him.

I grabbed his wrist, and my power ignited, wild and

urgent, ready to blast into him, but he dug his fingers into my skin and the hellfire in his eyes blazed.

"Don't you dare let the queen know your power," he gasped. "She'll imprison you and the others will kill themselves trying to free you."

I opened my mouth to argue with him, but he was right... well, maybe not about Sebastian trying to save me, but Cassius definitely would do whatever it took for me to escape.

Except I couldn't let Hawk die. My power wouldn't let me and neither would the rest of me.

I strained to hold my magic back enough that my hands didn't glow and raked my gaze over the crowd. But I couldn't see any of the other guys and there wasn't time for a more thorough search.

Save him. Save him.

The wind ruffled my hair, gaining strength but not nearly as strong as it had been when I'd been facing Deaglan, and my power swelled. It had barely awakened and already it roared through my body, straining for release, promising an excruciating backlash if I didn't save him. Now now now.

God, I had to save him.

But I couldn't endanger the others.

And really the best way to heal Hawk was to give him sexual energy. Using my magic on him was worse than using my magic on myself.

Except my power didn't care. I had to use it, had to save him, no matter that it was better to do something else. Even if I did manage to shove it aside and give him sexual energy, I couldn't do it in the ballroom with everyone watching... well I could, but I really didn't want to.

Behind us was an unguarded dimly lit hall. Statues in shadowy alcoves lined the walls on either side blocking my view of any possible doors, but surely we wouldn't have to go far to find a room.

I wrapped an arm behind his waist to help support him and we hurried to the hall.

"Amiah—"

"Don't you dare tell me to stop," I hissed as my power burned up my forearms, hot and sticky, and the pressure in my chest continued to grow. "There has to be a room somewhere."

Please, let it be close. Please. I have to save him.

He stumbled, his weight yanking me forward, and the wind gusted, helping me catch my balance. His breath was ragged and sweat slicked his skin. He hadn't been poisoned more than a minute ago and already it was overwhelming his natural healing. I didn't have a lot of time left. I had to do something. Now.

There. A recess in the wall that didn't have a statue. Was that a door?

I hauled him toward it. His legs barely held him up and his head lolled forward. Pressure screamed in my chest and my power burned not just around my hands but around my heart as well. I had to use it. If I waited any longer the backlash would tear through me and possibly knock me out and then I'd definitely lose Hawk.

But the recess wasn't a door, just a deeper alcove.

Hawk tensed and he released a strangled cry. The

poison had flooded his heart. We were out of time. There wasn't anywhere else we could go.

I shoved him into the alcove. It was wider than the opening, and with the court wind's help, I heaved him into the front corner so the only way we'd be seen was if someone caught a glimpse of us while heading to the ballroom or if they purposefully looked in the alcove — but we'd only remain hidden if we were standing.

He groaned and his eyelids fluttered open. His hellfire was barely visible, tiny red pinpricks that sparked with sudden erratic flashes of light, desperate to stay lit and keep him alive.

God, I had to save him.

My power burned stronger, heaving against my control and lighting up my palms. It wrenched my hands over his racing heart, the place where it had the easiest access into his body, and I leaned in, using my body to help brace him against the wall.

"Don't... waste... your magic."

"I don't have a choice." All I could do was pray it would be enough to save him. "This will hurt."

His eyes rolled back and his lids shut again. "Already... does."

I released my magic, straining to control it, so it wouldn't hurt him as much as it could, but it blasted out of me, drawing a sharp scream.

Shit. Hold it back. I had to hold it back. Except I couldn't. My magic howled to save him — n*ow now now* — fast before the poison killed him, and I couldn't resist it.

I tried to move one of my hands to his head to draw

his lips down to mine and stifle his cry, or even just cover his mouth, but my power held tight, locking both of my palms over his heart.

Fear churned with my power's desperate need and the wind picked up strength tugging at my dress and hair. Someone was going to hear us. We were going to get caught. The queen would learn the truth and everything would get worse.

No, nothing could be worse than Hawk dying.

My throat tightened. It didn't make sense. I barely knew him and I'd lost patients before, even lost a few I was close to. The idea of losing Hawk shouldn't crush me. And yet it did. I felt safe with him, wanted to spend more time with him, learn who he was—

No, it was my natural angelic sense of duty and justice. He didn't deserve this. He'd been in the wrong place at the wrong time and had gotten caught up in this mess. He hadn't volunteered like I had by rushing to save Titus's life.

My power swelled into a massive weight crushing my chest and stealing my breath.

Save him. Save him.

Another scream escaped his clenched jaw.

Hold. It. Back.

Just enough so it wasn't agonizing.

I gritted my teeth against the rising pressure of trying to control it so it wasn't blindingly painful, yet having to shove my magic into him because his natural healing fought me as well as the poison. I should be kissing him or giving him a handjob or a blowjob. That would have been more effective, but I couldn't move my hands from his heart, couldn't resist my magic's compulsion.

Save him. Now. Now.

I wouldn't be able to give him any kind of sexual energy until I'd used up all of my power or I'd healed him. Except for every molecule of poison I burned away, two more appeared, and for every damaged cell I healed, the poison destroyed three.

His body shook and his breath had become shallow, desperate gasps.

I was going to lose him. I couldn't lose him. The wind turned frigid with my fear and my soul screamed, panicked, desperate.

I had to work faster. I couldn't afford to hold back.

Save him.

I wrenched my power into a ball in my palms, holding it against the burning, howling need to push it into his body. If I could do a powerful enough blast, I could burn out the poison and then his natural healing could save him — *please let it be enough to save him* — but I had to blast all of my remaining power all at once. Fast. Explosive. Painful.

The pressure in my chest grew, threatening to rip me apart if I didn't push my power into him, but I held on, spinning it tighter and tighter until my hands and forearms felt as if they were on fire with Cassius's magic.

With a strangled sob — my attempt at holding back my own cry of pain — I slammed all but a glimmer of power into Hawk.

He wailed. My compulsion released me — because I had nothing left to give him — and I grabbed his head and smashed his lips against mine, stifling his scream, even as the court's wind whipped it away.

I could only pray no one had heard that and that it had worked.

Hawk wrapped his arms around me, clutching me to his trembling body, his forehead against mine, and exhaustion flooded me, weighing down my limbs. The world darkened, turning the alcove almost pitch black for me and what little I could see slowly spun.

Only a glimmer of power flickered in my palms and I couldn't catch my breath.

But neither could Hawk. And his pulse didn't slow.

"You shouldn't have done that." His grip on me tightened and the remaining wisp of my power connected with him... and the poison.

No.

My throat tightened. It hadn't been enough. Except I knew it wouldn't be. It would have taken almost everything I had just a heal a few broken ribs in an incubus. I had no hope of eradicating such a powerful poison. All I'd done was bought him a little time... and released myself from my compulsion so I could heal him properly.

"My power had locked onto you. It wouldn't have let me go until you were no longer dying or I was out of power," I said in my clipped doctor voice and leaned back to look him in the eyes, but my vision wavered and I couldn't get it to focus. "Let's finish this. Kiss me."

"Amiah—"

"I'm not letting you die." I reached between us and with trembling, numb fingers worked to unlace him from his pants.

He cupped the back of my head and captured my lips in a searing kiss that made me forget I was trying to unlace him. It stole all breath and thought, and I melted into his embrace. Even dying his kiss could inflame my desire and make me forget about the exhaustion threatening to overwhelm me.

But his hold on me tightened and his fingers dug into my scalp and waist. He tipped his head back against the ice wall, gasping, and groaned in pain. The kiss wasn't enough, not even if we kept going. He needed stronger energy.

I fumbled with the rest of his laces and slid my hand inside his pants. I didn't know if a hand job with kissing would be enough, either, but I didn't think he was in any condition to have intercourse, he could still barely stand.

"Hey," he gasped, his gaze sliding to the alcove's opening. "We're in here."

My heart leaped into my throat and the Winter Court's wind gusted with my fear of getting caught and then Sebastian stepped into the alcove. Oh, thank God. Someone else who could help.

"What the hell?" he hissed. "Why did you leave the party?" Then his gaze landed on me and his eyes flashed wide. "Your eyes. Where's your power."

"He's been poisoned. Help me." I knew Sebastian didn't want to have sex with me, but maybe a little foreplay with Hawk drawing energy from both of us would be enough to save him.

"Fuck." Sebastian jerked close and pressed one hand over his hip where he had his sound blocking glyph and the other on his shoulder. "I've blocked sound and put up a veil behind me. We don't have a lot of space, but no one will see or hear us."

Hawk moaned in agony, his body trembling, and turned my head back to him to capture my lips again. The poison was growing again, painfully destroying his cells as if I hadn't just pushed all of my power into him. I wrapped my fingers around his penis, but he was only partially erect. That wasn't good. An incubus had control of his erection, and Hawk knew he needed sex to survive.

Sebastian drew up behind me, the clasps on his jerkin cool against my bare back. He slipped one around my waist and over my belly and drew my hair aside with the other.

Except I didn't react to his touch. Not even a glimmer of desire.

God, what was wrong with me? I'd been fantasizing about being with Sebastian and Hawk since I'd first met Hawk.

But I couldn't get my thoughts to focus on anything other than the fact that Hawk was dying and I had no magic left. I was also still selfishly hurt over Sebastian's words in our suite. He didn't want me again. He'd made that perfectly clear.

"This isn't going to work," I said. "If neither of us can muster up any desire, we won't be able to save you."

"Bane isn't the problem," Hawk gasped. "He's been wanting to make love to you again since you ran out of his bed." Hawk tensed and moaned. "And that dress is driving him crazy."

"But I'm not the one you're supposed to be with,"

Sebastian murmured against my neck his voice soft and strange. "I'm not in love with you. Cassius is."

For the love of—!

"I don't want you to be in love with me," I snapped, making the wind gust. "I just want someone to have sex with."

"But now your reasons are different," he replied.

"Yes. Hawk is dying." *Dying! Save him.* I had to save him. But what Sebastian had really meant was that my brand was gone and I could be with Cassius without fear of being permanently bound to him.

"And you need to relax for this to work," Sebastian said. "Hawk, can you give her a jump start?"

"I'll try," Hawk groaned against my lips.

A whisper of sensual heat slid down my throat, a teasing promise of what Hawk's power could be. It made my heart ache, churning with the growing fear in my gut and filling my chest with pressure again.

I couldn't lose him.

Except I had no idea why I couldn't lose him. Why?

Sebastian's hand on my belly slipped beneath my dress, gliding to the edge of my curls, while his other hand cupped my breast. Hawk pushed his tongue into my mouth, deepening our kiss, and I tried to forget he was in agony, or that I desperately needed to save him, or that my limbs were heavy with exhaustion.

I needed to relax, feel good, forget about everything.

Sebastian dipped his fingers into my curls.

This was the fantasy. Caught between both of them, having both of their hands and mouths on me.

Sebastian brushed tauntingly close to my folds,

trying to work up the sexual tension and make me ache for him. And I did. I hadn't stopped aching for him even after having sex. But I was also still too afraid, my mind and body out of habit clinging to stern professionalism and shoving my feelings deep down so I could appear calm.

Just forget about the poison.

I sucked in a ragged breath, released it, and tried to relax in Sebastian's embrace. Hawk had held me like that only a few hours ago. He'd slowly built up my desire and let his magic swell inside me.

I focused my whirling thoughts on the memory of that, of how he looked at me with such heated need, or how he'd caressed me, teased me, brought me pleasure. He'd built up the tension inside me until I was aching with want then twisted it tighter and tighter until I'd exploded.

Sebastian moaned against my neck and brushed his cool fingers through my folds, drawing a shiver of desire.

Yes. Focus on that. Focus on how Sebastian's body is cool and Hawk's is hot.

Except the moment I thought about Hawk's body, my mind jumped to his condition. Sebastian and I had given him more power and slowed the poison's spread, but it still burned through him, his sweat-slicked body still trembled, and his erection was still only half hard. He was barely holding on.

I pulled away from him to look him in the eyes again. His hellfire was barely lit. Even the sparks had died down. "We have to give you more." A lot more.

"Come for me," he gasped, and Sebastian slowly slid a

finger inside me, giving me a teasing reminder of what it had felt like to have him there filling me.

I groaned, my need surging with the memory of him pushing inside me, but I wasn't even close to coming, I was barely wet. It was going to take a lot more than that to make me come.

Then a strong thread of sensual magic slid down my throat, ratcheting up my desire. My breath hitched half in need and half in fear.

"Stop using your magic," I said, my voice low and breathy. "You need it."

"You need a strong orgasm for this to work," he said, his grip tightening and his face scrunched in pain.

Except I wasn't sure if just me orgasming would be enough.

But if Sebastian also came—

"You need two," I said. "I've never seen a poison this potent before. One isn't going to be enough."

"I don't have time for you to have two," he gasped.

"Not from me." I couldn't believe I was going to say this, but we were out of options. If Sebastian still desired me, I could make this work. I had to make this work. I couldn't lose Hawk.

"Sebastian, we have to have intercourse." The words came out sharper and colder than I intended, but we didn't have time to be polite. Hawk was dying.

"I—" Sebastian withdrew his fingers from me and shifted away.

"I know you don't want to. I know you think I should have sex with Cassius instead, but he's not here and Hawk is barely holding on. It has to be you." I turned to face him, to kiss him and get things started, but Hawk whimpered, grabbed my head, and turned me back to him, making the world lurch with the sudden movement.

"Don't stop kissing me," he begged.

Crap.

Fine. Sebastian and I still needed to have sex, so I reached behind my back and drew my dress aside, offering Sebastian my naked rear end. "Not anal. I'm not ready for that yet."

Hawk's trembling grew. His breath had become shallow and I had no idea how he was still standing. If we waited any longer, Hawk would start bleeding out.

The court wind turned cold and gusted with my fear, stinging my bare skin. I sucked in a breath that did little to calm me.

Come on, Amiah. Relax. You can do this. Think about when you had sex with Hawk, when you had sex with Sebastian.

Sebastian didn't draw closer or say anything.

What was he waiting for? Had Hawk lied and Sebastian didn't really desire me?

"Sebastian, we're running out of time. Are we clear?" I glanced at him from the corner of my eye. He stared at me with a strange look on his face, but his image was out of focus so I had no idea what his expression meant. "Please. He's dying. Have intercourse with me."

He ran a hand over his spiky white and silver hair. "Fuck me."

"No, Sebastian," I begged. "You're supposed to fuck me."

AMIAH

Sebastian groaned. "Fucking hell. I'm going to regret this."

"I won't make you do it again," I promised.

"That would be the problem." He unlaced himself, and used his body to sandwich me against Hawk. "I didn't want to stop the first time, but I also don't want to be burned to a crisp."

"Cassius wouldn't burn you," I said, as he pushed aside the fabric over my breasts and roughly worked my nipples into taut peaks.

My breath picked up and his erection hardened against the swell of my rear, but I trusted he'd respect my wishes. While I didn't know Sebastian well, I'd never seen him do something to purposely hurt someone, and forcing me into a sexual act I didn't want would hurt me and Hawk, because if I wasn't into it, Hawk wouldn't get the sexual energy he needed.

I fought to stay focused on the sensation of Sebastian's hands on me and his hard body pressed behind me along with the memory of having sex with him. His desire had barely been contained, just like mine because of Hawk's magic. I had ached for him, ached for his hands and mouth, ached for him to fill me. And he had. God, the things he'd done with his mouth had been amazing, the way he'd brought me to climax then worked me back up to crash over the edge again... it had been everything I'd hoped sex would be and so much more.

I moaned into Hawk's mouth, remembering the throbbing desire that had swelled through me just before Sebastian had filled me and imagined that need pulsing in my core now, growing stronger than my fear and exhaustion.

Hawk deepened his kiss, and Sebastian's breath picked up. He dipped a finger back inside me then slid the slickened tip over my clit. My focus jerked to the sensitive nub and the real throb building there.

Oh, yes.

Another moan slipped out, and Sebastian's hold around me tightened.

"That's it, sweetheart," he murmured. His thumb replaced his finger on my clit with a delicious firm pressure that made my desire twist tighter, and two of his fingers pushed inside me. "Show him how fucking hot you are."

He worked his fingers, sliding them in and out, and rubbed his thumb against my clit as Hawk devoured every gasp and moan. His tongue pushed inside me like Sebastian's fingers, claiming my mouth and fueling my desire. It overwhelmed the memories of them making love to me, pushing me into the here and now, and stole all conscious thought. There was no past, only present, only the feel of their sculpted bodies boxing me in, their hands and mouths bringing me pleasure, and the growing need building inside me.

Hawk's erection grew firmer in my grip, but with my whirling thoughts and the flood of sensation, all I could do was hold on.

Oh wow. This was the fantasy, the feeling I'd been craving. And oh my goodness! It was so much hotter than I imagined.

My desire twisted tighter and my breath grew ragged. If Sebastian kept doing what he was doing I'd orgasm soon, and even though it was possible for me to come and then Sebastian, I really wanted to come with him inside me. I wanted to feel that connection again, the thrum of his life force caressing my senses that was enhanced when we joined.

"Sebastian, I'm close," I gasped. "I want you in me."

Sebastian groaned, pulled out his fingers, and tugged my hips back to offer him better access then pushed part way into my opening, making me tense in anticipation.

"Oh, fuck," he panted and inched farther in, his girth stretching me, making me whimper. "Sorry. I know you need slow. But—"

"It's okay. Hawk needs this."

"Right," he said with a sudden sharpness. "You're just doing this to save Hawk." He fully sheathed himself with a quick push and my essence sang, despite the whisper of pain. Sebastian filled me, body and soul, his life force thrumming, drawing me to vibrate in harmony with him.

God this felt so good. His essence, his life, and him inside me.

I pulled away from Hawk's lips so I could look at Sebastian. The world was still out of focus and spinning, but I met his pale almost colorless gaze as best as I could, determined to show him how serious I was. "I'll never get tired of how you make me feel. I was momentarily confused last time, but I know what I want now. I don't want this to be the last time we have sex."

"Fucking hell," Sebastian growled, his voice dark and husky, and he slowly started to pump inside me, reconnecting me with my desire.

"But you have to be willing to share." Hawk drew my lips back to his.

"You have to ask her first," Sebastian said.

"Hey, Amiah..." Hawk said into my mouth.

"Yes," I moaned, saying it to the feeling of Sebastian moving inside me and Hawk's request.

"It's not fair to ask her while she's distracted."

Sebastian's thrusts picked up speed, twisting my need closer to the edge, and my desire and essence roared with his life force. I didn't even need Hawk's magic to feel that glorious pressure building in my core, promising to crash through me.

"Oh, God, Sebastian."

His thrusts grew harder and my orgasm rolled through me. I threw my head back with a gasp and a throaty moan, and Sebastian grunted low in his throat and tensed with his own release.

My connection to his life force swelled, adding to the

bliss rushing through me, stronger than the last time we'd made love.

I never wanted this feeling to stop, but no matter how good it felt, we were still doing it to save Hawk.

I dragged my whirling thoughts to focus on him and concentrated on my weak thread of power still connected to him. There wasn't a hint of poison left, and his hellfire blazed, strong and healthy, licking his cheeks. He looked at me with the same awe that I'd seen the last time we'd made love, as well as with a heated desire that made my breath hitch and my body ache.

God, I needed him in me, needed to feel his life force like I'd felt Sebastian even though my magic told me he was fine.

I captured his head and pulled his lips to mine with a hungry kiss.

He lifted me off Sebastian, and I hooked my legs around his waist and aligned him with my entrance. He plunged into me, a curl of his seductive power turning the pain of the sudden invasion into breathtaking pleasure.

I clung to him as he clutched my hips and drove into me with hard wild thrusts. The ferocity of his passion filled me, igniting already hyper-sensitive nerves and ratcheting up my need to new panting heights.

His life force sang inside me, so powerful, so sure, and I gave into the feeling of him moving inside me, giving him full control of my body.

God, yes.

This. This was the way it was supposed to be, what I'd been denying myself for far too long.

"Open your eyes and look at me, gorgeous," he gasped. "I want to watch you come."

I open my eyes and was drowning in hellfire and need and that soft awe that I'd seen before. I still had no idea what it meant, but it sang to something deep in my heart and my power made my essence stutter and matched my pulse with his, entwining our life forces with a breath-taking swell.

Then he pushed a whisper of magic into me. It wasn't much, but it sparked an explosion inside me, crashing me over the edge.

I tried to keep my eyes open. I really did. But every muscle gloriously contracted and I wasn't sure what I did after that. All I knew was that I cried out his name as his release took him and he moaned mine and the court's wind whipped around us. The most amazing sensation rushed over me, stealing my breath, and the world went black.

Once again, I was whirling, floating, swept away on bliss, stunned at the force of Hawk's power and the overwhelming sense of life from both him and Sebastian. It was as if a new sense had awakened within me, one that could only be felt when I joined with someone.

Panting, Hawk held me in a firm embrace as if he never wanted to let me go. His breath was heavy and his pulse raced, but he was healthy. All of the poison was gone. He was going to be okay.

Thank God, he was going to be okay.

As if thinking those words gave me permission to relax, the adrenaline rushed out of my body. It left me with an exhaustion that dragged at my limbs and even with my eyes closed, I could feel the world spinning.

"Thank you," Hawk murmured, his lips brushing my neck sending glorious aftershocks rushing through me. "God, you're amazing. Thank you."

"Jesus, Amiah," Sebastian groaned, and he drew close and pressed a tender kiss to the back of my neck. "I wish I could let you pass out and enjoy that, but we have to get going."

"Come on, give her a minute," Hawk replied. "She just gave all of her magic and her body to save me."

"I can't. Deaglan and my mother started talking. That's why I came looking for you. We need to leave before he convinces her to jump straight to the night's grand finale." Sebastian kissed my neck again. "As much as I really want a repeat of what we just did, I don't want us to have to do it in front of an audience."

My heart skipped a beat and the fear about the night's plans that I'd managed to momentarily forget flooded back with a vengeance.

"Okay," I said, my voice still shaky and soft. "We should go."

"I'm not sure you can walk, gorgeous," Hawk murmured. "And you didn't just drain your magic. I took a lot of life force from you, too."

I knew that. I was just too exhausted to remember. That was why incubi couldn't be monogamous. One lover wasn't enough to sustain them because they needed to feed faster than a single person could restore their life force, and that lover slowly emaciated until they withered to a husk and their organs failed.

"And neither of us should carry you through the ballroom," Hawk said. "That would definitely draw attention."

"I can walk. Put me down." God, I hoped I could walk.

I unwrapped my legs from Hawk's waist. He lowered me to the floor and I sucked in a few deep breaths to try to get the alcove to stop spinning.

"See. I'm fine."

Hawk's eyes narrowed. "I haven't let go yet."

"If she needs help, I'll help her. That will be believable. I can say you're still too weak and spending time at the party has exhausted you." Sebastian closed his eyes and his full body glow undulated around him.

Something whispered across the inside of my thighs, drawing a shiver of desire, and the ejaculate slowly oozing down my legs vanished.

Sebastian groaned — and not in the good way — and he grabbed the wall to keep standing, his breath suddenly ragged. His glow dimmed, and even in the weak light, I could see that his complexion had turned gray. Then his glow flared again, back to its normal luminescence.

"Whatever you cast, you shouldn't have," Hawk said. "Especially after casting the sound block and veil spells. I took life force from you, too."

"Amiah can't walk into the ballroom dripping our cum. She needed a clean-up and we don't have time for her to go to a bathroom." With another groan, Sebastian straightened, then reached for my breasts and slid them back into my dress.

Jeez. I was so dizzy I hadn't even thought to fix

myself... and so dizzy I'd just stood there and watched while Sebastian had tucked me back in instead of insisting I could do it myself like I usually did.

I drew in another breath then another as Sebastian laced himself back into his pants. The dizziness of having used all of my magic and being drained by Hawk would pass... eventually. I just had to power through until then.

"Okay." I ran my fingers through my wind-blown hair. "I'm good." Or as good as I was going to get in the next minute or so.

Sebastian offered me his arm and I took it, drawing close and using him to help me keep my balance, and Hawk released me.

The hall's spinning picked up and I gritted my teeth.

I won't pass out.

My body trembled and the hall's dim light darkened.

I. Will. Not. Pass. Out.

Hawk laced himself back in and we stepped out of the alcove and headed back to the ballroom — which was farther away than I expected. I hadn't thought Hawk and I had gotten very far, but I'd been so desperate to save him, I hadn't been paying attention. And now a part of me regretted that. I was already exhausted and we hadn't even gotten to the end of the hall, let alone crossed the ballroom to the hall leading to the Winter Forest.

But passing out would draw attention and the queen would either revive me and jump to her grand finale or send me back to the suite where it would be harder to escape.

I forced myself to keep moving, determined to keep my back straight and my expression calm, but my body and mind were heavy and numb as if I was walking and thinking through water.

Around me, the hall heaved in and out of focus, and the bright light from the ballroom ahead of us got dimmer and dimmer.

Come on. Don't pass out.

We were halfway to the ballroom when my feet tangled and I lost my balance. I tried to tighten my grip on Sebastian's arm but my hands and fingers were weak.

"Amiah—" Sebastian gasped as he caught me and pulled me into a firm embrace.

"I'm okay. I just need a minute," I said, clinging to him and squeezing my eyes shut, desperate to get the hall to stop spinning.

"You're not." Hawk placed a warm hand on my back and my senses instantly connected with his life force, strong and sure. "You need at least ten minutes, ideally more and something to eat."

Except the longer we stayed the greater the chance I'd have to have sex with Sebastian with everyone watching.

That thought made my stomach churn. Yes, I wanted to have sex with Sebastian again, but I wanted the next time to be because we wanted to not because we had to, and I certainly didn't want to do it with a bunch of strangers watching.

"I can do this." I tried to push out of Sebastian's arms and stand on my own, but he wouldn't let go. "I can't do sex in public for your mother's entertainment."

"It's better to wait and risk it," Sebastian said. "You're not going to make it to the ballroom let alone to the other side."

"Well," a dark masculine voice purred from the direction of the ballroom, sending a shiver of fear racing down my spine.

Sebastian stiffened and I dragged my attention up to see Deaglan and his demon-vampire hybrid between us and the ballroom.

AMIAH

Deaglan and his hybrid stood in the darkness a few feet away from the edge of the bright light spilling into the hall from the ballroom, blocking our way and threatening our escape. Their faces were cast in shadow and only my night vision and the simmering hellfire in the hybrid's eyes allowed me to make out their features.

"Trying to sneak away?" Deaglan asked.

"Letting my wife have a quiet moment," Sebastian replied. "She's not accustomed to court functions and she's not fully healed."

"Of course." Deaglan flashed a wicked grin. "I'm sure there are a lot of things she'll have to get accustomed to." His dark gaze slid over my body his meaning clear. I'd have to get used to having sex in public and soon. "You should really have your incubus warm her up."

"That's my business," Sebastian said.

"Just giving you a warning," Deaglan said with a shrug. "Your mother will be unimpressed if she just lies there, especially since we know she's a wild cat."

My pulse beat faster and a hint of the court's wind fluttered around me. Except it was a soft breath compared to the gale it had been the last time I'd faced Deaglan. But then I'd been filled with fear and adrenaline before, and now I could barely keep from passing out...

And Deaglan didn't know that. I'd scared him last time. Maybe if I showed a little backbone, I could get the wind to gust stronger and make him go away.

Please, just go away so we can get out of here.

I straightened my back as best I could in Sebastian's embrace and leveled my sternest, iciest glare on Deaglan, but the court's wind didn't gain strength. In fact it vanished, taking with it some of the air around me.

I forced my expression hard, praying I could carry through with my bluff and not let the fear of suffocation brought on by having been caught by the leash spell make me gasp. "Do I need to remind your majesty who's court we're in?"

"Not yours," Deaglan said and his shadows exploded from the darkness around us as a blast of shadow slammed into me and Sebastian.

Sebastian stumbled and the hybrid leaped forward so fast that with my spinning, wavering sight I could barely see him. He grabbed my arm and wrenched me from Sebastian's grasp while he was off balance.

Deaglan's shadows shoved between us, knocking Sebastian back seconds before he burned it away with a blast of light, but it was enough for the hybrid to wrap a strong arm around my waist, yanking me farther from

Sebastian and Hawk and pinning my back against his cool bare chest.

The sense of cold lifelessness shuddered across my senses and the hall whirled and darkened around me.

Don't pass out. Please. Don't pass out.

Hawk jerked forward to help me, but a shadow wrapped around his neck and wrenched him off his feet. Gasping, Hawk clutched at the shadows choking him but couldn't rip the darkness apart and free himself.

"Get your hands off her." That sounded like Cassius.

I dragged my gaze to the mouth of the hall. Cassius and Titus stood in the bright light pouring in from the ballroom. Smoke curled from Cassius's hands and Titus snarled, his lips curled back showing his extended canines.

"This isn't a fight you want to have," Sebastian said, and a glyph on his left arm and one curling around his neck lit up with power. "Let go of my wife and my guard."

"I think you've forgotten who holds the queen's favor," Deaglan sneered, his shadows writhing around Sebastian but not attacking. "You've been gone, Seireadan, and someone needed to reassure your mother that you'd eventually be found."

"What a load of shit," Sebastian shot back. "You tried to ki—"

"Her majesty won't stand for you abandoning your duties again," Deaglan interrupted as if he thought someone else was listening instead of gloating like he had before. "You can't run out on this like you ran out on the Winter Court three hundred years ago."

"I said let her go," Cassius repeated and flames swept

over his hands.

"Enough," the Winter Queen commanded as she strode into the hallway, her blood red dress billowing around her. The werepanther who'd pleasured her when she'd first tried to get Sebastian to sleep with me was one step behind her along with two other fae men — neither man the fae who'd joined the werepanther pleasuring her. They all wore the red leather pants of her harem.

Ice enveloped Cassius's hands and a frigid wind blasted down the hall, stinging my skin and pasting my gauzy dress to my legs — and thankfully not flashing my privates to Deaglan.

Titus jerked forward and wind slammed him into the hall wall and pinned him there, as Cassius's fire melted the ice containing his power and he tensed, about to stand and fight.

"Stand down, Cas and T," Sebastian said, the light in his glyphs fading. "Mother—"

"Don't 'Mother' me," she snapped. "Deaglan said you'd try to slip away and if he's holding your man and your wife then he was right."

"We weren't. Amiah just needed a moment to rest," Sebastian insisted, as Cassius sucked his fire back under his skin but didn't relax and Titus continued to heave against the queen's wind.

"Then what is this?" Deaglan clenched his fist.

Sebastian stiffened and his full-body glow flared, his eyes narrowing in concentration for a second before squeezing tight in pain, and he released a strangled scream. The small shimmering orb of magic that Karthick had pushed into Sebastian to protect him from the Wilds after he'd removed my mating brand, emerged from his chest with a sickening tearing sound and floated into Deaglan's outstretched hand. "You've protected yourself from the Wilds. It sure looks like you're trying to sneak away."

"I won't let you run away from your duty again," the queen said and the wind gusted around us laced with pieces of ice that sliced shallow stinging cuts across my skin. "If you hate this court so much, you can leave once your heir makes a connection to the Winter Court. All I want is the child."

"Amiah just needed a moment," Sebastian gasped, his hands pressed to his chest where the orb had been.

"If she's so exhausted, your majesty," Deaglan said, turning to the queen, "it would be best to conceive the next Winter Court heir now."

My pulse stuttered and I weakly pushed at the demon-vampire's grip but he held tight.

No.

No no no.

Sebastian had to buy us time, find a way for us to slip away. I had to. Someone did. Please.

"There's no need to rush and ruin your party," Sebastian said.

"No, the King of the Shadow Court is right," the queen said. "It's time for you to sleep with your wife."

I had to think of something, anything for us to get away, but I couldn't get my thoughts to focus beyond the exhaustion threatening my consciousness and the fear of being naked and exposed in front of everyone.

"Perhaps he needs more incentive," Deaglan said.

The queen's eyes narrowed. "My constructs say you're friendly with your bodyguards. How friendly?"

The court's frozen wind whipped around Cassius's neck and jerked him to his hands and knees. His fire roared up his arms but was extinguished by more ice.

Titus snarled and the wind capturing him against the wall pounded into him with crushing force, drawing a guttural scream of pain.

"Fuck your wife or I'll kill your men," the queen said.

No, please.

My pulse tripped and the court's wind gusted for me, frozen and flecked with ice. But the Winter Queen flicked a finger and it vanished.

"This is my court," she said, stalking toward me, frost crackling over the floor with each step and inching closer to my bare feet. "My power. You can't use it against me. My will is stronger than yours, little angel."

Sebastian stepped between me and his mother. "There's no need for this."

"Fuck your wife." Darkness swept over the Winter Queen's eyes turning them black. "I'll even help you along. Deaglan, have your hybrid bite her to get her going."

Deaglan's eyes lit up with dark pleasure. "Rin."

"Let her go," Titus growled. He heaved against the wind and it snapped his head back into the wall with enough force his eyes rolled back and his eyelids fluttered shut for a second.

A few feet beside him Hawk gurgled and gasped for breath, his feet skimming the floor, while Cassius tried to stand, but the wind whip yanked him back to the floor and another wave of ice swept over his hands and up his forearms.

"She's weak," the hybrid said, his voice barely more than a whisper. "Blood loss won't help her."

I dragged my attention over my shoulder and met black eyes with a smoldering pinprick of hellfire and an emotionless expression that told me nothing about why he hadn't immediately obeyed.

"I didn't ask for your opinion," Deaglan snapped and he clenched his fist.

The hybrid tensed and what little magic I had left connected with him.

Pain. Agonizing breathtaking pain burned through his veins for a blazing second then vanished, leaving me gasping.

"Yes, my lord," the hybrid said his voice still that emotionless, barely audible whisper with no indication of the agony that had just burst through him.

He tangled his fingers in my hair, jerked my head to the side, and sank his fangs into my neck without further hesitation.

More pain, a fraction of what I'd felt from him moments before, sliced into my neck.

"No, please." I weakly pushed against his grip, my heart pounding. I didn't want this, didn't want a stranger holding me in an intimate embrace, consuming my blood. And I didn't know how much I could take before I collapsed. I was already weak, my magic and life force drained, and what little magic I had left snapped, a dying flame in a ferocious wind, desperate but unable to save me.

Titus howled and bucked against the wind, while Hawk strained to break free of Deaglan's shadows, and Cassius clutched at the wind whip choking him, his face turning red with effort and lack of oxygen.

Then the hybrid took a long, hard pull on my vein and bone-melting bliss swept through me, rushing straight to my core, filling me with sudden aching need, and dragging at my already weakened limbs.

The hall darkened, my pulse stuttered and slowed, and for a terrifying moment there was nothing, not even the bliss of the hybrid's magic.

Then panic seized me and wrenched me back to the hall. My muscles had given out and only the hybrid's grip in my hair and around my waist kept me upright.

"Fucking hell," Sebastian hissed. His cool hands cupped my cheeks and he urged my head up the fraction of an inch needed to meet his pale gaze, suspending me in a cold, clear nothingness, the heart of the Winter Court captured in Sebastian's almost colorless eyes. For a second, sparks of magic flashed in his irises and I could see a vast, breathtaking expanse of power there.

Then he blinked and the endless expanse vanished and the hybrid's power surged drawing a throaty moan that I tried but couldn't keep back.

My body throbbed, aching for a release I didn't want, and I shivered at every sweep of wind against my suddenly too-sensitive skin. I was hyperaware of the feel of Sebastian's cool hands on my cheeks and the thrum of his life force, as well as the hybrid's hard body pressed against mine, his breath a little too fast, his arms trembling, and the cold absence of his life force. His fangs slid from my neck and he replaced them with his lips in a barely-there kiss. The warm flicker of heat of his miniscule healing magic — a magic all vampires possessed — sealed the puncture wounds shut and sent an aching shudder racing through me.

"Your highness," he said and he eased me into Sebastian's arms.

"Now fuck your wife," the Winter Queen said.

"Jesus." Sebastian hooked an arm under my knees and lifted me, cradling me against his chest. "You're not going to get much of a show now."

The queen's eyes narrowed. "My original offer to have the court fuck her first still stands."

"Your majesty, Rin and I will be happy to show him how it's done," Deaglan said.

Sebastian's grip on me tightened and Hawk made desperate choking sounds, his rapid healing the only thing saving him from suffocation.

Titus growled low in his throat. He extended his claws and the massive muscles in his arms and neck bulged with the effort to break free of the Winter Queen's wind.

"Amiah," Cassius gasped, his breath short and ragged, every muscle straining to break free and his fire racing over his arms as more ice encased him over and over again. His angel glow blazed and his eyes were filled with ferocious determination.

He was going to fight and so was Titus and there was a chance, a good chance, they wouldn't survive, because even if they could break free of the Winter Queen's power there was still Deaglan and all of the queen's guards.

I met Cassius's gaze, begging him with my eyes. *Don't.*

Please don't. Remember your promise.

He tensed and I dragged my gaze away from him before he could respond and leaned into Sebastian, the hall still spinning and dim and the hybrid's magic throbbing low within me, making my stomach churn with frustration and fear that my body craved something the rest of me didn't.

"I'm waiting." The queen wrenched her hand down and Titus smashed face-first onto the floor.

Blood rushed from his now-shattered nose and from a gash above his right eye. My power stuttered, still too weak to do anything but twist my compulsion to heal tight in my chest.

"What's more compelling?" the queen asked, her voice dark and dangerous. "Avoiding the pleasures of the King of the Shadow Court and the rest of my court, or saving your soldiers?"

Cassius released a strangled cry and blood oozed down his neck as the wind whip tightened and cut into his skin. His eyes bulged and his mouth opened for a breath he couldn't draw.

No, please.

My power stuttered stronger, desperate to help them, but it was still a weak useless glimmer in my palms.

The Winter Queen sent another wind whip around Hawk and wrenched him free of Deaglan's shadows and slammed him onto the floor beside Titus with crushing force, drawing a sharp scream.

Please stop. Just stop.

"This isn't necessary," Sebastian said, his body tense and his grip on me tightening.

The wind gusted stronger around us, filled with thick snowflakes and sweeping through the queen's hair and dress making her look ferocious and dangerous. "Make your choice."

Cassius's eyes rolled back and Hawk released another sharp scream.

Stop. Please, God, stop.

My throat tightened. I couldn't lose them. I couldn't be responsible for their deaths.

I had to do it. I had no choice.

"Just do it, Sebastian," I begged, "before the hybrid's magic wears off." *Before she kills them.*

Because the hybrid's magic would wear off. I wasn't bite-locked which meant I didn't need an orgasm to release his magic, it would just naturally fade away and then I wouldn't even have that to distract me from what was going to happen.

"Amiah—" Sebastian whispered.

"Please. You promised. You all promised." I couldn't let them die. It was just my body. It wasn't my soul and it was with Sebastian. I could do this. I had to do this.

The court's wind stuttered then snapped colder than before. My fingers and toes grew numb, my teeth started to chatter, and the hall grew darker.

"Please," I gasped. "Don't let her kill them."

Sebastian's expression turned sad and soft, and my throat tightened. This wasn't the way we were supposed to have sex again. It was supposed to be beautiful, purposeful, not because we needed to save Hawk and certainly not desperate and on display to save Cassius, Hawk, and Titus.

"Okay," Sebastian murmured against my forehead.

Titus howled and all three of them wrenched against the queen's control, but the wind picked up, slamming their heads into the floor, stunning them, and Deaglan's shadows wrapped around their necks, choking them.

"After you," the queen said, her wind slamming the guys against the floor again.

Sebastian jerked away from them and marched down the hall to the ballroom. The Winter Queen and Deaglan, arm in arm, strode behind us with the hybrid a few steps behind them, while Cassius, Titus, and Hawk, barely conscious, were behind the hybrid, dragged along by the court's wind, and guarded by the queen's three men.

Sebastian stepped into the ballroom and headed straight to the bed, while the queen and Deaglan led everyone else to the raised throne at the back of the room.

Cassius, Titus, and Hawk were wrenched to the floor in front of the dais's steps with the rest of the queen's men standing guard on either side of them, and if any of the queen's guests noticed, they didn't react to the bleeding, stunned men being held captive at her feet.

The light in Cassius's eyes blazed so brightly I could barely make out his facial features and smoke billowed around him. Beside him, Hawk gasped for air, clutching the wind whip around his neck, while Titus heaved and snarled, his eyes wild, blood on his face from the cut above his eye and his shattered nose.

Stop. Please stop. They had to stop fighting. They couldn't win and I couldn't lose them. I could get through this if I knew they were safe.

The queen sat on her throne, raised her hands, and the room went silent. "The time has come to welcome a new heir to the Winter Court."

The room burst into wild cheers and all eyes turned to me and Sebastian as we drew closer to the center of the room.

Oh God oh God oh God.

My pulse pounded so fast my chest hurt and I couldn't catch my breath.

The room grew dimmer, and the beam of moonlight shimmering from the skylight onto the bed grew brighter.

I couldn't do this. I couldn't.

But I had to.

Please. I couldn't be responsible for their deaths. I couldn't lose them.

Sebastian paused at the edge of a thin, barely visible sparkling line encircling the bed. "Amiah—"

"Just make it quick."

He pressed his lips to my forehead and murmured, "If we don't loosen you up more it'll hurt and Hawk won't be able to help you."

"I don't care. I just want this over with. This doesn't count. It's not real. We'll get real again when this is over and we're safe."

The muscles in his jaw flexed and the grief in his eyes deepened. "She'll want a show."

"Then pick an interesting position."

"You're too weak for that." But he still squared his shoulders and stepped across the sparkling circle.

A whisper of ice shivered through my veins and the

hybrid's magic billowed. I tried to hold back my moan, but it still escaped, low and breathy.

Sebastian sat me on the bed, knelt in front of me, and captured my cheeks between his palms.

I tried to stare into his almost colorless eyes, tried to find that vast expanse of power and lose myself in his gaze again, but I couldn't focus and couldn't concentrate past the exhaustion and fear and throbbing desire of the hybrid's bite.

I can't do this. They're all looking at me. They're all going to see me. I can't, I can't.

I have to. Please.

"I won't make it if you draw it out." I wasn't sure I could make it now. "Just rip off the bandage. Hard and fast. Make me cry, that'll make your mother and Deaglan happy."

"I'm not making you cry." He captured my lips in a tender kiss filled with such concern and gentleness that it broke my heart and my wavering vision grew glassy with tears I didn't want to cry.

The court's wind gusted around us, ruffling my hair and another shiver of ice swept through my veins.

I tried to find my strength, my resolve to do what had to be done, and appear brave, but a tear frustratingly rolled down my cheek.

"I'm going to cry anyway," I said. "I'm crying now. I don't want this. I don't want your mother to kill the others. I can't—" My throat tightened and I couldn't catch my breath. If he treated this like we were actually making love I'd shatter. I wouldn't be able to get through it.

I captured his face with my palms and pressed my

forehead against his. "Please, Sebastian. Just make it quick. Get me through this as fast as possible."

He stared into my eyes as if he could see into my soul for a long, terrifying moment. He had to do it fast. I wasn't going to make it if he didn't. I didn't know how to convince him. All I could pray was that he could sense my desperation and just do it.

Then he gave a tight, barely-there nod.

"Okay," he murmured back, his voice heartbreakingly soft. "I don't mean any of this."

"I know."

He seized a handful of my hair, painfully jerked my head back, and smashed his lips against mine in a bruising kiss. It happened so fast, the room darkened for a second, then another shiver of ice swept through me and the skylight lurched back into sight.

He shoved his tongue into my mouth and his hand between my thighs. One finger slid inside me, testing how far the hybrid's bite had gotten me, making the magic inside me twist tighter in my core. But the hybrid's magic had only gotten me started. Sure, I was mostly lubricated, but even with that I wasn't relaxed enough to accommodate Sebastian's size without still taking it slow.

And still I shuddered at the invasion, my body aching for more even as my pulse raced with shame and embarrassment.

They were all watching me, all waiting for Sebastian to shove himself inside me, all thrilled that they got to see us like that.

My stomach churned at the thought. Didn't I like the idea of being watched? Wasn't that what I'd wanted in

Hawk's tent when I'd seen Sebastian's desire at my reaction to Hawk's magic? But this wasn't like that at all. Intimacy didn't just have to be between two people, it could be between three or four — or, oh my goodness! five people — that I cared about and desired. There was nothing intimate about what was happening right now. Even if I remained clothed, I was still being exposed and violated. Both of us were.

I dragged my wavering gaze to the throne. The queen smirked with satisfaction while Deaglan watched with dark desire. At least the aggressive kiss seemed to be satisfying her.

Then my gaze dipped to the guys and my throat tightened and another tear escaped. Titus wrenched against the wind again and again, his eyes were wild with rage, and fire sparked from Cassius's arms even though they were encased in ice. His breath was hard and fast and his angel glow had sharpened into a cold fury.

The court's wind gusted stronger, whipping my hair to the side and stinging my skin.

They were still fighting. They had to stop. They were going to make this sacrifice pointless and get themselves killed.

Sebastian had to hurry this up, not just for me, but for them. If we finished there'd be no reason for them to fight. But he roughly rubbed his slick finger against my clit, trying to build on the hybrid's magic.

Except it wasn't going to be enough. Nothing would be enough, not to get me to relax or forget everyone was watching or that the Winter Queen was going to kill the others.

I grabbed the front of Sebastian's jerkin and weakly struggled against his grip, trying to tell him to just get it over with. But he wouldn't let me go and wouldn't ease up enough on his kiss for me to speak. All I could do was gasp shallow shuddering breaths.

He kissed me as if he was furious, as if he could vent all of his frustrations out through his lips, and I couldn't tell if it was an act or not. He twisted my neck to a painful angle, dug his nails into my scalp, and bit my lip, drawing blood.

I whimpered against his mouth, not needing to pretend it hurt, and he snarled back at me.

The Winter Queen's smirk deepened and Deaglan's breath picked up.

Then Sebastian yanked his hand out from my thighs, quickly unlaced himself one-handed, and shoved me back onto the bed, the sudden movement making my head spin. My gaze caught his and my heart broke at the pain in his eyes. This wasn't him. It wasn't us.

"It's okay," I murmured, trying to hide my terror and give him the strength to get through this. Because if he couldn't, I couldn't. I didn't have the willpower to shut myself away from what was happening. I needed him strong, steadying me, needed to cling to the strength of his soul and his compassion to survive. "Make it good so we never have to do this again."

Titus's struggling grew frantic, desperately bucking and heaving against the wind, the Winter Queen sat forward, and Deaglan's hand slid inside his pants.

My stomach churned with a nauseating mix of fear and unwanted desire. More ice crackled through my veins, stronger than before, and the court wind gusted, picking up speed.

I dragged my attention back to Sebastian.

It's okay. We can do this.

Sebastian aligned himself with my opening, his gaze locked with mine.

We can do this. We can save the others. Because this isn't really us. Not our souls, just our bodies.

He seized my hips.

Not us. Not us. This doesn't count.

Then he plunged into me with a forceful thrust.

I cried out, my body tensing, and tears spilled down my cheeks at the pain of his savage invasion and the horror of what was happening, as the people in the room cheered.

The court wind whipped into a gale that tore through the room and swept inside me, following the ice in my veins to explode around my heart in a wild, ferocious torrent that threatened to tear me apart.

Titus howled, a great bellowing roar, that carried through the gale. He wrenched against the wind holding him and his body swelled, his muscles and chest growing enormous and his hips and thighs tearing through his leather pants. Red and gold scales swept over his neck and hands and raced over the rest of him. With another great howl, he tore through the Winter Court's wind and shifted...

Into a massive, furious dragon.

Don't miss the next book in the series!

FATED FEAR
Angel's Fate: Book Three

She'll sacrifice anything to protect them... whatever the cost.

The Winter Queen had me and my guys where she wanted us, forcing me to make a terrible deal with the Winter Court itself, and even then, we barely escaped with our lives. Now we're all being hunted. Especially Titus, whose rage tore the lid off the one secret that could spell his doom.

Among all of us, he's the biggest prize — the only one with a connection to a magic so powerful that whoever controls it, controls the realm. His fight to stay free digs its talons into my soul, because I know the fear of imprisonment and have spent my life determined to never be trapped again. Except something I never thought I wanted is wrapping itself around my heart — ties between me and my guys that are starting to feel less like chains, and more like home.

But now the Winter Court's frozen magic courses through my veins, an icy tether that could yank me back into its trap at any moment. And when the next disaster strikes, the ties between me and my guys may not be enough to save us all.

OTHER BOOKS BY TESSA COLE

NEPHILIM'S DESTINY

Destined Shadows, prequel story

Destined Darkness, book 1

Destined Blood, book 2

Destined Fire, book 3

Destined Storm, book 4

Destined Radiance, book 5

ANGEL'S FATE

Fated Bonds, book 1

Fated Winter, book 2

Fated Fear, book 3

Fated Despair, book 4

Fated Resolve, book 5

Fated Heart, book 6

THE GRECIAN GODDESS TRILOGY

Kiss of the Goddess, book 1

Power of the Goddess, book 2

Bonds of the Goddess, book 3

ENSNARED BY THE PACK